CANYONLANDS CARNAGE

Also by Scott Graham
in the National Park Mystery Series

Praise for the National Park Mystery Series

"Graham's winning fourth National Park mystery uses Yosemite as a backdrop for a host of shady dealings and dangerous power struggles. This zippy tale uses lush descriptions of natural beauty and twisted false leads to create an exciting, rewarding puzzle."
—*PUBLISHERS WEEKLY*

"As always, the highlight of Graham's National Park Mystery Series is his extensive knowledge of the parks system, its lands, and its people."
—*KIRKUS REVIEWS*

"Intriguing . . . Graham has a true talent for describing the Rockies' flora and fauna, allowing his readers to feel almost as if they were trekking the park themselves."
—*MYSTERY SCENE MAGAZINE*

"Graham has crafted a multilevel mystery that plumbs the emotions of greed and jealousy."
—*DURANGO HERALD*

"Graham has created a beautifully balanced book, incorporating intense action scenes, depth of characterization, realistic landscapes, and historical perspective."
—*REVIEWING THE EVIDENCE*

"Masterfully plotted in confident prose, *Arches Enemy* is not only an adventurous and fascinating mystery you can't put down, it delivers important insight on ancestral cultures and their sacred lands. Scott Graham proves yet again that he is one of the finest."
—CHRISTINE CARBO, author of
A Sharp Solitude: A Glacier Mystery

"A winning blend of archaeology and intrigue, Graham's series turns our national parks into places of equal parts beauty, mystery, and danger."
—EMILY LITTLEJOHN, author of
Shatter the Night: A Detective Gemma Monroe Mystery

CANYONLANDS CARNAGE

A National Park Mystery
By Scott Graham

TORREY HOUSE PRESS

Salt Lake City • Torrey

This is a work of fiction set in a real place. All characters in this novel are fictitious. Any resemblance to actual events or persons, living or dead, is entirely coincidental.

First Torrey House Press Edition, September 2021
Copyright © 2021 by Scott Graham

Published by Torrey House Press
Salt Lake City, Utah
www.torreyhouse.org

International Standard Book Number: 978-1-948814-46-1
E-book ISBN: 978-1-948814-47-8
Library of Congress Control Number: 2020946749

Cover art by David Jonason
Cover design by Kathleen Metcalf
Interior design by Rachel Leigh Buck-Cockayne
Distributed to the trade by Consortium Book Sales and Distribution

Torrey House Press offices in Salt Lake City sit on the homelands of Ute, Goshute, Shoshone, and Paiute nations. Offices in Torrey are on homelands of Southern Paiute, Ute, and Navajo nations.

ABOUT THE COVER

"The Toroweep Overlook is an iconic view of the Grand Canyon. Although I've painted it on numerous occasions, the scene always feels fresh and never fails to inspire."

Acclaimed Southwest landscape artist David Jonason painted "TOROWEEP OVERLOOK," a portion of which appears on the cover of *Canyonlands Carnage*. Combining a keenly observant eye and inspiration drawn from a number of 20th century art movements, including Cubism, Futurism, Precisionism, and Art Deco, Jonason achieves a uniquely personal vision through his vividly dreamlike oil paintings of the American Southwest. Jonason connects on canvas the traditional arts and crafts of the Southwest's native tribes with the intricate patterns in nature known as fractals. "For me as a painter," he says, "it's a reductive and simplifying process of finding the natural geometries in nature, just as Navajo weavers and Pueblo potters portray the natural world through geometric series of zigzags, curves, and other patterns."

"Toroweap Overlook" (30×24 inches, oil on canvas, 2020) is used by permission of The Jonason Studio, davidjonason.com

For my son Taylor,
with thanks for sharing his deep
knowledge of water with me

PROLOGUE

Four rusted screws fastened the locked hasp to the face of the rock wall. He slammed the screws with the loaf-sized chunk of sandstone he held in both hands, bending the screw heads downward. His second blow freed the screws from the rock, and the iron gate swung away from the wall with a rusty screech, the secured padlock still hanging in the hasp.

He dropped the stone and clicked on his headlamp, lighting the opening of the head-high tunnel that disappeared into darkness behind the gate. Entering, he took long strides down the passage. He had to move fast. He'd slipped away from the riverside camp during the initial chaos of unloading the boats and setting up the tents and kitchen, but his absence would be noticed before long.

Veins of salt striped the walls and ceiling of the tunnel. Piles of the white grains rested on the floor of the passageway. The veins grew thicker and the piles higher as he strode farther underground.

Everything was as he'd hoped—the easily broken hasp, the level passage deep into the side of the canyon, the preponderance of salt.

The piles formed perfect pyramids, built up over time by grains dribbling from the veins in the ceiling and walls of the drilled passage. If the rumor was true, somewhere ahead he would come upon a mound of salt that no longer formed a flawless cone, but instead was disturbed, having been shoveled and rearranged to encase and preserve the artifacts he sought.

He sped up, nearly breaking into a run, and directed his headlamp down the dark tunnel. He passed another salt pile. Another. Ten feet ahead, his light flickered across the largest mound he'd yet encountered. The pile of salt covered the floor of the tunnel from wall to wall and rose nearly to his waist. The sides of the mound were pocked and indented, its apex uneven rather than coming to a pristine, unadulterated point.

He grinned. Someone had dug up and reformed the salt pile—and he knew exactly why they'd done so.

He hurried forward, noting a slender, sword-like length of wood protruding from the top of the pile. He stepped around the mound of salt, admiring it from all sides. In the beam of his headlamp, the length of wood threw a thin, dark shadow across the shimmering white crystals.

He set to work, scooping aside handful after handful of salt, intent on uncovering what had been buried away in the pile so many years before.

PART ONE

"We have an unknown distance yet to run,
an unknown river to explore."

—John Wesley Powell

1

Chuck Bender snugged the straps of his personal flotation device tight around his chest. He thrust his feet against the whitewater raft's round aluminum foot bar, straightening his legs and pressing his hips into the low-backed captain's chair positioned at the center of the big, inflated boat.

Counterweighted oars extended through bronze oarlocks from the sides of the raft into the calm water of the Colorado River. He lifted the oars out of the water. Droplets sparkled in the midday sun as they dribbled from the oar blades into the brown, silt-laden river.

Clarence Ortega, Chuck's brother-in-law, sat in front of Chuck on an oversized plastic cooler strapped with inch-wide nylon webbing to the raft's metal frame. Clarence's jet-black hair, secured in a ponytail beneath his whitewater helmet, lay over the back of his life jacket. The heavyset young man, twenty years Chuck's junior, gripped the nylon webbing, his fingers curled around the thick straps at his sides. He stared downstream along with Chuck at bursts of water spouting into the air from a rapid three hundred feet ahead. The churning whitewater was the first of Cataract Canyon's two dozen unforgiving rapids over the course of fourteen torturous miles in the heart of southeastern Utah's remote Canyonlands National Park.

The roar of the roiling whitewater nearly drowned out Chuck's words as he leaned forward and said in Clarence's ear, "We're all set. Hold on tight and we'll be through this first one in a heartbeat."

"It's my heart I'm worried about," Clarence replied. He bent forward, peering ahead, his neck stiff. "Look at that. The water's shooting straight up in the air. *Jesu Cristo*." He turned an ear to the whitewater. "You didn't tell me it would be this loud."

Chuck dipped an oar into the smooth water above the rapid and spun the big raft a few degrees, aligning the boat with the flow of the river. "Loud doesn't necessarily mean terrifying."

"I'm way more than terrified, *jefe*. I'm scared to death. That *rápido* sounds like some sort of crazed beast that's been let off its chain and is looking to swallow us whole."

"That's what twenty-three thousand cubic feet of water sounds like when it plunges through a rapid."

"Plunges is right," Clarence said, his voice shaking.

Chuck peered downstream past Clarence's hunched frame. They would enter the whitewater in less than a minute, last in a procession of eight boats—two hardshell kayaks and half a dozen inflatable rafts—on a two-week river journey down Cataract Canyon called the Waters of the Southwest Expedition. The kayaks led the way, followed by the matching sky-blue rafts positioned a hundred feet apart in the center of the river.

Seated in their highly maneuverable playboats, one electric yellow, the other lime green, the group's two safety kayakers dug their dual-bladed paddles into the water, powering toward the head of the rapid. The kayakers, Liza and Torch, would run the rapid first and station themselves at its bottom, ready to rescue any expedition members tossed from the rafts by the force of the surging waves.

Liza and Torch were guides for Colorado River Adventures, the outfitter for the expedition, as were the captains of all the rafts except the one at the end of the line helmed by Chuck.

The expedition's lead inflatable boats were a pair of fourteen-foot paddle rafts—small, lightweight watercraft that carried little in the way of gear. Three paddlers lined each side of the rafts, six to a boat. The paddlers hugged the rafts' air-filled thwarts with their thighs, like rodeo riders atop saddle broncs. Five paddlers in each boat held paddles aloft, ready to dig their blades into the water at the command of the captains positioned at the back right corners of the boats.

Unlike the paddlers, the captains of the two rafts thrust their paddle blades downward into the water beside them and swung the blades in the current, using them as rudders to direct the lightweight boats straight downstream as they approached the turbulence.

"Less than a minute till we drop in," Chuck told Clarence.

"It's like slow motion."

"The water piles up and almost comes to a stop before rapids."

Three sixteen-foot oar rafts trailed the paddle rafts. Seated at the midpoint of the larger boats, the captains gripped heavy oars with fiberglass shafts, propelling the boats through the slow water above the rapid with steady forward strokes. Four expedition members rode in each of the rafts, one at each corner—save for the last of the three boats. The final oar raft, captained by head CRA guide Tamara Fisher, lacked a passenger at its right rear corner, opposite Joseph Conway. Joseph, the senior water analyst for the Intermountain West office of the US Bureau of Reclamation, was stationed at the left rear corner of the boat.

The expedition members at the front corners of the three oar rafts gripped paddles, set to aid their captains by stroking through the whitewater. Joseph and the other expedition members at the rear corners were tasked merely with hanging on and avoiding being thrown into the frothing water as the boats heaved and bucked through the rapid.

Chuck captained the expedition's so-called gear barge at the end of the procession. He'd signed on as the naturalist for the expedition, offering concise lectures at lunch and after dinner that covered the Colorado River Basin's geology, plant and animal life, and—his specialty—the basin's archaeological and anthropological past.

Clarence was the expedition's unpaid swamper, performing all manner of grunt work in return for his free trip down the river. He set up and dismantled the expedition's portable toilet, erected and stowed the group's tents and cots, and prepared food and scrubbed dishes before and after meals in the camp kitchen.

The gear raft was eighteen feet long and half again as wide, its inflated tubes more than two feet in diameter. The gargantuan boat carried the group's camping and kitchen gear—sturdy tables, collapsible chairs, cooking supplies, steel fuel tanks, aluminum dry boxes packed with food and drinks, and two coffin-sized plastic coolers filled with meat, cheese, and produce.

All told, the gear raft and its load, strapped fore and aft and along the sides of the boat, weighed more than three-quarters of a ton. The oversized thwarts of the massive boat rode so high above the surface of the river that any paddlers stationed at the boat's front corners would not have been able to reach the water with their paddle blades, leaving Chuck to control the boat on his own. The immense raft had proven challenging for him to pilot over the previous seven days on the initial, eighty-mile, flatwater portion of the journey. The slightest of breezes had forced the boat sideways despite his best efforts to keep it in line with the current. The raft would be infinitely more difficult to control in the first of Cataract Canyon's rapids just ahead and in the remainder of the rapids—a fact that, for reasons of selfish pride, he had yet to share with Clarence.

The procession tightened up in the sluggish water before the river poured over the lip of the rapid, the space between the boats diminishing to fifty feet.

Chuck's attention was drawn to the unoccupied rear corner of the raft directly in front of him. He shivered despite the blazing desert heat of the late-May day. The spot should have been occupied by Ralph Hycum, the esteemed emeritus professor of water policy from the University of Nevada-Las Vegas School of Law who'd been coleader, with Chuck's friend Wayne Coswell, of the Waters of the Southwest Expedition.

The expedition was comprised of water-policy experts and corporate representatives voyaging together down the Green and Colorado Rivers through Canyonlands National Park. The participants were to experience the park's magnificent red-rock landscape by day. Then, around the campfire each night, they were tasked with debating the contentious government policies for water use in the arid American Southwest, discussing how to improve rules and methods for allocating water among residential consumers and agricultural and industrial users, while ensuring enough water remained in the rivers to keep the threatened riverine ecosystem of the Colorado River Basin alive and well, too.

Chuck had enjoyed sipping scotch and chatting with Ralph late into the evening hours over the first three days of the journey—until two nights ago, when Ralph climbed into his tent at bedtime and never came out, his death the result of an apparent heart attack. Ralph's body had been airlifted out of the canyon the following morning, leaving Wayne as sole leader of the river trip.

Ralph's death had cast less of a pall over the expedition than Chuck had anticipated—until he reminded himself the policymakers on the trip comprised the Southwest's top field experts on water use and conservation, most of whom were seasoned outdoors people familiar with the risks associated with wilderness travel. Like Chuck, they doubtless had lost friends over the years to whitewater drownings, mountaineering accidents, avalanches, rockfalls, and the like. To die as Ralph had—in a tent in the backcountry near the end of his natural life—likely was the dream of many members of the expedition.

After dinner the last two nights, Ralph's closest friends had recounted tales of past journeys they'd taken with the professor. The trips had ranged from a treacherous rafting trip down the desolate Yarlung Zangbo River deep in the Tibetan Himalaya to a raucous party boat excursion on the crowded Hudson River in

New York City, and included numerous expeditions down the Southwest's magnificent desert rivers. At the end of the tales, the water experts hoisted their drinks—cans of beer, tumblers of whiskey, mugs of herbal tea—in hearty toasts to their departed colleague.

Chuck glanced away from the empty spot at the back of the oar raft and stared downstream at the rapid's horizon line, which extended straight as a ruler from one side of the river to the other above the upcoming stretch of whitewater. He tightened his grip on the oars and mentally reviewed his strategy for running the first rapid.

For weeks leading up to the expedition, he'd studied online videos of rafts navigating Cataract Canyon's rapids, committing to memory the moves required of him to successfully row the gear boat through each stretch of whitewater. Cataract Canyon's twenty-four rapids were spaced so closely together that they were named simply by number in downstream order, from Rapid 1 to 21, until the canyon's last three stretches of whitewater, named Big Drop One, Big Drop Two, and Big Drop Three. Rapid 1 called for a mid-river entry, a hard left pull away from a center hole, then a push back to the middle of the river.

Ahead, Liza and Torch entered the rapid. First the safety kayakers' boats, then their upper bodies, then their helmeted heads disappeared from view as they dropped over the horizon line and into the whitewater beyond.

The lead paddle raft reached the top of the rapid seconds after the safety kayakers. Its captain rowed forward and called out, her command carrying over the thunder of the whitewater, "All ahead full!" The paddlers dug their paddles into the water in unison, as they'd practiced on the calm river over the preceding days. The paddle raft plunged over the horizon line and out of sight after the kayakers. The second paddle raft, with the captain and paddlers digging hard into the water together, dropped into the rapid close behind the first.

Clarence said something unintelligible as he faced downstream in front of Chuck.

The rapid was less than three hundred feet away, its deep-throated growl increasing with each passing second, the spouts of water glittering in the sunlight.

"What's that?" Chuck asked, his voice raised so Clarence would hear him over the thundering whitewater.

Clarence turned his head and spoke loudly as well. "I said, there are a lot of forces at work."

Chuck looked from Clarence to the geysers of water shooting above the horizon line ahead. He grimaced. He did not need this right now.

"The rapid has so much power, so much force," Clarence continued. "It's got me thinking."

The roar of the whitewater was loud as a jet engine. The first of the three oar rafts dropped into the maelstrom behind the paddle rafts and kayakers.

"Thinking about what, for Christ's sake?" Chuck shouted.

"Ralph wasn't that old—in his early seventies maybe—and he seemed to be in good physical shape." Clarence turned forward and hunkered over the cooler, gripping the straps at his sides.

"So?"

"So, I've been picking up on some *fuerzas*—forces—that I hadn't mentioned to you." The wind whipped off the rapid, moist and cool despite the desert heat, carrying the words back to Chuck. "Ralph was too healthy," Clarence said. "Seeing this rapid and the forces involved, it's got me convinced that what I've been thinking is right: no way did that dude just up and die."

2

Chuck gaped at the back of Clarence's helmeted head. "What in God's name are you saying?"

"I mean, consider the odds," Clarence yelled back at him.

"You really think—?"

Clarence nodded, his plastic helmet bobbing. "I do. The power—the force—of this first rapid made me realize I needed to say something."

Chuck grimaced and rowed backward, adding space between the gear boat and the remaining two oar rafts still in sight above the rapid. "Now is not the time, Clarence. In fact, now is the very worst time."

"Sorry, *jefe*," Clarence shouted back. "I just had to say it."

Chuck gritted his teeth. They were seconds from dropping into the whitewater.

"Plus," Clarence said, "there's the penny."

Chuck huffed.

A tiny object had fallen from Ralph's supine frame into the sand when Tamara's guides had removed the professor's body from his tent. The guides hadn't noticed the object, but Chuck had. While the guides wrapped Ralph's body in a plastic tarp, Chuck had retrieved the object from the ground. It turned out to be a dull copper penny. He'd tucked the penny in his pocket and mentioned it to Clarence.

"People carry coins in their pockets all the time," Chuck hollered over the roar of the rapid. "Especially older people. The penny fell out of Ralph's pants when the guides moved him, that's all."

"You sound awfully sure of yourself."

"Because I am."

"Well, I'm not all that sure I agree with—"

"Enough," Chuck commanded, cutting Clarence off. "There's no more time."

Rapid 1 was a hundred feet ahead. He had to focus on running it—and, in particular, avoiding the hole at its center.

The whitewater in Cataract Canyon formed where flash floods swept boulders into the river from side canyons. The boulders gathered in invisible heaps beneath the surface, roiling the water above.

The least threatening of the canyon's rapids were those composed solely of standing waves. Because of their constant downstream flow, standing waves offered relatively safe, roller-coaster-like fun, with passengers whooping in delight as rafts reared up and over them.

In contrast, waves known as holes formed in the steepest, toughest rapids. Holes were waves that fell backward upon themselves, creating dangerous pits in the middle of whitewater runs. To enter a hole in a raft was to risk flipping and flinging passengers into the recirculating maw of the depression, where they could be trapped under the overturned boat or sucked deep beneath the surface of the water. Numerous holes lurked in the whitewater stretches of Cataract Canyon. The most treacherous of the canyon's rapids featured two or more holes, requiring captains to oar their boats back and forth across the river in the midst of the seething whitewater to avoid them.

Rapid 1 was challenging but not necessarily death-defying, rated Class IV on the Class I to V scale of whitewater difficulty. The rapid featured only one hole, but the hole was situated in the center of the river at the base of the entry tongue, making it difficult to avoid.

Ahead, the second and third oar rafts had plunged over the horizon line one behind the other, leaving the gear boat alone in the calm water, fifty feet from the start of the rapid. Chuck pushed forward with his oars once, twice, three times. The sour smell of perspiration rose from his armpits as he shoved the oars hard away from his chest, adding speed to the raft for use as momentum during the upcoming move to avoid the Rapid 1 hole.

As the gear raft crested the horizon line, the rapid's four-hundred-yard stretch of turbulence came into view. Chuck noted the kayaks and paddle rafts bounding through the boisterous tail waves at the bottom of the rapid a quarter mile downstream. The kayakers peeled off, one to each side of the river, while the paddle rafts coasted into the calm eddy at the end of the whitewater.

Upstream from the kayaks and paddle rafts, the first two oar rafts were successfully below the recirculating hole and coursing through the standing waves in the middle of the rapid. The paddlers at the front corners of each boat dug their paddle blades into the river, while the captains strained at their oars from the seats in the center of the two boats. Behind the guides, the passengers at the rear of the boats lay on their stomachs, clinging to looped straps to remain aboard.

The third and final oar raft floated down the center of the rapid's entry tongue. Tamara pushed forward with her oars while her front paddlers stroked with their paddles. She had replaced the battered, straw cowboy hat she customarily wore with a plastic helmet. Her paddlers, also temporarily helmeted for the rapid, worked with her to complete the lateral move required to break the boat out of the V-shaped entry tongue before reaching the hole, which lurked at the base of the tongue like a dark, menacing portal to the underworld.

Together, Tamara and her paddlers punched the raft nose-first through the lateral waves and safely away from the hole.

Behind Tamara's boat, the gear raft began its descent down the smooth Rapid 1 entry tongue. Without paddlers at the front corners of the oversized gear boat, Chuck would have to oar the big raft out of the entry tongue on his own before reaching the hole, while Clarence clung to the cooler in the front well of the boat.

As the speed of the current picked up, Chuck spun the raft until it was perpendicular to the flow of the river. Seated sideways to the seething hole waiting at the bottom of the tongue, he reached forward with his oars and dropped the blades into the water. He pulled backward, enlisting his shoulder and back muscles to apply more power to the stroke than he could with a forward push.

His first pull on the oars would begin the process of powering the raft sideways across the tongue and away from the recirculating wave. If his attempt to break out of the tongue failed, he would have a few precious seconds to spin the raft forward and strike the hole's breaking wave head on. The key for all raft captains was to never enter a hole sideways, because the narrower side-to-side width of oval-shaped rafts meant entering in that position increased the odds of flipping exponentially.

Chuck heaved backward on his oars, initiating his first stroke in the center of the rapid's entry tongue. The oar shafts bowed where they passed through the oarlocks at the sides of the raft, transferring the power of his stroke to the oar blades. The blades began their forward sweep through the water. He strained harder, applying every last bit of his strength to the stroke. In response, the oar shafts bowed another inch—and the right oarlock snapped in two.

The freed oar straightened with a vibrating zing and skittered across the top of the raft's side thwart. The bronze oarlock's U-shaped top remained wrapped around the oar, while the bottom half of the oarlock poked from the head of the oar tower at Chuck's side, its sheered shaft glinting in the sun.

Chuck stared at the spot where, a second ago, his oar had been secured to the oar tower.

Oarlocks were made of soft metal, most commonly bronze, and thereby designed to break when rafts struck immoveable objects like rocks or cliff walls. At the same time, however, oar-lock shafts were fashioned to withstand many times more force than the strongest human could possibly apply to them with an oar stroke. Yet the gear boat's right oarlock had failed at Chuck's pull, leaving the boat—and Chuck and Clarence with it—at the mercy of the rapid.

The raft sped down the center of the tongue, seconds from dropping into the hole. There wasn't enough time before the boat reached the recirculating wave for Chuck to replace the sheered oarlock, or for him to resecure the loosed oar with a loop of webbing around the oar tower and return the oar to partial service. Instead, he had only the left oar at his disposal.

He let go of the right oar, grabbed the left oar handle with both hands, and pulled, pivoting the raft until it faced downstream. Thirty feet ahead, at the bottom of the entry tongue, the hole's backward-cresting wave surged into the air, a seething wall of water ten feet high.

Next to Chuck, the unsecured right oar slid off the thwart. When the oar blade dove into the water, the force of the current against the blade pinwheeled the oar's heavy shaft above the river's surface. The shaft swung across the front of the boat like a pendulum, and the iron counterweight, bolted below the oar handle, struck the side of Clarence's helmet a violent blow.

"Clarence!" Chuck cried out, too late.

Clarence collapsed across the cooler, his head cradled in his hands. The raft pivoted around the pinwheeling oar until the big boat once again floated sideways in the current. Chuck dug the left oar into the water and yanked the handle in desperation, but his effort was futile; the raft floated into the hole before he could reorient the boat downstream.

The raft rode sideways up the face of the wave. It slowed to a crawl, then came to a full stop, hanging in space, nearly vertical.

Clarence tumbled off the cooler. His big body slammed into a square, metal storage box strapped to the side of the raft frame.

Behind Clarence, Chuck toppled out of the captain's seat. The handle of the left oar, still secured in its oarlock, struck his ribcage a bruising blow as he fell. He wrapped his arms around the left oar tower and clung to it as water poured over the thwarts, filling the boat from all sides.

Still perpendicular to the current, the raft slid back down the face of the wave into the recirculating hole. Water sluiced over the bow, sweeping Clarence out of the boat. In a flash, he disappeared beneath the surface of the river.

The madly churning water at the base of the wave suctioned the raft's lower thwart, trapping the boat in the hole, while the collapsing top of the wave shoved the upper thwart so far over that the boat's massive load of gear hung directly above Chuck's head.

Before the raft flipped entirely, the water pouring over the side thwarts ripped Chuck's arms free of the oar tower and swept him out of the boat. He plunged into the swirling center of the hole and beneath the surface of the river.

The water closed over his head, instantly reducing his world to bubbling quiet and murky darkness.

3

Two Weeks Earlier

"They call it carnage when a raft flips in a rapid," Chuck explained to Rosie Ortega, his thirteen-year-old stepdaughter. "That's because gear and passengers get tossed every which way, like a bomb going off, when a boat capsizes."

"Cool!" Rosie exclaimed. She stood at Chuck's shoulder, bouncing on her toes, animated as ever.

Chuck sat at his desk in his study at the back of their small, Victorian house in the Rocky Mountain town of Durango in southwestern Colorado. He'd bookmarked links on his computer to some of what were termed the "sickest" and "most heinous" whitewater rafting accidents ever captured on video, from multi-passenger spills in thundering rapids on Zimbabwe's Zambezi River, to frame-snapping end-over-enders in infamous Lava Falls Rapid on the Colorado River in Grand Canyon.

He clicked on the links, playing clip after clip of rafts overturning in surging whitewater and flinging passengers hither and yon like so much confetti.

Rosie oohed and aahed at the scenes of disaster. "You have to see this, Carm!" she called down the hall to her sister, Carmelita, who'd celebrated her sixteenth birthday and the receipt of her driver's license a few weeks ago.

No reply came from the living room, where Carmelita had been stretched out on the couch, her phone before her eyes and her thumbs flying across its face, when Chuck had invited her and Rosie to his office to check out the videos he'd lined up.

Rosie's curly black hair brushed the side of Chuck's head as she leaned forward and whispered in his ear, "Carm hates you. That's why she won't come."

"No, she doesn't," he protested.

He wore his customary long-sleeved flannel shirt and camel-colored work jeans in the drafty house on this cool day in early May. Diffused light through the study window reflected a faint image on the computer screen of his clean-shaven face, the wrinkles at the corners of his eyes and mouth set deep in his sun-seared skin, his short hair, brown peppered with gray, thinning at the temples.

Pasta Alfredo, the now-plump house cat Rosie had discovered as an emaciated, semi-feral stray in Arches National Park two years ago, curled in her customary lounge spot on the wide window sill beside his desk.

"Oh yes, she does," Rosie maintained. She straightened and nodded her head vigorously, her body rocking along. "She told me so."

In contrast to Chuck's lean frame, Rosie was chunky and big boned, her Four Corners Dance Team T-shirt stretched tight across her plump midsection.

Chuck kept his tone neutral, aware that Carmelita almost certainly was listening from the living room. "Why would she say that?"

"She says you never let her do anything she wants."

"It's part of being a parent. I have to say no sometimes."

"You say no all the time."

"Is that you talking, or your sister?"

"Umm. Both."

"If you're speaking for both of you, then I'll respond to both of you." Chuck spun in his office chair to face the open door to the study and raised his voice, sending it down the hallway. "Your *mamá* has gone from working part-time to full-time with Durango Fire and Rescue. She's not around as much as before, which leaves the three of us to figure things out on our own sometimes. Last night just happened to be one of those times. One of the first times, actually."

Yesterday evening, with five minutes to spare, Carmelita had informed Chuck that she was about to be picked up by her friend Skye, in Skye's car, to attend another friend's birthday party. Like Carmelita, Skye had received her driver's license only recently. Therein lay the problem for Chuck, who had familiarized himself with Colorado's new-driver rules—one of which forbade teenage drivers from having other teenagers in their cars as passengers during their first six months as licensed drivers.

Chuck cited the rule in explaining his discomfort with Carmelita's catching a ride to the party with Skye. Carmelita immediately requested a second opinion from Janelle. But Saturday evenings were one of the busier times of the week for ambulance callouts, and Janelle didn't respond to Chuck's text.

He offered to drive Carmelita to the party himself. "You can stay as late as you want. I'll come get you whenever you call."

His suggestion earned him only a look of loathing from Carmelita. "Nobody follows the stupid no-teenage-passengers rule," she said, glaring at him. "It's idiotic. It's...it's subterranean. Nobody else's parents even care. Skye is, like, the best driver ever. Her mom made her take the extra-hours driving class and everything."

Carmelita stood with her feet planted on the kitchen floor, her fists on her hips. She was already decked out in her party outfit: flowered blouse with wide lapels, hip-hugging black jeans, and shiny leather boots. An orange scarf secured her long, black hair in a silky smooth ponytail at the back of her neck.

Chuck shuddered. This argument should not be happening. He and Carmelita weren't adversaries; they were best buddies.

During a visit to Yosemite National Park three years ago, he had introduced Carmelita to rock climbing, the sport that had consumed him as a young man, providing welcome escape and new friends for him after his lonely childhood spent in a profoundly broken home in Durango with his single mother and her string of odious boyfriends.

Carmelita had turned out to be a rock-climbing wunderkind. With her slender frame, extraordinary athleticism, and keen sense of balance, she had eclipsed Chuck's climbing abilities in a matter of days. Now, at sixteen, she was the champion sport climber in the region for her age, and she earned spending money coaching younger climbers at the local rock gym.

Unlike brash Rosie, Carmelita was soft-spoken, a true introvert. But she was quietly confident nonetheless, with a strong competitive drive that served her well in climbing contests.

Chuck traveled with her to competitions in cities around the Southwest—Denver, Salt Lake City, Phoenix—cheering her on as she took home trophy after trophy.

Her success was a result, in no small part, of the hard training she put in with him. They climbed rock faces outside town together on the weekends, and he belayed her on weekday evenings at the local indoor climbing gym, where she worked out on the gym's expert-level inverted wall after completing her coaching duties. During their climbing sessions, Carmelita confided in Chuck her worries about upcoming school tests—despite the fact she'd never gotten anything less than a B on any of her report cards. She even revealed to him her crushes on boys at Durango High School.

Chuck relished the close bond he shared with Carmelita. "This stepdad thing," he boasted to Janelle in the kitchen one day while the girls were at school, "I'm the *man*." He twirled a dishtowel above his head in triumph.

"Enjoy it while it lasts," she advised him.

Janelle's comment had proved prophetic last night, as Carmelita glowered at Chuck in the kitchen.

"Sorry, but you're not driving with Skye," he concluded, failing to come up with anything better.

"You…you *stink*," Carmelita sputtered.

Rosie sniffed the air from her seat at the dining table. "Like Pasta Alfredo's poop. I hate how that stuff smells."

Carmelita marched down the hall and pounded up the stairs to her low-ceilinged bedroom tucked beneath the eaves of the story-and-a-half house.

"Wow," Rosie said from the table, widening her eyes at Chuck.

"Yeah," Chuck acknowledged with a heavy sigh. "Wow is right."

In the end, Skye drove to their house in central Durango from her rural home, and she and Carmelita walked the several blocks to the party.

"Be sure you stick with Skye all the way there and back," Chuck admonished as Carmelita departed. "Your *mamá* and I don't want you on the streets alone after dark."

"Fine," she said with a sniff.

Chuck had stayed up until Carmelita returned home a few minutes after her midnight curfew. He continued to fly solo with Carmelita and Rosie this morning, while Janelle slept at the station after her twenty-four-hour shift.

Carmelita had stayed in her bedroom until late this morning, and she had addressed Chuck only in monosyllables when she descended the stairs and plopped on the couch, phone in hand, half an hour ago. Not even the videos of whitewater carnage Chuck offered up for viewing had enticed her down the hall to the study.

"I'm sorry about last night, Carm," he said through the open doorway. "I don't make the driving rules. But I can't ignore them, either, not without an okay from your *mamá*." He leaned back in his chair and gripped the armrests, Rosie at his side.

A subdued creak issued from the sofa, signaling Carmelita's rise. Footsteps sounded across the scarred oak floor of the living room, and the front door opened and slammed shut with an echoing bang.

4

"Well, that's not very nice," Rosie said as the echo of the slammed door died away.

"It's not easy being a teenager," Chuck replied, spinning to face her in his chair.

"I'm thirteen; I'm a teenager. It's easy for me."

"It'll get harder as you get farther into your teen years."

"How come?"

"It can be difficult to figure out who you are when you're sixteen, especially with your parents hanging around all the time, telling you what you can and cannot do."

"I already know who I am, and I always will."

Chuck grinned. "With you, that might well be true."

"Does Carm hate you because she doesn't know who she is yet?"

"I don't think she hates me."

"It sure seems like she does."

"Actually, for the most part, she and I have been having fun with the whole driving thing. She's been practicing a lot with me—going in reverse, parallel parking, working her way through tight places like parking lots. She's getting to be a good driver really quickly."

"I'm going to be a good driver, too. Just you wait." Rosie's gaze returned to the flipping rafts and flying passengers on the computer screen. "Why do you even want to do something like that?"

Chuck glanced at the screen. "Because it's fun."

"It doesn't look fun to me."

"That's kind of what makes it fun, if you know what I mean."

"Like how Carmelita likes rock climbing?"

"Yes, like that."

"But I don't."

"You're into dance instead."

Rosie had begun dance lessons a year ago, throwing herself into the local dance scene with her characteristic reckless abandon.

"I'm the most out-there dancer of them all." She gyrated her hands above her head and swiveled her torso, her feet twisting on the wood floor. "Everybody says so."

"I can see why."

Rosie was such an unabashed ham on the dance floor that her instructor had recommended she give Durango's youth improvisational comedy team a try. On the improv team, Rosie delivered her punchlines with exaggerated facial expressions and abrupt movements of her chunky frame, using her low, sandpapery voice to full effect.

"You're the most out-there comedian of all, too," Chuck said.

"I love improv almost as much as I love dance." She stopped moving. "But I'm never going on a rafting trip, not in my whole life."

Chuck aimed a thumb at the screen behind him. "Maybe I shouldn't have shown you the videos. I assumed you'd think it was exciting."

"Well, I don't. If that's what's going to happen to you and Uncle Clarence, why are you even going?"

"First, that's not what's going to happen to us—not if I can help it, anyway. Second, we're going because it'll be fun for me to do again after a long, long time, and it'll be entirely new for your uncle. Plus, we'll be part of something that hopefully will be good for everybody who lives in this part of the country."

"How can a rafting trip be good for everybody?"

"Because of all the super-smart people going on the expedition. They're rafting down the river together to make decisions about how best to use and conserve the water that flows out of the mountains and down into the deserts of the Southwest."

"You mean like the Animas River in Durango?"

"Yep. The Animas flows into the San Juan River, and the San Juan flows into the Colorado River. We'll be floating down the Colorado through Cataract Canyon."

"That's where all the rapids are, right?"

Chuck nodded. "They're famous because they're so big. But your uncle and I will be okay. Guides with lots of experience will be in charge of the expedition. I'll be working on the trip. So will your uncle Clarence. One of the expedition leaders is a friend of mine. He asked me to be the trip naturalist."

"What's that?"

"I'll give talks about the canyon—the rocks and plants and, of course, the archaeology."

Rosie was an avowed archaeology buff. She raised her eyebrows. "There's old stuff by the river?"

"Some, but not a whole lot. There aren't many ancient habitation sites because Cataract Canyon is in the middle of the desert. The only year-round water is the river itself. With the high canyon walls on each side, there's not much bottomland for growing food."

"It's in the middle of nowhere, right?"

"More or less, yes. It's in Canyonlands National Park, one of the most remote national parks in the country. John Wesley Powell explored the canyon back in the 1800s. His team ran into all sorts of problems in the rapids with their boats. Later on, the government looked into building a dam there, but the canyon was protected when the national park was created. It's a rugged place. No roads reach all the way to the river. There's no phone service, no people, no houses, nothing."

"So you'll be like a teacher on the trip, telling everybody about it."

"That's a good way to put it."

"And Uncle Clarence is going with you."

"I'm looking forward to taking him through the canyon."

"What do you mean, 'taking him through'?"

"I'll be rowing the gear boat. Clarence will be my passenger. He'll be the swamper on the expedition, doing all the extra work that needs doing. That's why he gets to go on the trip for free."

"He's lucky."

"He'll earn his way, believe me. He'll be busy the whole time. The amount of work that has to be done on a river trip is never-ending."

Rosie pointed at a capsized boat on Chuck's computer monitor. "What if that happens to you?"

"The gear boat is the biggest one on the expedition. It's almost impossible to flip."

"But Uncle Clarence has never been on a river trip. I bet he's scared, like I would be."

"I'm not sure your uncle is ever scared of anything. Besides, he can take care of himself. He's a big boy."

Rosie nodded gravely. "He sure is."

"I didn't mean it that way."

"He is, though," Rosie insisted. "If he went in the river, he'd float like a balloon, like, *no problema*."

Chuck smiled. "For his sake, I hope you're right."

Three days passed, during which Carmelita addressed Chuck only in one- or two-word phrases. By then, however, the ongoing rift between them wasn't Chuck's biggest concern, which instead was his growing sense of unease regarding the rapidly approaching expedition.

The initial invitation from his old friend Wayne Coswell to serve as naturalist and additional oarsperson on the trip had stirred recollections in Chuck's mind of his formerly independent bachelor self, and he'd responded to Wayne with a quick and hearty acceptance.

In the aftermath of his turbulent childhood in Durango, Chuck had crafted a quiet and even-keeled—if solitary—adult life for himself over the course of more than two decades, building a successful career as a self-employed archaeologist conducting digs and site surveys in national parks and on government lands across the West from his home base in Durango. Then he'd hired Clarence to assist him with a dig, and Clarence had introduced him to Janelle, Clarence's older sister.

Janelle and Chuck had married following a brief courtship, after which Janelle moved with Carmelita and Rosie from inner-city Albuquerque, New Mexico, into Chuck's aging Victorian in Durango. Overnight, nonstop chatter filled his formerly silent house, charger cords clogged the wall plugs, and salves, lotions, sprays, and gels overloaded the bathroom shelves.

Janelle took courses to become a paramedic and, upon earning her certification, found part-time work as an ambulance crew member with the Durango Fire and Rescue Department. A few months ago, as the girls grew older and increasingly independent, she had accepted a full-time position with the local emergency services provider.

After his many years of confirmed bachelorhood, Chuck relished his role as husband and stepfather. He particularly appreciated the increased parenting responsibilities he'd taken on these past months since Janelle had begun working full-time. He drove Rosie to her dance and improv practices, cooked basic meals for everyone, and washed, dried, and folded heaps of clothing in the musty basement, all while spending late nights in front of the computer, keeping up with his archaeological work.

The invitation to join the Waters of the Southwest Expedition had struck him as a welcome opportunity for a brief sabbatical from his satisfyingly frenetic life as a family man. He'd rafted Cataract Canyon twenty-some years ago, and the opportunity to run it again as he neared fifty initially had filled him with excitement. Now, however, with a week to go until the start of the journey, his excitement had turned to dread.

What had he been thinking when he'd accepted Wayne's invitation and secured a position for Clarence on the trip as well?

Once upon a time, Chuck had been an accomplished river runner. But he was long out of practice. On the expedition, he'd be an out-of-form rower facing some of the most challenging rapids in North America. Moreover, he'd be away from Janelle for two full weeks, their longest separation since they'd married.

At this point, the only solace he could find in the rapidly approaching trip was that, while he'd be away from Janelle for half a month, he'd be away from Carmelita for the same length of time—long enough, he hoped, for her anger at him to dissipate.

Chuck confessed his concerns to Janelle late in the afternoon. They were overturning soil in their raised-bed garden in the fenced backyard opposite the one-car garage, prepping to plant their usual smorgasbord of vegetables at the end of the month, after the risk of late-season freezes had passed.

"I never should have said yes to Wayne," he concluded, his stomach tight.

Janelle rested her gloved hands on the top of her shovel handle. "Well, then, don't go."

She wore jeans and a faded blue T-shirt bearing the logo of a boy band Carmelita had adored a couple years ago. A red bandanna circled her forehead, directing her long, black hair down her back.

"It's not that simple."

"Sure, it is. You've told me how lucky you were that Wayne invited you on the trip. I'm sure there are all sorts of people who would go in your place."

"The trip is only a week away."

"Still, if it's such a great opportunity…"

Chuck pressed his tongue to the roof of his mouth. "You're

right," he admitted. "Wayne probably knows of somebody who would be happy to replace me."

"You've told me river rafters jump at the chance when they get asked to go on trips at the last minute. You said you did that lots of times yourself."

"That's true, I did. The best rivers are so popular, with limited permits given out by lotteries months in advance, that people make a habit of going on trips as last-minute replacements."

"Like you used to do."

"Not anymore. Not with you and the girls."

"You'd better not be complaining," she warned, her eyes sparkling.

He raised his gloved hands to her, smiling. "*Nunca, cariña mia.*"

"I imagine it would be easy enough for Wayne to find a qualified naturalist to take your place, what with all the big-name water people going on the trip. Sounds like it's a golden ticket."

Chuck clapped dirt off his gloves. "That's the reason part of me still wants to go. With the right people, rafting trips are magical things. You're away from the outside world, working together as a team to get yourselves down the river. It's a great adventure. That's why I was happy to get Clarence invited along, too. I know he'll love it."

"Well then, go," Janelle said simply.

Chuck studied his work boots. "It's just, I should have thought more about what it would take to row the gear barge down Cataract Canyon."

"You said there'll be safety kayakers to come to your rescue in the unlikely event—to use your words—you or Clarence end up in the water."

He raised his head. "I'd have thought you'd be more worried about us."

"I would have been a few months ago. But not anymore. If there's one thing I've learned from working at Durango Fire and

Rescue, it's that people's lives can be totally upended in a second. Car wreck, ladder fall, ruptured aneurysm. It's made me realize that all of us—you, me, the girls, Clarence—have to just get on with whatever it is we want to get on with." She looked Chuck in the eye. "You're nervous. I get that. I'm nervous for you, and for Clarence. But only a little." She aimed her dimpled chin at him. "You want to know what I think?"

He shifted his boots in the soft dirt of the garden. "I'm not sure."

"I think you're worried about being embarrassed if it turns out you're not as good at the oars as you used to be." She shrugged. "If that's the case, so be it. We talk to the girls all the time about not giving in to peer pressure. Sounds to me like you need to remind yourself the same thing."

Chuck straightened. "If you hear after the trip about what a bumbling loser I was at the oars, do you promise not to think less of me?"

"Just come back in one piece, that's all I ask. And keep Clarence safe, too."

5

A week later, Janelle passed the garden bed on the way to the garage. The bed remained fallow, but a warm front over the last few days had caused flowers and bushes to bloom all across town.

Spring gave way quickly to summer in the sun-drenched Four Corners region where Colorado, New Mexico, Utah, and Arizona met. Even so, the explosion of blossoming daffodils and lilacs in front yards throughout Durango had taken her by surprise. This morning, Rosie had capped off Janelle's late-spring surprise when she'd entered the kitchen with her stocky legs stuffed into a pair of Carmelita's stretchy polyester climbing shorts.

"Oh, no, you don't," Janelle said, wagging her finger at Rosie. "You're not wearing those to school."

"But it's hot out now," Rosie protested. "It's like it's summer already. Everybody's wearing shorts."

"Carm only wears those at the climbing gym. Besides which, they fit her."

Rosie stomped her foot. "Awww."

Janelle pointed at Rosie's fleshy thighs bulging outward where the shorts ended. "That look does not flatter you, *m'hija*."

"I'm not fatter," Rosie protested. "I'm full-bodied, that's what you always say."

"Fatter, flatter, whichever. Your body is too full for Carm's clothing. If you really want to wear shorts to school now that it's getting warmer, we can look for some for you. But those?" She shook her head. "Uh-uh."

Rosie dropped her chin and folded her arms across her

chest, her lips turned down in a pout. She spun and marched out of the room.

Janelle had won the shorts battle this morning. But as she crossed the backyard in the fading evening light, she wondered how long such victories would continue. Not long, she imagined. Rosie had been headstrong since she was a baby, leading Janelle to suspect her younger daughter's teen years would be stormy and filled with defiance.

Janelle plucked a freshly opened leaf from a branch of the healthy young catalpa tree she and Chuck had planted next to the garage a couple of years ago. She caressed the pliant new leaf between her thumb and forefinger. Chuck and Clarence were leaving on the expedition in the morning. She'd bunched her shifts to free herself from work for the next two weeks and was looking forward to the time on her own with the girls—a chance to reconnect with them after her last few months of full-time work, and, perhaps, get a sense of what lay ahead with Rosie as she barreled into her teen years in Carmelita's wake.

Janelle dropped the leaf and entered the small garage, which functioned as a combined storage unit and workspace. A sturdy wooden workbench lined the back wall, opposite the alley-facing garage door. Shelves on the far wall held Chuck's archaeological equipment: hand trowels, metal buckets, steel-mesh sieves, and transparent plastic storage containers filled with survey flags and spools of twine. Two lower shelves on the near wall overflowed with outdoor gear—tents, sleeping bags, cookstoves, and fuel canisters—called upon when Chuck overnighted in the field during work assignments and when he, Janelle, Carmelita, and Rosie camped or backpacked as a family. The top shelf, above the outdoor items, was stacked with climbing gear—ropes, seat harnesses, pulleys, and aluminum cams and nuts—used by Chuck and Carmelita on their weekend climbs outside of town. An overhead shelf, suspended from the rafters by bolted two-by-fours, normally held plastic storage containers coated with dust.

Every now and then, when the screech of the girls' hair dryers and the thump of their hip-hop music became too much for Chuck, he disappeared from the house. On those occasions, Janelle invariably found him in the garage involved in a maintenance task of some sort. He'd be standing at the workbench, sewing a rip in a work glove with fishing line and suturing needle, or kneeling on the concrete floor, cleaning a cookstove with steel wool and scouring powder.

Chuck regularly noted to Janelle and the girls how important it was for archaeologists to be well organized. His profession, he explained, involved carefully tracking one obscure discovery to the next, and from there to the next, until, ultimately, a pattern emerged that revealed a complete picture of the past in all its fascinating detail. The nearly fanatical level of organization required of archaeology matched Chuck's personal fondness for order, which, he admitted, was one of the many reasons he relished his chosen career. As a result, Janelle recognized how jarring her and the girls' arrival into his life had been six years ago, making it easy for her to accept his periodic escapes to the garage for a few hours of solitude.

Today, Chuck had been in the garage packing for the expedition since lunchtime. Janelle had checked in a couple of times throughout the afternoon as he'd first outfitted Clarence, then himself, with items from the dusty storage containers he'd taken down from the overhead shelf for the first time since she and the girls had moved in with him. Earlier in the afternoon, gear from the containers had covered much of the garage floor, barely leaving room to stand. By now, however, Clarence had departed with his allotment of gear, and the last of the items from the overhead bins took up less than a third of the floor space in the garage.

The remaining items were arranged in compact piles. Half a dozen dry bags made of heavy-duty rubber were rolled and stacked by size from small to large. Pairs of canvas river shoes, neoprene booties, and strap sandals rested next to the dry bags.

Beside the footwear, a sun-bleached life jacket lay atop a neoprene wetsuit. Waterproof pants with seals at the ankles and a splash jacket with gaskets at the wrists and neck sat next to the wetsuit.

Chuck turned to Janelle as she pulled the back door to the garage closed behind her. An unusual look filled his eyes, not quite fear but something close to it—uncertainty, perhaps, or trepidation, words Janelle rarely associated with her husband.

She studied Chuck. He was her beacon of confidence. He had championed her pursuit of paramedic licensure and had insisted she put her certification to use. He had supported her move from part-time to full-time with the department, and when she'd begun working her full-time allotment of shifts, he'd stepped up his family duties uncomplainingly, enabling her to fulfill the long hours the position required.

For the first time in her life outside of raising the girls, Janelle had, as a paramedic, found true confidence in herself. She appreciated the opportunity to give back in her small way to the big, wide world that had supported her as a young, single mother to Carmelita and Rosie and that magically and inexplicably had given her Chuck as well.

He was her rock, her safe harbor—except that, here in the garage right this minute, the look in his eyes gave her pause.

This wasn't the Chuck she knew.

6

Janelle crossed the concrete floor of the garage to Chuck. "What is it? What's going on?"

"I'm not so sure about this," he said.

"You keep saying you and Clarence will be safe, that even though it's been a long time since you rowed, you're sure you'll be able to handle the rapids."

"It's not the rowing. It's being away from you and the girls for so long."

"Us? I'm not sure I believe that. You take off all the time to work in the field."

"Never for more than two or three days at a stretch, unless you and the girls come with me. The expedition is half a month long, and you're still in the start-up phase of your new job."

She searched his eyes. "There's more, isn't there?"

He exhaled. "It's the trip itself," he admitted. "There's something about it I can't quite put my finger on."

She breathed slowly, in, out. "Finally, the truth."

"The smartest water minds in the Southwest are going on the expedition, along with the biggest money players. I understand the idea of getting all of them together on the river for a couple of weeks to hash things out, but they're a pretty fiery bunch, and there's a lot at stake."

"Like what?"

"In a broad sense, the very survival of the human race. There are seven billion people on the planet, and every one of them needs water every day to survive. With climate change, water scarcity is fast becoming one of the most pressing issues in the world. That's especially true here in the southwestern US. It's one of the driest places on earth, and average temperatures here have risen four degrees since climate change really got rolling a few decades ago. That's three times the average increase for the rest of the planet, because our elevation is so high and our air is so dry. The extra heat equals less precipitation and more evaporation year after year, while the cities that depend on the decreasing supply of water keep getting bigger. The people coming on the expedition are responsible for divvying up the Southwest's water before everyone starts killing each other over it."

"You're making things sound pretty bad."

"Because they are. Drought is a constant in the Southwest these days, while demand for water keeps going up. Multinational corporations have begun buying up water rights from farmers and ranchers. Legislators are worried the corporations will charge extortionate prices for the water when demand outstrips supply. And that doesn't even begin to factor in the environmental damage from sucking more and more water out of the rivers and underground aquifers for human use." Chuck nudged one of the dry bags with his toe, aligning it with the other bags. "So far, at least, the fighting between the factions has been limited to shouting matches."

Janelle was relieved to see that the more Chuck talked, the more animated he became, and the less worry showed in his eyes. "'So far'?"

"There hasn't been any gunfire yet. But water levels in the reservoirs in the Colorado River Basin are decreasing every year. Cities and farmers are digging deeper wells and sucking underground aquifers dry, too."

"How is it you know so much about this stuff?"

"Archaeology is directly tied to climate change. That's especially true for me, because I mostly study the Ancestral Puebloans who lived around here until the 1200s, when they abandoned the area—most likely because of a prolonged drought combined with population growth and overuse of resources."

"Like what's happening today."

"Precisely," he said. "The goal of the expedition is to figure out how to keep what happened to the Ancestral Puebloans from happening again."

"I don't see why that should make you so worried."

"Wayne and a friend of his, a retired law professor named Ralph Hycum, came up with the idea for the expedition because water in the Southwest is fast becoming a commodity—that is, something of value, like coal or gold or copper. And something of value is something worth fighting over, by those who control the water now, and those who want control of it. With the value of water in the Southwest increasing, more corporate players are coming after it. Extractive industry folks, mostly. Big mining conglomerates, and big ag, too."

"You mean, big agriculture?"

Chuck nodded. "Multinational farming and meat-production companies. They know how to get what they want, and what they want these days is water. There's someone from Consilla Corporation, the single biggest owner of farmland west of the Mississippi, coming on the expedition. On the extractive side, a bigwig from Amalgamated Mining and Minerals is coming, too."

"I've never heard of either of them."

"Not many people have. That's the way they like it. Both companies are privately held. If you could get a look at their balance sheets, though, you'd be blown away."

"Okay, I get it: big money."

"Versus the ones trying to do the right thing for we, the people. That would be government representatives and policymakers at universities and think tanks. The corporations are buying up water rights as fast as they can. The Colorado River is the biggest prize of them all. Cities like Los Angeles, Las Vegas, and Phoenix depend on it. The river is a public resource, or it should be. If the corporations get control of it, though, they'll be able to charge whatever they want for its water. They'll hold the citizens hostage."

"What's the expedition supposed to do about that?"

"Wayne and Ralph are billing the trip as a fact-finding mission, a chance for the two sides to experience the Colorado River together up close and personal. But Wayne told me he and Ralph are hoping for a lot more from the trip. They convinced the biggest policymakers to sign on first. That forced the corporations to sign on, too, so they wouldn't look bad. The plan is for the participants to debate each other in the evenings while they're in the canyon, away from the media, where they can lay their cards on the table. If things go as Wayne and Ralph hope, the sides could potentially come to basic understandings that would put an end to the squabbling that's been going on for decades over the Colorado River Compact."

"The Colorado River what?"

"Compact. It's an agreement signed in 1922 that divided the water in the Colorado River between the four Upper Basin states at the headwaters of the river and the three Lower Basin states at the downstream end. Problem is, the compact was based on a series of super-wet years in the early 1900s. The flow levels in the river decreased after the compact was signed, so its numbers have never worked. To make matters worse, California built a canal from the Colorado River to Los Angeles in the 1930s and planned to start pumping more than its share of water down it. In response, the governor of Arizona put two armed gunboats on the river to protect Arizona's interests. California finally backed down, but the disagreements between the states never went away. Now, with climate change turning the water in the Colorado River into liquid gold, the corporations have shown up with their checkbooks, too."

"What if the policymakers and corporate people don't come to terms with one another on the expedition?"

The look of concern returned to Chuck's eyes. "That's the multimillion-dollar question—literally."

"Why haven't you told me any of this until now?"

Chuck eyed the rafting items on the floor of the garage. "On the surface, this is just a simple river trip with a bunch of experts getting to know one another while floating through Cataract Canyon." His gaze came back to her. "As far as the discussions between the two sides go, the result of the trip might well be what Wayne and Ralph hope: honest communication that will lead to better cooperation between all the parties in the years ahead." He paused. "Or they might just go to war with each other right there on the banks of the river instead."

Janelle pooched her lips. "Just like Arizona was ready to start shooting at California."

"There's no love lost between the policymakers and corporate people, that's for sure. Policymaking is all about thinking long-term, while corporations are focused on their next quarterly profit statements."

"Sounds like a powder keg."

Chuck nodded, his mouth tight. "One that's been getting closer to blowing up ever since the compact was signed a century ago."

7

The washboarded dirt road to the put-in on the Green River at Ruby Ranch, sixty miles north of Moab, Utah, passed through a desolate landscape of gray hills studded with dry, brown switchgrass. The road ended at the river's edge, where a sandy ramp sloped into the calm water of the river. The expedition rafts floated in the water, rigged for launch and snugged against the shore, their bow lines running to aluminum stakes driven into the ground.

It was mid-morning. Already the day was broiling hot. The upstream breeze would start up in an hour or two, as it did every clear day, generated by the heat of the sun. For now, however, the air next to the river was still. The riverbank smelled of mud and decay. Cicadas buzzed in clumps of willows and Russian olive trees growing in the damp soil at the river's edge. A tall stand of cottonwoods towered over the smaller trees and bushes.

Chuck lifted his broad-brimmed hat and wiped his sweaty brow with the long sleeve of the cotton dress shirt he'd picked up from a thrift shop in Durango. The light blue shirt was crisp and clean. After daily use for the next two weeks, however, it would be grimy and torn, its underarms rank with body odor no matter how vigorously he scrubbed it in the river each evening.

The pair of matching passenger vans that had delivered the expedition's two dozen clients to the put-in trailed twin clouds of dust as they drove away from the river. The clients gathered in a semicircle beneath the shade of the cottonwood trees facing Wayne and Ralph, the expedition leaders, and Colorado River Adventures head river guide Tamara Fisher.

Chuck returned his hat to his head and tapped it down over

his brow. He, Clarence, and Tamara's team of half a dozen CRA guides stood in a group behind the trip's paying customers.

Ralph raised an arthritic hand to the assemblage. The retired professor's face was heavily lined, his shoulders stooped and bony. He wore a lightweight plaid shirt and khaki slacks cinched with a cracked leather belt high and tight around his narrow waist. His rheumy eyes were set deep in their sockets behind thick glasses, while a pair of sunglasses, oversized to fit over his clear-lensed glasses, hung around his neck. His sunhat sat back on his head, revealing a high forehead speckled with sun spots.

"What a pleasure it is to see so many familiar faces here today," he said. "Wayne and I are honored that you have chosen to spend the next two weeks with us, and with one another, as we float together through Canyonlands—the most beautiful national park in the country, as far as I'm concerned—and as we discuss the pressing water issues to which many of us gathered here today have devoted our professional lives."

Ralph lowered his hand.

"Many of you know one another well," he continued. "You've authored papers together as academicians. You've sat on the same panels at conferences. Some of you, I know, are godparents to each others' children." His eyes roamed the group. "Others of you, from the world of industry and agriculture, are relative newcomers to the world of water allocation."

He tipped his head forward.

"I welcome each and every one of you on this journey of discovery and, I sincerely hope, connection. There will be differences of opinion among us. Some of those differences will be stark and thorny and difficult to overcome. But overcome them we must, for the people who depend on the water flowing in the Southwest's rivers, and for the plants and animals in the river corridors that require a share of that water, too."

In front of Chuck, the expedition clients shifted their feet. Several shot sidelong glances at those around them. The group was an even mix of men and women, ranging in age from their thirties to their mid-sixties.

Younger members of the group wore T-shirts, shorts, and strap sandals. Older group members were dressed like Ralph, in long-sleeved shirts and long pants that ranged in color from tan to light gray. Rather than sandals, the older group members wore river shoes—lace-up sneakers with grippy rubber soles. Everyone wore broad-brimmed sunhats or baseball caps, their faces doubly shaded by the brims of their hats and the cottonwoods overhead.

Half the outfits worn by the clients were stained and bleached by the sun. Those who wore the well-used clothing made up the left side of the semicircle. Clearly, they were the trip's water-policy experts, veterans of countless river journeys. Most of those on the right side of the semicircle wore brand-new clothing, outing themselves as the trip's corporate representatives. Creases lined the legs of their pants, and the bright colors of their pristine shirts glowed in the shade beneath the trees.

Wayne pushed his hat up on his brow with his thumb. He was younger than Ralph, in his early fifties. His bushy, black-and-gray eyebrows matched his salt-and-pepper hair, which fell across his forehead and covered his ears. His faded yellow sun shirt featured epaulets for buttoning the sleeves at the elbows.

"Ralph is right—all of us come from differing backgrounds and represent different viewpoints," Wayne said. "We will share our varied ideas during our journey together over the next two weeks, with the goal not necessarily of changing each other's minds, but of opening our minds to what each and every one of us has to say."

A harsh chuckle came from a stout man in his forties on the right side of the semicircle. Unlike the new clothing of the corporate representatives standing around him, the man's long-sleeved sun shirt was bleached by the sun at the shoulders and stained with sweat beneath the arms. His straw-colored hair poked from the hat he wore low over his slate-gray eyes. "You mean, we even have to listen to Sylvia?" he asked Wayne.

"Leon," warned a cinnamon-haired woman standing among the river guides, her green eyes flashing. She was short and muscular, in her thirties, and wore tight shorts and a torso-hugging surf-shirt that revealed her bare, flat midriff.

Leon lifted his shoulders to the woman in a taunting shrug. "Everybody here knows you're the one we need to be worried about the most, Sylvia, because you never listen to anyone else's opinions but your own."

A twenty-something female guide standing near Chuck muttered beneath her breath, "That didn't take long."

The female guide was tall and willowy, with wispy blond hair. She wore a fitted cotton shirt and lightweight cargo pants. Voluminous pockets hung outward from the sides of her pant legs, which bunched at her ankles. Freckles dotted her face and the backs of her hands, the only parts of her skin exposed to the sun.

A male guide standing next to the blond guide replied to her, his voice barely above a whisper, "You got that right, Maeve."

The male guide was several inches shorter than Maeve and a few years older. He had a large, bulbous nose and wore shorts and a tank top, his bare legs and shoulders bronzed by the sun.

"Gonna be an interesting trip, Vance," Maeve said beneath her breath to the male guide.

"Ain't it, though," he agreed.

Sylvia raised her chin. "Everyone I've talked to says you're the one we should be worried about," she said to Leon, "now that you've gone over to the dark side."

The expedition clients stood silent and unmoving.

"My, oh my," Leon said with a sneer. "Hell hath no fury..." He let the sentence dangle.

Sylvia aimed a stiff finger at him, her face reddening. "It was me who divorced you, remember? *I* scorned *you.*"

At Chuck's side, Vance shifted his feet. "Leon and Sylvia were married? I never heard that."

"I thought everybody knew," Maeve whispered to him.

Leon put his hands to his chest and toppled backward. A man and woman on either side of him grabbed his elbows and stood him back upright, their faces set.

"Thank you," Leon said, nodding to each of them in turn. He made a show of brushing off his shirtsleeves with brisk whisks of his hands, and then addressed Sylvia, his voice cold. "I wasn't referring to us. I was referring to Consilla. They're the ones who scorned you, remember? Or have you forgotten that little detail?"

"That's *enough!*" Ralph growled before Sylvia could respond. "We'll have no more of this. Wayne and I convinced Tamara it would be all right for both of you to come on the trip. We promised her the two of you would get along."

Sylvia jabbed her finger at Leon. "He started it. You heard him."

"Not...another...word," Ralph commanded. "Do you hear me? Not from either of you." He looked around the semicircle. "This is a gathering of knowledge. We, all of us, have pledged to travel down the river together in peace and in search of mutual understanding." He shoved his glasses up the bridge of his nose and regarded Leon. "If you cannot live up to that pledge, you can leave the trip right now."

"I'll be good from here on out," Leon muttered.

Ralph turned to Sylvia.

"As long as he keeps his mouth shut," she said, glaring at Leon, "I'll do the same."

"I guess that'll have to do," Ralph said. Behind his thick glasses, his eyes were fierce and alive with purpose, offering no indication of the fate awaiting him only three days later.

8

Wayne resumed his welcome speech.

While he spoke, Chuck said softly in Clarence's ear, "I'd recommend you keep your distance from that guy, Leon."

"*Por supuesto*," Clarence whispered back, nodding. The thick silver studs festooning his earlobes wagged along. "Of course. I think I'll just stick with the river guides."

Clarence looked past Chuck at the CRA employees. His gaze lingered on a short, muscular woman in her mid-twenties. She was barely five feet tall, her shoulders broad and powerful. Beneath the brim of her woven-sisal hat, the woman's dark face was burnished by the sun. Her charcoal-black hair fell down her back in a thick braid.

The guides ranged in age from their twenties, like the woman Clarence had his eye on, to their forties. They were uniformly tanned, their arms and legs rippling with muscle.

Matching the man Chuck knew him to be, Wayne's tone was calm and reassuring as he spoke to the group. His voice retained the flat vowels of his New England upbringing. He'd left Massachusetts to attend Fort Lewis College in Durango, where he and Chuck had met, and he had gone on to make the desert Southwest his home. After earning a PhD in water resource management at Arizona State University, he had put together a career as an adjunct professor at Northern Arizona University in Flagstaff and as a private consultant overseeing water development projects and mediating disputes over water rights between federal agencies, Native American tribes, metropolitan districts, and agricultural and corporate interests. Over the years, Wayne had recommended Chuck's firm, Bender Archaeological, for many of the detailed archaeological assessments required before water pipelines were laid or canals dug.

The deep respect for Wayne and Ralph among those in the policy world had led the Southwest's top water policymakers to sign up for the expedition as soon as the two men announced its formation. Through his consultant contacts, Wayne had then reached out to the corporate side. In recent years, he had explained to Chuck, corporations had been buying up rights to larger allotments of water than they'd purchased in the past.

"Sounds like they're already in the driver's seat," Chuck noted. "Why would they bother coming on the expedition?"

"Their bigger purchases come with increased risks," Wayne replied. "State legislatures could pass laws demanding corporations hand over the water rights they control to the public. If the courts were to uphold those laws, the corporations would be left with nothing. They know they'll have to compromise along the way if they're to profit off the rights they're purchasing. They just want the compromises to be as favorable to their side as possible. Spending two weeks on the river with policymakers is a good way for them to gauge how far they can push things their direction."

"I imagine the corporate representatives who are coming on the expedition are the ones who drew the short straws in their offices."

"Most likely," Wayne agreed. "Except the Consilla representative. He's a former river guide who switched to the business side. When I called him, he jumped at the chance to come on the trip. His name is Leon Madsen."

Beneath the cottonwoods at the put-in, Wayne completed his opening remarks and, aiming a stern look at Leon, echoed Ralph's comments to the river-guide-turned-corporate-representative. "Of all the people on this trip," he said, "you, Leon, should know better than to start things off by attacking someone, your ex most of all."

"I was just giving her a hard time," Leon protested weakly.

"When Sylvia was put on the schedule to work this trip, Ralph and I decided to keep you on the client list because we felt your river experience made your inclusion worthwhile. Now, however, I'm not so sure. We have some tough discussions ahead of us. All of us will have to be on our best behavior, you included."

Leon held Wayne's gaze. "I will be. I promise."

Wayne pursed his lips. He turned his back to Leon and introduced Tamara, beside him, as one of the most experienced rafting guides in the Southwest, with more than twenty seasons on various rivers in the Colorado River Basin. "Tamara will say a few words about safety," he said, "after which we'll all have a chance to double-check our personal gear before we shove off."

Tamara was in her late forties, trim and fit. A few tendrils of gray showed amid the tawny brown hair framing her tanned face below her straw cowboy hat.

She addressed the expedition clients on the left side of the semicircle. "I know we have a great deal of experience on this trip, so I'll make this brief." She shifted her attention to the corporate representatives on the right. "With regard to safety, we'll hold a complete briefing when we get to the rapids next week. For now, I'll simply ask that when we're on the water, you do as your boat captains tell you, and that you remember the first two rules of flatwater river travel." She held up a finger. "One: always wear your PFD—that is, your personal flotation device, or life jacket." She raised a second finger. "Two: be sure to pee before you get on your boat."

She stared hard at Leon, then scrutinized the rest of the clients. "I've been told to expect a certain amount of friction between the whole lot of you as we travel downriver together. I understand that's part of the idea behind the expedition." She inhaled through her nose. "River trips can be pressure cookers, filled with argument and misunderstanding. Or they can be what they're meant to be: fun and relaxing and adventurous all at the same time. For the sake of the expedition, I hope what we just witnessed is the worst of the former we'll see over the next two weeks." She smiled, but her face was stiff. "The last thing we need on this trip is any of you trying to kill each other."

The group broke up, guides heading to the boats, clients lining up before a pair of portable toilets set beneath the trees.

At a tap on his shoulder, Chuck turned to face a stocky man with a thick, dark brown beard and mustache. The man wore a T-shirt bearing the Colorado River Adventures company logo—a cartoon river raft atop a standing wave—and khaki shorts. A compact leather holster for a folding knife was strapped to the black nylon belt that held up his shorts, and a blue bandanna was knotted around his neck. His collar-length hair was corralled beneath a battered ball cap. The brow of the cap bore a logo with the letters CSM surrounding a small, brown circle with rays emanating from it, overlain with the outline of a dump truck. "You're our trip naturalist?" he asked.

"That's me," said Chuck.

The man extended his hand. "Sam Rockwell, Tamara's senior guide, which puts me just a smidgen above the other guides. You can call me Rocky, like everybody else." Rocky spoke with a deep southern accent. His palm was hard with callouses. "Tam says you know your stuff."

"Wayne must've told her that. When it comes to my naturalist duties, I'd agree with her. But it's been a lot of years since I've been on a river."

"What are your concerns?"

"The size of the gear boat, mostly. Its lack of maneuverability."

"I hear you, partner. But when we get to the rapids, the size of the boat will be your best friend, on account of how unlikely it'll be to flip. Besides, you'll have a week before that to get yourself comfortable at the oars again. By the time we get to the meat of the river, you'll probably be the one giving me pointers rather than the other way around." Rocky grasped Chuck's shoulder. "I'm going to have you run sweep, at the back of the line, to stay out of the way of the paying customers. How's that sit with you?"

"That'll be fine. I want to stay out of everyone's way, too."

"I'll fall back to check on you every now and then. Rest assured, though, if the barge ends up being too much for you, we can always find a sub from the customer ranks. Like Tam said, this is an experienced group." He squeezed Chuck's shoulder. "I've got all the faith in the world in you, though, partner."

Rocky headed for the boats lined along the shore.

Clarence gripped Chuck's shoulder and mimicked Rocky's accent. "Ah have all the faith in the world in y'all, ya hear?"

Chuck grinned. "You don't do southern very well, you know that?"

"*Sí*," Clarence agreed. He continued in Spanish, then repeated the words in English, replacing Rocky's drawl with his own distinctively Latino accent. "*La verdad, jefe, es que*...the truth, chief, is that I'll have to be sure and hold on tight to my own *acento* on this trip, just to remind myself who I am around all these gringos."

Chuck regarded the expedition clients. Most were in line at the porta potties. Others slathered sunscreen on their exposed skin or filled personal water bottles from a five-gallon jug on a folding table next to the boat ramp. As Clarence noted, they were overwhelmingly white, with only a handful of people of color.

All the CRA guides were Anglo as well, except for the young guide who'd caught Clarence's eye. She knelt beside a bright yellow kayak at the river's edge, loosening a ratchet strap in the boat's compact cockpit.

Chuck tilted his head at her. "She's no gringa."

"No, she's not," Clarence said. He observed her with big, round eyes. "*Caramba*," he whispered.

"Do you know how awful you sound?"

"I sound like I'm in love. Because I am."

Chuck slapped Clarence's arm. "You're the swamper on the expedition. The grunt. The first thing you do is anything and everything that needs to be done. The last thing you do is anything and everything that needs to be done. You won't have much time, if any, for fraternizing. But if you do, you do it with respect. You got that?"

"You know me, *jefe*."

"That's the problem."

"I'll be good. I promise."

"You sound like Leon."

"I'm a way nicer *hombre* than him."

"I'm serious, Clarence. Privacy is a scarce thing on river trips. If you play Don Juan during the expedition, everybody's going to know about it."

"Don't you worry. I won't have to make any sort of play for her whatsoever." Clarence cracked a grin, his eyes twinkling. "My animal magnetism will attract her to me instead."

9

That evening, Chuck pitched his small, solo tent next to the two-man tent he'd given to Clarence to accommodate his brother-in-law's bulkier frame. His and Clarence's shelters and the rest of the group's tents lined the back of the point of sand selected by Tamara as the expedition's initial campsite, five miles downstream from the put-in.

As the sun fell in the west and the day cooled, Chuck sat in front of his tent, checking his notes in advance of his first naturalist presentation. A day removed from Janelle and the girls, he was surprisingly content. He'd forgotten how nice it was to camp on the shore of a gurgling river, away from civilization.

The expedition hadn't yet entered the high walls of the deep canyon farther downstream. Rather, the same low hills as those at the put-in stretched to the distant horizon from both sides of the river, the blue sky arcing overhead. The steady upstream wind that had required Chuck to augment the sluggish current by rowing the gear boat downstream through the middle of the afternoon had relented with the onset of evening. Mosquitos and biting flies hummed in the thicket of tamarisk trees that formed a dense wall behind the tents.

The insects did not venture out of the invasive tamarisk trees, which had been imported from the Middle East during the Dust Bowl years in an attempt to control erosion along the banks of the desert rivers in the Southwest. Unfortunately, the idea had worked too well. The bushy tamarisk overwhelmed the Southwest's riverbanks, shutting out the native willows and cottonwoods that formerly blanketed the rivers' riparian zones.

Today, tamarisk trees contributed significantly to the desertification of the Southwest, sinking their roots much deeper into the soil than native plants, sucking water from far underground, and perspiring the moisture into the dry air in prodigious amounts.

While Chuck worked on his presentation, Clarence helped the CRA guides prepare dinner in the camp kitchen, which consisted of three long tables set in a U-shape, the tables' metal legs pounded into the sand for stability. Cookstoves, utensils, and cutting boards topped the sturdy tables.

Clarence stood shoulder to shoulder with the female safety kayaker, chopping onions and chatting with her, his wide, sparkly smile filling his face.

Chuck stowed his notes when Tamara rang a bell, calling everyone to dinner. The meal was served buffet style, first to the trip clients, then to the guides and Chuck and Clarence.

"Her name is Liza," Clarence reported to Chuck as they ate. "I figured she was Latina, but she's not. She's Ute Mountain Ute, from Towaoc."

The tribal lands of the Ute Mountain Ute people abutted Mesa Verde National Park forty miles west of Durango. The small town of Towaoc was the capital of the Ute Mountain Ute Tribe.

"She's a fellow southwest Coloradoan with you," Chuck noted. "Almost your neighbor."

After dinner, Clarence washed dishes with Liza in the camp kitchen while Chuck stood before the clients at the water's edge. By now, the sun had set behind the hills on the far side of the river.

The clients sat in folding camp chairs in a half-circle facing Chuck. They remained divided as at the put-in, corporate representatives on one side, policymakers on the other. They sipped after-dinner drinks and scooped spoonfuls of the evening's dessert—cherry cheesecake crumble—out of bowls balanced in their laps.

Chuck began with Cataract Canyon's human history.

"A few Ancestral Puebloans settled along the Colorado River south of here a thousand years ago, farming and building stone homes and granaries," he recounted. "Another group, closely related to the Ancestral Puebloans, settled along the Green River and its tributaries at about the same time. They're known to anthropologists as the Fremont people, named after the Fremont River in central Utah that, in turn, was named for early white explorer John Fremont. The Ancestral Puebloans and Fremont people are renowned for the residences, granaries, and spiritual structures known as kivas they constructed out of stone and mortar, many beneath overhanging cliffs. Both groups dispersed in the 1200s, leaving their cliff dwellings intact for archaeologists like me to study. After the departure of the Fremont people and Ancestral Puebloans, the Ute people migrated into the region. They had the area pretty much to themselves over the centuries that followed—until 1869."

He looked around the semicircle, waiting.

"JWP," said Leon, slouched in his webbed seat, his hands wrapped around a steel tumbler in his lap.

"Right," Chuck said. "John Wesley Powell."

Leon raised his cup, congratulating himself.

"Major Powell was a one-armed veteran of the Civil War," Chuck told the group. "He was a cartographer and geologist. After the war, with a crew of eight men, he was the first known explorer to navigate the rapid-filled canyons of the Green and Colorado Rivers."

He waved his hand at the calm waters of the Green River flowing around the point of sand.

"The Powell Geographic Expedition floated right around this bend and on south to where the Green River meets the Colorado River. The team continued downstream beyond the confluence of the two rivers, as will we when we reach the confluence next week. The cataracts, or rapids, below the confluence constituted the toughest stretch of whitewater Powell and his men had encountered to that point, leading them to name the gorge Cataract Canyon. One of the team's wooden boats was pulverized in the very first rapid in the canyon. The wreckage of the boat, abandoned onshore, remained visible from the river for decades afterward."

"Until it disappeared," Leon interjected.

"What's that?" Chuck asked.

Leon straightened in his seat. "Don't play coy with me. All of us on this trip who have any sense at all know perfectly well why you're here." He blasted a derisive jet of air between his lips. "Naturalist, smashrulist. *Ha*. You're one of the best-known archaeologists in the country, what with your discoveries and published papers and finds displayed in museums all over the place. I know why you're on this trip. All of us do. You want to follow up on the rumor."

"I don't know what you're—" Chuck began.

"Oh, yes, you *do* know what I'm talking about," Leon said, cutting Chuck off. "The boat wreckage was there, then it was gone. Did a flood really wash it away, as the Bureau of Reclamation claims? Or—as many people believe, me included—did it never leave the canyon? You know as well as I do how important Powell's legacy is to historians, which means the wreckage of his boat would be headline news if it was ever recovered. Beyond that, it would be a career-defining find for any archaeologist—even a big-name one like you."

Chuck turned to the group. "Leon brings up an interesting point," he said, seeking to direct the conversation back to the expedition's overarching subject, water policy. "In recent years, people increasingly have come to recognize how forward-thinking John Wesley Powell was regarding the lack of water in the Southwest."

"What about the boat wreckage?" Leon urged.

"I like treasure hunts as much as anyone," Chuck admitted,

"and Powell's lost boat certainly would qualify as archaeological treasure. But the rapids where the boat was lost are still a week downriver from here. We'll have plenty of time to discuss the possibilities in the days ahead." He cocked his head at Leon. "In the meantime, if you'll allow me to bring everyone up to speed, we'll all be able to use that information to consider what might have happened to the Powell boat wreckage."

"I like it," Leon said with a nod. "That way everyone will be in on it together. But when we get below the confluence, it'll be each man for himself."

In the camp kitchen, Sylvia paused while drying a handful of silverware. "Herself," she said. "Each woman for herself and each man for himself."

Leon smirked at her. "Sorry. Didn't mean to leave you out, babe."

"Don't you dare 'babe' me," she snapped.

Leon grinned and asked those seated around him, "Or should I call her 'they'? Isn't that how we're supposed to refer to each other nowadays? No more he or she. Just they." He directed a thumb over his shoulder at Sylvia. "It'll be each person for *they* selves."

"Jerk," Sylvia muttered, slamming the silverware into a tray with a noisy clank.

Chuck cleared his throat, drawing attention back to his presentation. "Jumping ahead a century from the Powell expedition," he said, "how many of you have read the book *Encounters with the Archdruid*, by John McPhee?"

Several people raised their hands, all of them on the policymaker side of the half circle. Perhaps it was Chuck's imagination, but after Leon's discussion of the missing boat wreckage, everyone seemed more attentive than before.

He nodded approvingly. "That's more than I expected, considering the book came out in 1977," he said. "I'm mentioning it now, on our first evening together, because it bears many similarities to our own Waters of the Southwest Expedition. In the book, McPhee describes a series of meetings between government officials and the archdruid himself—David Brower, the first executive director of the Sierra Club. To this day, Brower is known as our nation's greatest environmentalist. He's credited with putting the environmental movement on the map in the US through sheer force of will. But even the most successful people don't succeed all the time. Those of you who've read the book will remember what Brower considered his most monumental failure."

Chuck aimed his chin down the river.

"Brower's failure occurred two hundred miles south of here, early in his career, when he made a deal with the Bureau of Reclamation that he shouldn't have. At the time, the bureau was damming rivers all across the West. One of their plans called for building a dam in today's Dinosaur National Monument. Another plan called for a seven-hundred-foot-high concrete dam between high sandstone walls in northern Arizona. Brower told the feds that if they abandoned their plans for the Dinosaur dam, he and the Sierra Club would not stand in the way of the Arizona dam, which would drown a two-hundred-mile stretch of the Colorado River north into Utah known as Glen Canyon."

The Green River murmured behind Chuck. The evening breeze sighed through the tamarisk branches. A canyon wren called from a crumbly wall of gray stone set in the hillside beyond the screen of tamarisk, its mournful, descending cry echoing in the gathering dusk.

"The problem was that Brower had no idea what he was giving up when he made the deal that sealed Glen Canyon's fate. When he finally got around to visiting Glen Canyon, he found a Garden of Eden in the desert. Trickling creeks. Trees and grasses and flowers amid the harsh, red-rock splendor of southern Utah's incomparable canyon country. Ancient homesites of the Ancestral Puebloans who'd lived in the canyon a thousand years ago. Modern-day homes and farms and fruit orchards of the San Juan Southern Paiute people who'd populated Glen Canyon for centuries after the Ancestral Puebloans left the area. Brower was astounded by the grandeur of what he saw. But it was too late by then. He'd already made his deal with the devil. Everything he saw was covered by water after Glen Canyon Dam was completed in 1963. Spurred by what he called the biggest sin he ever committed, he devoted every waking moment for the rest of his life to protecting the last of the West's free-flowing rivers. For those efforts, he became known as the archdruid—the high priest of the conservation movement in America."

Chuck looked around the semicircle.

"That's where all of you come in, whether you appreciate Glen Canyon Dam for its hydroelectricity generation and storage capacity, or hate it for what it drowned. You've been invited on this trip to discuss how best to allocate the Southwest's water resources while also preserving the fragile environment of the desert Southwest. In *Conversations with the Archdruid*, McPhee provided a written record of the age-old push-pull between development and conservation. He went along as a journalist on a rafting trip down the Colorado River that included Brower and Floyd Dominy, the head of the Bureau of Reclamation and Brower's arch-nemesis. While Dominy was working to dam every mile of every river in the western US, the environmental movement under Brower's leadership was growing increasingly powerful. By the time Dominy rafted the Colorado River with Brower, the Bureau of Reclamation was on the defensive, failing time and again to win public support for its proposed dams in the West—a string of failures that began when Dominy, just like Brower, suffered the greatest failure of *his* career."

Chuck pointed at the purple evening sky overhead. "Dominy's failure occurred up there in the air, directly above where we're sitting right now."

10

Ralph stirred in his camp chair. "Thank God for Dominy's screwup," he said. "Thank Stewart Udall, too."

Chuck nodded toward the retired professor. "If David Brower was the archdruid of the environmental movement, then Stewart Udall was the environmental movement's arch-*political*-druid."

Ralph returned Chuck's nod. "Stewart Udall is the only reason we're rafting down this stretch of river. Udall and his buddy, Bates Wilson, that is. I met Floyd Dominy once, at the very start of my career. He was retired, same as I am now. I interviewed him for a paper I was writing. He was so old he could barely get out of his chair to greet me. But there was still plenty of energy in his voice when he laid out his case for dams on every river in the West, no matter what would be drowned in the process. He never changed, even after the world passed him by—and even after *his* biggest failure." Ralph looked at Chuck. "But I'm stealing your thunder, aren't I?"

Chuck confirmed to everyone, "Dominy never saw a river he didn't want to dam. In fact, the only thing that excited him more than damming one river was damming two rivers at once. He succeeded at that with Glen Canyon Dam, which, in addition to backing up the Colorado River to the north, also backs up the San Juan River to the east. A twofer, as it were."

Chuck glanced at the Green River behind him.

"We left Moab, on the banks of the Colorado River, this morning, and drove west, up and over the Island in the Sky massif, to our put-in on the banks of the Green River. The Green flows south from its headwaters in Wyoming, while the Colorado flows west from its headwaters near Denver. The two rivers meet in the center of Canyonlands National Park. Their confluence divides the national park into its three distinct districts, which are not connected by roads within the park. The Island in the Sky District rises between the two rivers at the north end of Canyonlands, the Needles District is on the east side of the rivers, and the remote Maze District makes up the park's western third. Long before Canyonlands was created, though, Floyd Dominy had his eye on this area for what he was convinced would be his greatest triumph—a dam in Cataract Canyon, below the confluence of the Green and Colorado Rivers, that would block two of America's mightiest rivers in one fell swoop. In so doing, Dominy would create two giant pools of water, one stretching east along the Colorado River to Moab, the other north along the Green River to Interstate 70."

Chuck paused, allowing everyone to take in the stillness of the desert evening.

"The beauty of Dominy's scheme was that, like Glen Canyon to the south, the remote Utah canyons of the Green and Colorado Rivers were unknown to most Americans. Once the canyons were under hundreds of feet of water, it would be as if they'd never existed. By 1961, Dominy's Bureau of Reclamation engineers were in Cataract Canyon drilling test adits into the canyon walls to study the porosity of the stone. That year, enthralled with his idea, Dominy flew south in a small plane to a conference in Grand Canyon National Park with Stewart Udall, who'd just been named secretary of the interior in the Kennedy administration. Dominy directed the pilot to fly over Cataract Canyon so he could point out to Udall the sublime perfection of his proposed dam. But when Udall looked out the window of the plane, he saw something entirely different than Dominy."

"He saw a new national park," said Ralph.

Chuck nodded. "A spectacular one at that. In the expanse of deep canyons, high buttes, and jutting promontories that surrounded the two river corridors, all of it virtually undisturbed by human hands, Udall saw a landscape every bit as incomparable in its magnificence as Yosemite or Yellowstone or Grand Canyon. Right then and there, he decided to devote himself to convincing Congress to declare the region a national park—knowing full well it would mean going *mano a mano* with Dominy."

"Fortunately," Ralph noted, "Udall had Bates Wilson to help him."

"Wilson was superintendent of Arches National Park, outside of Moab, in the 1950s," Chuck explained to the group. "He fell in love with the remote canyon country beyond the boundaries of Arches to the west and south. Like Udall, Wilson concluded that the region deserved national park designation. Working together, the two men accomplished just that. In 1964, just three years after Dominy flew over Cataract Canyon with Udall, Congress created Canyonlands National Park, denying Dominy's dream of double-plugging the Colorado and Green Rivers."

"If not for Udall and Wilson," Ralph said, "we'd be in a houseboat right now—" he directed a finger skyward "—floating around up there somewhere."

"Would that really be so bad?" asked a slender, middle-aged woman seated among the corporate representatives. She wore a long-sleeved shirt and multi-pocketed cargo pants similar to those worn by the tall, blond guide, Maeve. "I've seen pictures of people cruising around Lake Powell in houseboats. That looks pretty good to me. Not to mention all the water Lake Powell stores for use downstream."

"It all depends on your definition of good, Greta," Ralph replied. "The evaporation rate of the reservoir behind Glen Canyon Dam is so extreme that studies show it perspires more water from its surface into the atmosphere than it stockpiles for later use. The same high evaporation rate would have been true of Dominy's confluence dam."

"I thought the idea of this trip was to be evenhanded. It sounds to me like you and your naturalist already have your minds made up."

"Because we do," Ralph said. "Or, speaking for myself, I do. I'm heartbroken by the drowning of the West's free-flowing rivers that resulted from the dams built by Floyd Dominy and his Bureau of Rec engineers, and I always will be. But the point of this expedition is not to change minds. It's to work together, regardless of our varying mindsets, to chart a course for future water use in the Southwest." With a glance at Chuck, Ralph said to Greta, "As for our naturalist, his job is to provide information about our surroundings for us to chew on. Given his job title, I'd fully expect that the information he provides would come from a conservationist perspective."

"As an archaeologist," Chuck said, "I study and document ancient human history. I'm as heartbroken as Ralph about Dominy's dams—in my case, because of the irreplaceable ancestral sites they drowned, human history I and other archaeologists never will have the opportunity to study."

Greta ignored Chuck and addressed Ralph. "I don't have a problem with your personal beliefs about dams. I'm just worried your notions concerning water use in the Southwest may be so unwavering that you're incapable of compromise."

"My *notions*, as you call them, are based on facts," Ralph responded. "For example, it is a fact that Glen Canyon Dam was the last concrete edifice built by the Bureau of Reclamation in this country to halt the free flow of one of our nation's largest rivers. It is also a fact that there are no plans afoot to construct any more big dams. Which is to say that, like it or not, we've moved on from building dams to other ways of dealing with the Southwest's mounting water problems, such as groundwater regeneration, riparian habitat restoration, and, most important of all, demand management—that is, simple, straightforward conservation."

"But the bureau's dams have driven the Southwest's economic boom," Greta said.

"Their storage capacity has been helpful from an economic standpoint, yes. But in today's West, where every drop of water increasingly counts, the dams' evaporative losses are fast offsetting their storage benefits. Besides which, much of the stored water of the Colorado River is used to irrigate water-intensive crops like cotton and alfalfa in 120-degree heat in the desert sands of Southern California's Imperial Valley. That is literally the most wasteful, unproductive, uneconomic use of water ever conceived by mankind." Ralph glanced back at Sylvia, in the camp kitchen. "Or, I should say, humankind." He studied the seated clients. "The agricultural scheme in the Imperial Valley doesn't help the general public at all. Rather, it enriches a handful of multinational agricultural corporations—one of which is represented here with us tonight."

Ralph's eyes landed on Leon. The Consilla representative looked away, his jaw set, as Ralph continued.

"Irrigation in the Imperial Valley uses more than half the water of the Colorado River each year. It enriches a handful of mega-corporations with holdings in the valley at tremendous cost to American taxpayers, not to mention the riparian habitat of the Southwest's rivers. US citizens paid for the construction of Dominy's dams decades ago. Today, taxpayers continue to pay the cost of transporting the water stored by those dams to the Imperial Valley via canals and pipelines. Yet the most prolific crop in the valley—alfalfa—is grown for no beneficial purpose whatsoever. Rather, it is used as worthless ballast in the bottom of empty cargo ships returning from the West Coast to China for more factory goods. In China, the alfalfa is fed to cattle simply to get rid of it." Ralph looked around the group. "In other words, much of the precious water of the Colorado River is entirely wasted, providing no value to the American people, but at tremendous taxpayer cost, and at tremendous environmental cost as well."

Greta sat still, clenching her knees with her hands, but Leon leapt from his chair.

"You convinced me to come on this trip under false pretenses," he challenged Ralph.

The professor clasped his hands over his stomach and looked up at Leon from his seat. "It appears you're offended by my judgment that your company profits at the expense of taxpayers and the environment." The professor looked past Leon at Greta and the other corporate representatives. "Does anyone else feel as Leon does?"

A beat of silence passed.

"Greta?" Ralph urged.

She let go of her knees. "Everything you just said is true," she conceded. "I've known it for a while now, and I recognize that the American public is becoming increasingly aware of it, too. My company, Amalgamated Mining and Minerals, sees water the same way it sees everything else it deals in—as a commodity. We're happy to have the water rights we own put to their most beneficial use. Whether for farms, cities, or the environment, it's all the same to us, as long as we get the return on our investment our shareholders expect. All of which is to say, I was sent on this trip for one reason and one reason only: I'm here to deal."

Ralph turned to Leon.

"I was sent on this trip by Consilla Corporation, the biggest agricultural player in the Imperial Valley," Leon said. "We grow lettuce to feed America, cotton to clothe America, and, yes, alfalfa that supports the American-Chinese supply chain. That is to say, Consilla uses the water of the Colorado River to keep America's economic engine running. I've been sent on this trip to make sure that keeps happening, and if that's a sin, then count me guilty as charged." His head swiveled between Greta and Ralph. "To hell with the both of you." His gaze stopped on Ralph. "But you, especially."

Two mornings later, when Tamara called out that breakfast was ready, Ralph did not emerge from his tent.

11

"Hey there, Ralph," Joseph Conway called as he approached the professor's small hoop tent.

Chuck sat in front of his solo tent thirty feet away, tugging on his river shoes and watching as Joseph stopped at the zippered door to Ralph's tent. The Bureau of Rec water analyst was in his mid-forties, with flabby arms and a pudgy midsection. In the shade of early morning, he wasn't wearing a hat. His brown hair was shorn in a crew cut, and his prominent ears stuck out from the sides of his head.

The expedition was camped on a narrow length of sand abutting the Green River. A cream-colored band of White Rim Sandstone etched the skyline. Below the belt of stone, a crumbly layer of reddish-brown Organ Rock Shale tumbled down the sides of the canyon to the green line of tamarisk trees along the shore of the waterway.

"Knock, knock," Joseph said, tapping the nylon roof of Ralph's tent. "Hey, sleepyhead. Wayne sent me over. It's time to get up."

The door to Ralph's tent was zipped shut. No sound or signs of movement came from within.

Chuck had spent the three previous evenings talking with Ralph late into the night. The retired law professor had sipped scotch and shared highlights of his past river trips with Chuck, and he and Chuck had exchanged stories about the many Southwest archaeologists they both knew. Joseph had joined Ralph and Chuck in casual conversation two nights ago, finishing a mug of hot tea before heading off to his tent.

The first night Chuck had visited with Ralph, the professor had leaned back in his chair and extended his legs, resting his heels in the sand of the broad beach lining the river's edge at that night's camp. "It's great that these beaches are still here along the Green River," he commented. "They've all but disappeared below Glen Canyon Dam in Grand Canyon, because the sand and silt from the Colorado and San Juan Rivers falls to the bottom of the reservoir above the dam. In fact, the lowest rapids in Cataract Canyon are gone now, with the underwater boulders that created the rapids covered in sludge."

"The sand from the two rivers used to replenish the beaches in Grand Canyon, right?"

"Yep, but not anymore. These days, the water flowing out of the bottom of Glen Canyon Dam is crystal clear, carrying no sand to replenish the beaches downstream." Ralph rested his elbows on the cloth arms of his folding chair. "The problem for beaches in the canyon only gets worse from there. The Bureau of Reclamation releases water from the bottom of Glen Canyon Dam based on demand for air conditioning in Los Angeles. Each day at noon, as the temperature rises and people turn on their coolers, the engineers open valves to make more hydroelectricity, sending a surge of water downstream in the process. When evening comes and LA's electricity demand decreases, they shut down the valves, reducing the amount of water flowing down the canyon. Basically, the river level in Grand Canyon rises and falls like an ocean tide every twenty-four hours, in direct response to the demand for electricity in Los Angeles. The resulting surge of water eats away at whatever sand is left along the shore, destroying the beaches and eroding the canyon's riparian habitat."

"But it's a national park."

"The Bureau of Reclamation doesn't answer to the National Park Service. It answers to politicians in California. The people of California get their peak daytime electricity from Glen Canyon

Dam virtually for free. The last thing they want is to have to pay more for their peak power from some other source."

"Damn the dam, then," Chuck said.

"It's a few decades too late for that, I'm afraid." Ralph pulled his feet back and straightened in his chair. "The tidal surge has non-environmental effects, too. For one, it makes things really interesting for rafters. The surge rolls down the river at a steady pace. Rafters calibrate when it will reach their camps and plan accordingly, making sure their rafts aren't left high and dry on shore when the river recedes overnight. They even plan their runs through various rapids based on the surge. Some rapids are more difficult to run at higher water levels, others are easier."

"As I recall, the most difficult rapid in the canyon, Lava Falls, is easier to run at lower levels, isn't it?"

"That's correct. The surge reaches Lava Falls rapid every day around noon. Rafters try to run the rapid before the surge hits, making for crowded campsites just upstream of Lava Falls, and crowds at the rapid every morning."

Chuck shook his head. "All because of a concrete plug between the canyon walls upstream."

"All because of that," Ralph agreed with a nod.

The second night, Chuck and Ralph talked about the pros and cons of life on rivers.

"I considered a career as a river guide at one point, when I was a lot younger," Chuck told the professor. "I loved the freedom of river trips. But, ultimately, I decided I couldn't handle the isolation that comes with the job. I was a pretty solitary guy to begin with. I realized removing myself fully from regular society wouldn't be good for me."

"I can tell you from my own experience that you made the right choice," Ralph said. "The team aspect of river trips—the esprit de corps—is a great thing. But for river guides, it's a whole new team every expedition—a different group of guides, a new bunch of paying customers. Besides which, river guides are paid next to nothing. They have to work year-round to make any sort of living at it. Most don't have permanent homes off the rivers to go back to. They're true nomads."

The professor took a sip of his scotch, the woody aroma of his drink prickling Chuck's nose.

"Tamara told me that while she loves guiding, she still regrets not having children," Ralph went on. "Rocky mentioned how hard it's been for him to get over the death of his father without close friends to lean on. As for me, I never worked as a guide, but there was a time when you could say I was almost addicted to river trips. I said yes every time the opportunity came along for me to join an expedition. It was the freedom of it, like you said, and the camaraderie, fleeting as that was. I ran rivers in Tibet, Nepal, Chile, Honduras. I went everywhere. But when I came home from one of my trips, my wife wasn't there anymore. She'd taken our kids and left." Ralph stared into his cup, then looked at Chuck. "I'm glad you've managed to find yourself a family. From what you've told me, it sounds as if you've got a good thing going with them. Be sure you don't make the same mistake I did."

Chuck warmed at the thought of coming home to Janelle and the girls rather than the empty house he'd returned to after his long-ago river trips in his previous life as a bachelor. "Never," he said.

Late last night, Chuck's conversation with Ralph had turned to John Wesley Powell, whose 1869 journey down the Green and Colorado Rivers had opened the way to the colonization of the Southwest by white Americans from the East.

The Waters of the Southwest Expedition was deep in Still-water Canyon, a calm stretch of the Green River that wound between high, vertical walls of blood-red Wingate Sandstone before the Green met the Colorado River and the combined waters of the two rivers plunged through Cataract Canyon. Stars shone between the cliff walls above, and a slight breeze sifted down the canyon, flowing downstream above the cool surface of the river.

"John Wesley Powell was a fascinating and driven character," Ralph said. "Actually, his wife, Emma Dean, was cut from the same cloth. She nursed John Wesley back to health over four grueling months after he gave his arm, and nearly his life, to his anti-slavery convictions in the Battle of Shiloh during the Civil War. She received a special dispensation to stay with Powell for the rest of the war, working as a Union nurse in brutal conditions for two years during the Vicksburg Campaign down the Mississippi River. After the war, Emma Dean accompanied John Wesley on his first expedition, an overland trip through the Rocky Mountains. That was extremely unusual for a woman in those days. She overwintered in a small cabin with John Wesley and his otherwise all-male team, then supported his river expedition the following year despite the immense risks involved. She was one of the first known summiteers of Pikes Peak, and she was quite a scientist in her own right, specializing in ornithology." Ralph swirled his drink. "John Wesley was Emma Dean's intellectual equal. He was fluent in Greek and Latin, and he formed an organization for scientific and theoretical discussion called the Cosmos Club that exists to this day. As a geologist, he was fascinated by the Canyonlands region. He was a superb cartographer. The maps he created of the Colorado River Basin were remarkably accurate. As one of America's earliest conservationists, his observations about how much the lands of the Southwest could support in the way of human capacity were spot-on."

"But those observations weren't well received, as I recall," Chuck said.

"Not well at all," Ralph agreed. He took a swallow of his drink, then wiped his mouth with the back of his hand. "His explorations opened the Southwest to colonization—that is, to the taking, by force, of the land and water of the Native Americans who lived in the region. After his expeditions, Powell was appointed the director of the US Geological Survey. He was tasked with surveying the Southwest to determine its potential for development through colonization. He reported that only two percent of the region was suitable for agriculture. The railroad barons didn't like his finding one bit. They'd received nearly two hundred million acres of western lands from Congress in return for laying tracks across the country, and they wanted to make money by selling off those lands. The railroads pushed the false notion, known as 'rain follows the plow,' that increased agriculture in the region would increase precipitation. Congress went along with that harebrained idea and opened the arid Southwest to unrestricted exploitation."

"While Indigenous tribes were shoved aside."

"More like genocide. Some Native Americans survived, of course. But Europeans poured into the region even as Powell was warning Congress that opening the Southwest to unrestricted homesteading was—" Ralph made air quotes "—'piling up a heritage of conflict and litigation over water rights, for there is not sufficient water to supply the land.'"

"You've got his words memorized?" Chuck asked, incredulous.

"Of course. Powell was entirely correct. He resigned in protest after the results of his survey were rejected. But by then the damage was done. The unrestricted exploitation of land and water spurred by the Homestead Act led directly to the destruction of the Oklahoma and Texas grasslands. The decimation of the grasslands caused the Dust Bowl during the 1930s. Since the Dust Bowl years, continued development in the Southwest has led us to where we find ourselves today—approaching war between the Upper Basin and Lower Basin states over the limited water in the Colorado River Basin, with concerns about the riparian habitat of the basin's rivers literally left in the dust. All of which is exactly as Powell predicted."

"He really was ahead of his time, wasn't he?"

"That's why knowing about him is so worthwhile." Ralph took another sip of his scotch. "Here's a second quote for you. Powell grew increasingly frustrated near the end of his tenure with the US Geological Survey. In one of his speeches before he submitted his resignation, he said the government was acting criminally by encouraging people to move to where there wasn't enough water. He predicted water shortages would plague the Southwest in the future, and people would end up at each other's throats. 'Years of drought and famine come,' he said, 'and the climate is not changed with dance, libation, or prayer.'"

"Pretty prophetic."

"For him, it all came full circle, back to the deadly end to his 1869 expedition."

"Ah, yes," Chuck said. "Separation Rapid."

Ralph tipped his cup to Chuck. "Powell's team made it through the rapids of Lodore Canyon on the upper Green River, through Cataract Canyon on the Colorado River, and on into Grand Canyon. In the Grand, his team worked their tails off in the brutal heat of summer, lining their boats down rapid after rapid after rapid. Finally, in late August, thinking they were still in the heart of the canyon, three of Powell's men had had enough. They abandoned the expedition and hiked away from the river at what is now known as Separation Rapid. Two days later, Powell and the remaining members of his team floated out of the canyon and returned to civilization."

"Meanwhile, the three men who left the expedition were killed, weren't they?"

Ralph nodded. "By Indigenous people living in the area, most likely. The story is that the local Native Americans believed Powell's men had murdered one of their tribal members. Still, some people believe to this day that Mormon colonists killed them, or that the men died of thirst. If the latter was the case, their deaths were a foreshadowing of what Powell predicted would eventually come to pass for the entire region."

"Is there really not enough water these days, though?" Chuck asked Ralph. "You're the one who talked about the wasteful use of water to grow cotton and alfalfa in the Imperial Valley."

"The answer is, it's complicated. The amount of water from the Colorado River used for agriculture should be carefully controlled, that much is beyond question. Take away agricultural irrigation and there's enough Colorado River water for current residential, tribal, and commercial uses, with some left over to preserve the riparian habitats along the river."

"What's the answer then?"

"Exactly what's happening on this expedition—talk, discussion, compromise, all leading to changes in the way water is allocated in the Southwest. Right now, water rights are assigned on a use-it-or-lose-it basis. Nothing could be worse for the people or the environment of the region."

"You have to figure Powell would approve of what you and Wayne are doing on this trip. A century and a half after his team first came through here, another team is floating down the river, trying to decide how best to use the limited water supplies in the Colorado River Basin."

"And it only took a century and a half for it to happen," Ralph said ruefully. He glanced at the moon, high in the sky, and pushed himself stiffly to his feet. "Time for some shuteye."

"What about the wreckage of the boat from the Powell expedition?" Chuck asked, rising with the professor.

"What about it?"

"Leon's pretty keen on it."

"He's not the first and he won't be the last. He mentioned the rumor. I'm sure you've heard it, too. Lots of people have. But no one has ever come up with anything."

"You think it's just a rumor, then?"

Ralph's eyes glinted in the moonlight. "You're the big-time archaeologist. Why don't you tell me?"

12

Seven hours later, Chuck looked on as Greta walked across the beach, coffee mug in hand, and joined Joseph in front of Ralph's tent.

"Is the old man in there?" she asked, aiming her mug at the tent door.

"If he is, he's sound asleep," Joseph replied.

She scanned the deserted beach. "Maybe he's taking his morning constitutional. Or he went for a pre-breakfast stroll."

Joseph's gaze fell on Chuck. "How about you?" he asked. "Have you seen him?"

Chuck stood up and brushed sand from the seat of his pants. "Not this morning." He pointed at the bare patch of sand in front of Ralph's tent. "I don't see his shoes. I bet he's already up and around."

Joseph rested his hand on the roof of the tent. "Should we check inside?"

"I don't think he'd mind."

Joseph squatted, unzipped the tent door, and peered through the opening. Blood drained from his face and he lurched backward, knocking against Greta's legs.

"Careful!" she cried, coffee flying from her cup.

Joseph collapsed at Greta's feet, facing the open tent, his hand to his mouth. He moaned, staring inside.

Greta bent and looked into the tent. Her eyebrows shot upward and she dropped her cup in the sand, splashing her legs with the last of her coffee.

"Ralph," she murmured, tears springing to her eyes. "Oh, dear, Ralph."

Chuck scurried to the tent and looked through the opening. Inside, Ralph lay on his back atop his sleeping bag, his arms at his sides. He was fully clothed, his river shoes still on his feet. His face was white as chalk, while his ears were deep purple, filled with gathered blood. Behind his glasses, his eyes were open, milky gray and shrunken in their sockets, staring unseeing at the tent ceiling. The tip of his tongue showed between his parted lips. A trail of dried saliva ran from the corner of his mouth to his sleeping bag.

Ralph was dead. Clearly, he'd been so for hours.

Chuck's legs gave out and he crumpled to the sand next to Joseph, staring at the professor's blanched face. He reached a trembling hand toward the professor. "He never even got undressed."

He rocked forward, reached through the tent opening, and tugged the top of the sleeping bag over Ralph's bloodless face, covering the professor's vacant eyes and slack mouth.

He summoned Wayne and Tamara, who took the places of Joseph and Greta. Tamara lifted the sleeping bag from Ralph's face, verifying his death, then gathered with Chuck and Wayne in front of the tent.

"This isn't the first death I've dealt with on a trip," she said, her tone matter-of-fact, "and I don't imagine it'll be the last. More and more elderly people are signing up for our trips these days, checking it off their bucket lists, I suppose."

"You don't even seem to care," Wayne challenged her.

"I don't mean to be callous," she said. "I'm not, believe me. It's just that the desert is a harsh environment. The heat, the dryness. It takes its toll—on older folks, in particular."

Chuck took in the bare rock walls of the canyon, the jumbled boulders below. He drew a breath of the parched air in the gorge. Much as he wanted to contradict Tamara, he knew what she'd said was true.

Wayne's voice shook. "Ralph is, was, a good man. He was

doing so much for the world. He was one-hundred-percent alive."

"He was a decent guy, I'll grant you that," Tamara replied. "But death is a part of life. No matter how alive you are, you're still only that way until you're not." Her tone softened. "We're all headed to the same place, Wayne. The only question is when each of us will get there."

Wayne blinked. A tear escaped his eye and trickled down the side of his face. "I know you're right," he admitted. "It's just... it's..."

"You'll do fine leading the rest of the trip on your own," she assured him. "I'll have your back. All my guides will."

"So will I," Chuck told him.

"But for now," said Tamara, "we need to get to work—the sooner the better for the good of the expedition."

She strode to the boats lined along the shore, retrieved the satellite phone from its waterproof container on her raft, and made several calls. Then she gathered everyone on the beach, the small, black phone in her hand.

"You've heard by now that we've lost Ralph," she announced. "I share my sympathies with all of you." She lifted the phone, displaying it to the group members, who stood in silence before her. "There's a protocol for what's happened, and I've put it into action. A helicopter is on its way from Grand Canyon National Park. It'll be here within the hour. We'll postpone breakfast to prepare the landing zone and secure camp for its arrival."

Tamara directed the clients to break down their tents, stow their belongings in their personal dry bags, and leave the tents and bags in front of the rafts. The guides dismantled their tents, too, then smoothed a broad section of sand at the head of the beach. In the middle of the smoothed patch of sand, Rocky placed a large cross consisting of strips of bright orange plastic weighed down by rocks.

Maeve and Vance removed Ralph from his tent. Chuck retrieved the penny, worn and coppery, that dropped to the ground as the guides carried Ralph's body to a tarp waiting on the sand. He tucked the coin in the zipper pocket of his lightweight river pants while Maeve and Vance wrapped Ralph in the tarp.

A white helicopter with a yellow stripe and a black tail flew low over camp thirty minutes later. The brown, arrowhead-shaped National Park Service insignia emblazoned its doors.

Rocky tugged the orange plastic cross from beneath the rocks, tossed the rocks aside, and scurried away from the section of smoothed sand with the plastic sheeting wadded into a ball and pressed to his chest.

The chopper hovered over the landing zone, now cleared of the indicator cross. The helicopter's rotors blasted sand in all directions. Chuck covered his nose and mouth with his forearm and watched through squinted eyes as the chopper landed on the beach.

The helicopter's spinning rotors slowed and two helmeted rangers in olive-green flight suits hopped out of its side door. Ducking beneath the rotating blades, they scurried to Tamara and Rocky, who waited beside Ralph's tarp-wrapped body. The rangers and guides exchanged a few words, cupping their mouths with their hands, then carried Ralph to the helicopter and placed him inside.

Tamara and Rocky retreated. The rangers climbed back into the helicopter and slid the side door closed. In the glassed cockpit, the pilot revved the engine. The rotors picked up speed. The pilot saluted Tamara and Rocky as the chopper lifted off the beach, once more blasting sand into the air.

The helicopter flew upriver, climbing out of the canyon, the deep-throated *chuff-chuff-chuff* of its engine dying away as it departed.

In the quiet that followed, Chuck unzipped his pocket and fingered the penny. He already missed his nightly conversations with Ralph—the professor's stories of his past river trips, the water-related truths and opinions he expressed in his gravelly voice. Tamara was correct that death was a part of life, but Ralph's death was so sudden, so jarring.

Chuck released the penny and zipped his pocket shut, grateful to at least have the small token of Ralph to accompany him for the rest of the expedition.

The penny was still zipped in his pocket two days later, when the surging water of the Rapid 1 hole sluiced him out of the gear boat and beneath the surface of the river.

13

A moment of stillness followed the initial shock of the water closing over Chuck's head. He'd managed to grab a lungful of air as he was flushed out of the raft. In place of the roar of the rapid, the underwater world was silent, almost serene. A stream of tiny bubbles escaped his mouth and floated upward past his face. Thin rays of sunlight pierced the shifting water, darting past him like green lasers into the depths of the hole.

The surface of the river was less than a foot above his head. A kick with his feet and a thrust of his arms, aided by the buoyancy of his PFD, would return him to the surface in no time.

As he prepared to kick, however, the circulating water in the hole drew him downward, deeper into its center and away from the air and sunlight above. The surface of the river grew distant, then disappeared entirely.

A whirling surge of water tumbled him head over heels, like clothing in a dryer. He swung his arms and kicked his legs, but the churning water spun him relentlessly, holding him captive deep in the hole. He pressed his lips together, preserving the last of the air in his lungs.

Suddenly, as if deciding playtime was over, the roiling water in the hole shot Chuck upward. The water brightened with filtered sunlight. He extended his arm. His hand broke the surface and his head quickly followed. He sputtered and drew a blessed breath of air deep into his lungs. Looking about, he found he was halfway up the face of the hole's breaking wave—precisely where the raft had halted before sliding back to the bottom of the depression in the middle of the river.

The wave fell over him from above, and the force of the

falling water drove him beneath the surface and into the maw of the hole once more.

Chuck knew what he was up against this time: a recirculating monster that sought to hold him in its swirling bosom for all eternity. He clamped his mouth shut and drew his knees to his chest, his arms tight around his legs and his chin tucked to his PFD, assuming the shape of a cannonball.

The downward shove of the breaking wave drove his balled body far beneath the surface of the river. Pressure built in his ears. Near total darkness enveloped him. He gyrated wildly, like a spinning toy top. Bubbles flew from the corners of his mouth, luminescent in the gloom.

He counted to himself, one-one thousand, two-one thousand, three-one thousand, growing increasingly lightheaded as his count lengthened. His lungs threatened to burst. He fought the urge to give up his tucked position and swim for the surface. But every additional second he remained underwater provided more time for his body to be drawn downstream, beyond the clutches of the recirculating wave, while he was in the depths of the river.

He maintained his curled position, trusting the buoyancy of his PFD to return him to the surface when the hole lost its grip on him. He tightened his arms around his shins and clenched his teeth. Gradually, the pressure in his ears decreased. Shards of light appeared, flashing past him as he tumbled. His diaphragm spasmed. He was desperate for air, but he forced himself to keep his mouth clamped shut.

Finally, unable to hold out any longer, he released his grip around his legs and clawed toward the light. His head broke the surface and he drew a breath of half air and half liquid. He coughed, spewing water. He threw back his head, his face to the sky, and took another breath. This one was pure air, saturating his lungs with life-giving oxygen.

He raised his head and looked around, the roar of the rapid loud in his ears. He was downstream of the hole, coursing through the standing waves in the middle of the rapid. The surging whitewater rotated him until he faced upstream. The massive gear boat, somehow still upright, launched to the top of the hole's breaking wave as if fired from a slingshot. Almost imperceptibly at first, then with increasing speed, the unmanned boat slid off the downstream side of the wave and on into the heart of the rapid, trailing Chuck.

The current spun him away from the boat. Facing downstream, neck-deep in the water, he searched for Clarence, his eyes darting.

Rosie's prediction that Clarence's bulk would provide him additional buoyancy if he wound up in the river was factually correct. Fatty tissue was less dense than muscle. That meant Clarence would float higher in water than, say, Chuck, with his sinewy frame. In the Rapid 1 hole, however, Clarence's corpulence may well have worked against him.

Earlier during the trip, Chuck had explained to Clarence the act of tucking into a ball to descend beneath a recirculating wave in a rapid. But the physics associated with Clarence's higher fat content combined with the buoyancy of his PFD would have rendered any attempt to sink beneath the hole problematic—unless the shock of being swept overboard had caused him to inhale involuntarily beneath the surface, filling his lungs with water.

If that had happened, Clarence's waterlogged body would have been driven deep beneath the hole and carried far downstream, his liquid-filled lungs providing no lifesaving air while he was beneath the surface.

At least a minute had passed since Clarence had been swept into the river along with Chuck.

The clock was ticking.

"Here!"

The cry came from downstream, cutting through the noise of the rapid.

Chuck crested a standing wave. Thirty feet ahead, Tamara's raft was poised in the middle of the river, its stern facing him. Tamara pulled hard on the oars, arching backward in her seat, her strokes slowing the boat's downstream movement almost to a full stop.

Joseph perched on his knees and right hand at the back of the raft, his left hand extended upstream toward Chuck. The boat floated up and over one of the standing waves in the rapid. Chuck swam after it. Tamara twisted and looked back at him, then turned forward and heaved on the oars, digging the blades deep into the water.

Joseph leaned from the rear of the raft, his hand outstretched. Chuck kicked forward, reaching for Joseph. But Joseph suddenly tilted outward, threatening to topple off the back of the boat and into the river. He withdrew his hand and grasped the boat frame, steadying himself. At the same instant, the surging current swept Chuck away from the raft, tacking him diagonally across the river.

He topped a wave. Downstream, the expedition rafts lined both sides of the calm pool at the end of the whitewater. Liza and Torch waited in their rescue kayaks at the bottom of the rapid as well, their double-bladed paddles gripped in their hands.

The current drew Chuck underwater once more. He resurfaced and lay on his back, his face to the sky. He took a deep breath, counting on the buoyancy of his PFD to keep him afloat until the safety kayakers paddled out to meet him at the foot of the rapid.

Buoyancy.

The word cut through his exhausted brain like a sliver of broken glass.

And: *Clarence.*

Chuck lifted his head and surveyed the boiling surface of the river.

Surging waves. Spraying water. Nothing else.

Then, in the midst of the turbulence, a flash of deep blue. The spot of blue disappeared beneath the water for a second, then returned to sight. The blue was the back of Clarence's PFD, floating at the surface of the river. But Clarence himself was out of sight, underwater, facedown and inert.

Clarence was drowning.

14

The blue PFD was fifty feet downstream in the middle of the river. Chuck swam after Clarence, scanning the river as he kicked and stroked. The unmanned gear boat bobbed through the rapid, its left oar still in its oarlock, its right oar hanging in the water next to the side thwart, leashed to the boat's aluminum frame by its tether. Tamara faced forward in her raft, pushing on her oars to power the boat to the bottom of the rapid. Having missed the opportunity to reach Chuck amid the standing waves, she now was clearly intent on getting to the end of the whitewater as quickly as possible and aiding in the rescue operation from there.

That left Chuck to deal with Clarence on his own.

The PFD sank beneath the surface of the river as Clarence's body disappeared into a standing wave. Chuck fixed his eye on the spot and stroked hard downstream. When he reached the wave, the same hydraulics that had drawn Clarence beneath the surface sucked Chuck underwater. A second later, he shot out of the far side of the wave as if fired from a howitzer. He landed back in the water and swam on downstream.

He again spotted the blue flash of the PFD, now twenty feet ahead, as Clarence was sucked into the next wave in the rapid. Chuck drew a breath before he was drawn through the wave as well.

He blasted out its other side. The back of Clarence's PFD floated a few feet in front of him. He threw himself forward, grabbed the life jacket, and gave it a powerful yank.

Clarence's helmeted head rose out of the water and flopped backward against Chuck's chest. Chuck put his feet to Clarence's back and pushed, laying Clarence's body out on the surface of the river, with his head nestled against Chuck's shoulder.

Clarence's eyes were closed, his face ashen. He convulsed. Water gushed from his nostrils.

Chuck clasped his hand over Clarence's nose and mouth as the next wave drew them beneath the surface. Clarence struggled, his body twisting and his arms flailing, but Chuck maintained his grasp while they were underwater.

They shot out the downstream side of the wave and Chuck released his grip. Clarence drew a breath of air—a heartening sign. But his eyes remained closed, his face drained of blood. He did not take a second breath.

Chuck peered downstream, his arm around Clarence's chest. They were nearing the rapid's end. He waved his free hand at Liza and Torch, who waited in their kayaks on either side of the river. The two safety kayakers were tasked with using their small, maneuverable boats to come to the aid of "swimmers"— passengers tossed from rafts in the midst of rapids. At Chuck's wave, the kayakers dug their paddles into the water, driving their short, squat boats toward him and Clarence.

Chuck tightened his arm around Clarence's chest and kicked his feet, making for the nearest shore. Liza paddled up to them, her arms windmilling. From the other side of the river, Torch powered his boat toward them with equally turbocharged strokes.

Liza clipped her oversized, D-shaped rescue carabiner around the shoulder strap of Clarence's PFD and spun her yellow kayak away from Chuck without a word. The cord connecting the rescue carabiner to her PFD unspooled to full length, and she tugged Clarence's unconscious body behind her as she paddled across the pool at the foot of the rapid toward the rocky shoreline.

Chuck lay back in the calm water, his face to the sky, utterly spent.

Torch reached him. "You okay?"

Chuck nodded wearily. Torch spun in his green kayak with a deft paddle stroke. Chuck grabbed the boat's rear handle and Torch towed him behind Liza and Clarence to a short stretch of sand between a pair of waist-high boulders at the river's edge.

Liza ran the bow of her boat onto the small beach, popped her elastic spray skirt free from the rim of her cockpit, and hoisted herself out of her boat. She waded into the river, grasped the shoulder straps of Clarence's PFD, and tugged him onto the sand to his waist. He lay on his back, water lapping at his legs, his mouth slack.

Chuck's shoes struck the rocky bottom of the eddy. He let go of Torch's kayak and scrambled to the river's edge.

Water coursed from Clarence's nose and mouth. A burst of air escaped his lungs and he drew a ragged breath, his PFD rising along with his chest. Chuck drew a deep breath in emotional support, fear curdling his stomach.

Torch unfolded himself from his boat and teamed with Liza to tug Clarence fully onto the shore. Like Liza, Torch was short and stout. Tendrils of wet hair plastered his forehead, and his muscular shoulders bulged beneath his dry top.

Liza knelt next to Clarence. When he did not immediately draw another breath, she unzipped his PFD and pressed hard on his sternum, thrusting with the full weight of her upper body. Clarence gagged and inhaled, his hands rising at his sides.

Chuck dropped to his knees in the shallow water at Clarence's feet.

Clarence's eyes sprung open. He looked up at Liza and took another breath, deeper this time. Liza stared down at him, her gaze piercing.

"*Dios mío,*" Clarence muttered.

He opened his eyes wide, focusing on Liza.

"*Eres bonita,*" he said. "*La más bonita de todos.*"

15

Relief surged through Chuck.

Liza turned to him, her thick, black eyebrows drawn together in question.

He translated for her, unable to stifle the smile climbing onto his face. "He says you're beautiful. The most beautiful of all."

Liza looked down at Clarence, her face an inscrutable mask. Raising her hand, she slapped him hard on the cheek, leaving a sandy imprint on his blanched skin.

"*Oom-mé, mahnomah*," she said. The Ute expression was guttural, issuing from the back of her throat. "You are beautiful, too," she repeated in English. "Because you are alive, not dead." She inhaled, her breath catching in her throat.

Clarence dug his fingers into the sand beside him and raised his head, struggling to sit up.

But Liza pressed him back to the ground. "Not so fast. We don't need you to go out on us again."

Chuck crawled around to Clarence's side. It looked as if he was going to be all right. "You gave us a pretty good scare, you know that? How's your head?"

"What do you mean, my head?" Clarence asked, looking up from where he lay.

"The counterweight on the oar smacked you a good one."

"Oh, yeah. I remember now." Clarence put his hand to his helmet. "I think this thing did what it's supposed to do." He glanced at Liza, then back at Chuck. "She *is* beautiful, isn't she?"

Chuck grinned, his teeth pressed hard together to keep them from chattering. Thank God Clarence was alive and still himself.

Liza's face flushed. She raised her hand, threatening to slap Clarence again, the corners of her mouth ticking upward in the start of a smile, just as Tamara rowed her raft up to them through the circling eddy at the bottom of the rapid. The gear boat trailed her raft, attached by its bow line to the stern of her boat.

"Everybody okay?" she asked.

Torch patted the top of his helmet with the flat of his hand, making the universal whitewater sign that all was well. "A bit of a scare," he said. "But we're good now."

"May I?" Clarence asked Liza, who lowered her hand.

She nodded and he sat up. Immediately, he dangled his head between his knees, taking big gulps of air.

Chuck stood and grabbed Tamara's raft, holding its bow at the river's edge.

"We nabbed your boat," she told him. "Looks like you snapped an oarlock." She frowned. "We put new oarlocks on all our gear boats before every trip. It's cheap insurance—or it's supposed to be, anyway. There's no way yours should have broken."

"It snapped when I put everything I had into my first stroke at the top of the rapid," Chuck said. "There must have been an imperfection in the bronze."

Tamara's mouth twisted. "That'd be awfully unlikely. I can't think what else it could be, though." She shrugged. "Anyhow, I'm glad we were able to grab your boat. We'll pop in a new oarlock and get going."

She pointed at a green, metal, army-issue ammunition can strapped to the back of the boat frame and addressed Joseph on the stern thwart. "Grab one of the extra oarlocks out of there, would you?"

Rather than respond, Joseph glared past Tamara at Chuck, his face beet red and his jaw set.

"*You*," he spat. "You killed Ralph."

Chuck took a stumbling backward step, his shoes slipping on the muddy shore. "What are you talking about?"

"He was fine until you started spending all that time with him every night. Ralph wasn't young, and he wasn't getting enough sleep. I brought it up with him. 'You have to slow down,' I told him. 'You need to get more rest.' But did he listen? Of course not. Not with you all over him like his new best friend."

"I hung out with him in the evenings, that's all," Chuck said. "Mostly, I listened. He told great stories. Any subject that came up, he knew all about it. Any place I mentioned, he'd been there a bunch of times. Every idea we discussed, he could analyze it from every angle imaginable."

"He drank with you every night, like a fish."

"He drank his own scotch, from the personal supply he'd brought for the trip. I had nothing to do with that."

"He wanted to impress you."

"Impress *me*? You have to be kidding. It was the other way around. *I* was impressed by *him*."

Joseph's jaw swung from side to side. "I know who you are. It's exactly as Leon said—just because you're playing the role of naturalist on the expedition doesn't fool any of us."

"I'm on this trip because I want to be on it. I couldn't pass up the chance to listen in on the smartest water people in the Southwest. That's what I was doing with Ralph—listening, learning. That's *all* I was doing." Chuck narrowed his eyes at Joseph. "Why are you bringing this up right now?"

The jug-eared official sat up straight on the rear thwart. "JWP."

Chuck jerked back his head. "What, you're channeling Leon now?"

"John...Wesley...Powell," Joseph said, emphasizing each word. "I know all about the rumor, too. I know exactly what you're up to. We all do."

"Why don't you enlighten me, then?"

"You helped Ralph drink himself to death. But I'm sure you got what you wanted from him before he died. Maybe you've forgotten that Ralph and I shared the back of this boat at the start of the trip. We did a lot of talking together, too."

"What did he say to you?"

Joseph sucked a sharp breath and looked sidelong at Tamara and the others, as if suddenly realizing he and Chuck weren't alone. "We'll talk later," he muttered, his eyes hooded.

Tamara dipped her helmeted head at him. "You're damn right you'll talk later. Right now, you'll do as you're told."

Joseph glared at her for a long second, then turned and loosened the strap securing the rectangular ammunition can to the raft frame. He opened the waterproof ammo can's hinged lid, pulled out a new oarlock, and handed it to Tamara. She tossed it to Chuck.

Joseph strapped the ammo can back in place and, tugging the gear raft's bow line, floated the big boat to Chuck, who climbed aboard and replaced the sheered oarlock with the new one.

"All set," Chuck reported to Tamara, glancing at the bottom half of the snapped oarlock as he tucked it in his pocket.

From her boat floating a few feet from the river's edge, she observed Clarence, still seated in the wet sand with his head between his knees. "Ready to get back in the saddle?" she asked him.

He lifted his head, his eyes bloodshot, his face drained of blood. "Not much choice, is there?"

"The good news is that Rapid 1 was today's only whitewater. We're making an early camp at Betty Beach, around the next bend, so we can hike up to the Maze this afternoon." She addressed Chuck, seated in the gear boat. "Are we good?"

At his nod, she backed her raft away from shore with steady pulls on her oars. "I'll let the group know you're okay," she said as she departed.

The stern of her boat reached the eddy line. She dipped her upstream oar in the water, pirouetting the boat into the current, and pushed forward with both oars, heading downriver.

Liza and Torch hoisted Clarence to his feet. He wobbled and leaned against Liza. She wrapped an arm around his waist, steadying him.

"You saved my life," Clarence said to her. "How can I ever repay you?"

"All I did was haul you to shore," she replied. "Chuck's the one who got to you in the middle of the rapid. If he hadn't reached you when he did, I bet you'd be dead right now."

"Well, thank you all the same." He looked at Chuck. "Thanks for getting to me in the *rápido, jefe.*"

"No thanks necessary," Chuck said.

"Actually, you're probably right that I don't need to thank you," Clarence said, his eyes glittering, "seeing as you're the one who dumped me in the river in the first place."

"Don't blame me, blame the broken oarlock." Chuck extended his hand from the captain's seat. "Need any help getting into the boat?"

Clarence waved him off. "I think I can manage." He turned to Liza. "With your help."

Leaning against her, he threw a leg over the bow. She lifted his other leg into the boat and leaned over the front thwart, maintaining her grip on him until he sat down heavily on the cooler.

She rested a hand on his knee. "I'll see you at the beach."

"Can't wait," he replied.

She and Torch slid into their kayaks and paddled downstream, leaving Chuck and Clarence alone at the edge of the river.

"I thought I was a goner," Clarence admitted. Water from his wet clothing pooled on the cooler lid. He wrapped his arms around himself, shivering.

"I thought you might be, too," Chuck admitted.

He settled the loose oar in the new oarlock and rowed gently forward, keeping the bow of the boat pressed against the shore.

He shook himself, terrified at the realization of how close Clarence, his best friend and his wife's brother, had come to dying. What if he hadn't seen the flash of Clarence's PFD in the midst of the rapid? What if he hadn't reached him in time?

"I remember going under," said Clarence, "then lots of bubbles, then...nothing."

"The hole sucked you under. Thank God it spit you out and I saw you."

Clarence glanced at the new oarlock. "What the hell happened?"

"It snapped at the worst possible time. We went into the hole sideways. The boat dumped us out, then flopped back down right-side up and floated on through the rapid."

"I've never been more scared in my life."

"Me, either."

"Remind me again, how many more rapids are there?"

"Twenty-three."

"Please tell me you're lying."

"No more today, though, like Tamara said. Betty Beach is right around the corner."

Clarence's teeth chattered. "That sounds *muy bueno* to me."

"Want to put on some dry clothes?"

"Nah. The sun will warm me up. Or thinking about Liza will do it."

Chuck rowed backward away from shore, the movement adding a hint of warmth to the muscles in his arms. "Here's to neither of us ending up like Ralph before the end of the trip."

Clarence turned to him. "How could that guy on Tamara's boat possibly think you had anything to do with that?"

Chuck lifted the oar blades out of the water and tucked the oar handles beneath his knees. The boat floated in the eddy. "It seemed as if he was trying to shift the blame somehow. He talked with Ralph and me the night before Ralph died. He didn't say anything about Ralph's drinking or lack of sleep then."

"Why didn't you remind him of that just now?"

"I didn't want to clue him in to what I was thinking."

Clarence's mouth fell open. "You honestly believe he might have had something to do with Ralph?"

"You're the one who said you don't think his death was natural. You said there are forces at work on the trip that you can't quite put your finger on."

"True, I did say that. *Fuerzas.*"

Chuck pulled the lower half of the broken oarlock from his pocket, handed it to Clarence, and pointed at the sheered end of the shaft. "Check that out."

Clarence squinted at the oarlock. "What am I supposed to be seeing?"

"Look close, right where it snapped."

Clarence brought the oarlock close to his face. His eyes grew large. "*Jesu Cristo,*" he whispered.

PART TWO

"Years of drought and famine come…and the climate is not changed with dance, libation, or prayer."

—John Wesley Powell

16

Janelle stared at the computer screen in Chuck's study, then sat back abruptly, rolling away from his desk and across the worn hardwood floor in his wheeled office chair.

"Carm!" she called through the open study door. "Come here, would you? I want to show you something."

Janelle wheeled herself back to Chuck's desk. A few minutes ago, she'd left Carmelita at work on a homework assignment on her laptop at the kitchen table.

"What is it?" Carmelita asked, entering the study and looking over Janelle's shoulder at Chuck's monitor.

"I'm keeping an eye on Chuck's emails while he's gone," Janelle explained.

Carmelita clicked her tongue. "He should've set an auto-reply saying he was out of town."

"He told me he might be able to hike out of the canyon and get a signal at some point. If so, he wanted to know if there was anything pressing he should hear about."

"And…?"

Janelle pointed at the screen. "This just came through."

Carmelita tossed a loose lock of hair over her shoulder and leaned forward.

The monitor displayed an email message with the subject heading, "Death of Ralph Hycum," from someone with the email handle "oldindian." The body copy was a two-word question, "Seen this?" followed by an online article from a website called Concerning the Law about the death of an emeritus professor from the University of Las Vegas School of Law during a Cataract Canyon rafting trip.

"Few details about Hycum's death are available at this point, as the trip is still underway," the story noted. It went on to summarize the professor's long career as an expert on water policy in the southwestern US.

The article named Ralph as coleader of the Waters of the Southwest Expedition, along with Chuck's friend Wayne Coswell. It outlined the potential compromises between policymakers and corporate representatives that might result from the trip and included remarks from two western state governors. Janelle recognized the governors' quotes, which were taken from the Waters of the Southwest media release Chuck had shared with her before the trip. One of the governors led the Upper Colorado River Basin state of Colorado, the other the Lower Basin state of Arizona.

"I hope discussions during the expedition will bring a dose of sanity to what for decades has been a needlessly contentious issue between Upper Basin and Lower Basin states," the governor of Colorado said. She concluded ominously, "Lower Basin states would do well to remember that precipitation in the Upper Basin states supplies virtually all the water in the Colorado River Basin."

The Arizona governor offered a starkly different take. "With increasing drought due to climate change in the Lower Basin states of Nevada, California, and Arizona," he was quoted as saying, "our three states are in desperate need of the water that has flowed down the Colorado River since time immemorial. That water is every bit as much the property of Lower Basin states as it is the Upper Basin states."

A lengthy thread of emailed comments followed the article. Janelle recognized several of the respondents from Chuck's archaeological work. Carmelita reached forward and scrolled through them, and Janelle reread them as they ran up the screen:

"Looks like the grim reaper finally came for old man Hycum. Too bad."

"Like it'll come for all of us someday. At least he went out on a river trip!!"

"That's how I'd want to depart this earthly paradise if I had the choice."

Only one respondent alluded to the possibility of anything untoward regarding Ralph's death: "Wonder if Ralph said the wrong thing to the wrong person, like he was prone to do!"

Despite the respondent's obvious attempt at humor, the comment still made Janelle cringe.

Carmelita reached the end of the thread and straightened. "So?"

Janelle spun in the chair to face her. "I'm wondering how worried I should be."

"Worried?"

"About Chuck."

"It was just some old guy who died. No biggie. Besides, Chuck can take care of himself. You know that better than anyone."

"I'm worried about Clarence, too."

"Chuck will protect him."

"From what, do you suppose?"

Carmelita frowned and put a finger to her chin, clearly taking Janelle's question seriously.

Janelle appreciated the sister-like bond she and Carmelita shared—in distinct contrast to the wall she'd erected between herself and her Mexican-immigrant parents during her own teen years.

Like many immigrant Americans, Janelle's mother and father had placed heavy expectations on their two children, demanding of Janelle and Clarence perfect school attendance, top grades, and adherence to a strict curfew. In response, Janelle defied her parents, taking up with a rough crowd in her family's low-income neighborhood in Albuquerque's South Valley. Her rebellion culminated in her pregnancy with Carmelita at seventeen, the result of her relationship with an unsavory South Valley drug dealer.

The elder Ortegas doted over newborn Carmelita, providing countless hours of childcare while Janelle continued to run with her bad crowd—until the demands of single motherhood with two young daughters, after her second pregnancy with Rosie, set her on a new path. She ended the relationship with her boyfriend, earned her high school diploma, and went to work as an office receptionist while her parents continued to provide free babysitting services.

With Chuck's concurrence, Janelle did not place the sort of academic demands on the girls that had provoked her rebellion against her own mother and father. Rosie remained a work in progress when it came to schoolwork. Carmelita, on the other hand, poured herself into her classes, just as she did climbing, excelling at both.

Carmelita tapped her chin, eyeing the computer screen. "Chuck will protect Uncle Clarence from whatever he needs protecting from," she said finally.

Janelle nodded to Carmelita. "Fair enough." She turned back to the computer. "According to what it says here, the man who died was one of the expedition leaders. There's no word on how it happened."

"Everybody dies," said Carmelita. "It's not like they have to do it at home or something."

"True." Rising from her seat, Janelle drew Carmelita close and said in her ear, "Thanks, I needed that." She stepped back. "I thought I'd be okay with Chuck being gone this long. Turns out I'm not."

"But he goes away for work every few weeks or so."

"Never for more than two or three days at a time, though. He says he can't stand being apart from us any longer than that."

"What's it been now, a week?"

Janelle nodded.

"With another week to go?"

"*Sí*. Two weeks total."

"Seven more days, that's not so bad."

She waved her hand at the computer screen. "If it weren't for this."

17

Janelle replied to the email from oldindian, explaining that Chuck was on the Waters of the Southwest Expedition. She provided her phone number and asked oldindian to call her in Chuck's absence. Her phone buzzed half an hour later, while she was in the kitchen. The number began with New Mexico's 505 area code. She gave Carmelita a thumbs-up and headed for Chuck's study.

"Is this oldindian?" she asked, dropping into the office chair.

"That's me," said the rough voice of an elderly man, followed by a gravelly chuckle. "I'm that one."

The tempo of the man's words was unhurried, his tone formal.

"Are you Navajo?" she asked, naming the most populous Native American tribe in New Mexico.

Again the man's low chuckle came over the phone. "Oh, no, I'm not *Diné*," he said, using the Navajo term for the Navajo people. "I'm Jicarilla Apache."

Much of Chuck's archaeological work focused on federal lands, including national parks, national forests, and Bureau of Land Management tracts. He worked regularly on Native American land as well, most often that of the four tribes with reservations near Durango. Since marrying Chuck and moving to Colorado, Janelle had grown familiar with the four neighboring tribes—the Southern Ute people, whose reservation abutted Durango to the east; the Ute Mountain Ute people, whose reservation lay west of town; the Navajo, or *Diné*, whose large reservation encompassed parts of New Mexico, Arizona, and Utah to the south and west; and the Jicarilla Apache, whose large reservation encompassed a rugged swath of New Mexico mountains to the south across the Colorado-New Mexico border.

The Jicarilla Apache economy was based on proceeds from natural gas wells and a small casino popular with dedicated gamblers who made the three-hour drive north into the mountains from Albuquerque. Chuck had worked several contracts for the Jicarilla people in the years since Janelle had come into his life, including a job a few months ago assessing the archaeological significance of proposed well sites for a newly approved natural gas operation on the Jicarilla Apache reservation.

Janelle rolled herself up to Chuck's computer, her phone to her ear and her eyes on the email from oldindian. She knew some Native Americans considered the term "Indian" outdated and offensive, while others embraced it as part of their complex American heritage.

In response to oldindian's kindhearted chuckle, she risked a joke. "Are you related to Geronimo?" she asked, naming the famously elusive leader of the Chiricahua Apache Tribe in Arizona in the late 1800s.

The old man's voice grew grave. "Every Apache is a part of every other Apache, from the beginning of time. That's what we believe. I am a part of Geronimo, just as he is a part of me, and just as you are a part of your people. You're Chuck's wife, is that correct?"

"Yes, I'm Janelle. Janelle Ortega," she replied, unconsciously falling into oldindian's formal cadence.

"*Or-te-ga*," the man repeated, giving the *r* the hard trill of a native Spanish speaker. "I can hear your Iberian roots in your voice. My people journeyed from the plains into the mountains many years ago, just as your people and others journeyed across the ocean to come here and conquer these lands—and my people." Over the phone, the man's voice grew forlorn. "The Jicarilla Apache people have been working ever since to recover from that time."

"I hope your recovery has been successful."

"The pain will always be there. But I know there is pain in your people as well."

Janelle pictured the gang-ridden streets of Albuquerque's South Valley. "You're a wise man."

"The younger ones say that about me sometimes. But I don't believe it, because I still have a lot to learn."

"What's your name?"

"Henry Lightfeather."

"How do you know Chuck?"

"I was the cultural preservation officer for the Jicarilla Apache people. It was my job to select the companies that performed archaeological work on our lands. Once, a long time ago, I hired a young man who was just starting out in his profession."

"Chuck?"

"Yes. He was grateful for the opportunity I gave him. He worked hard and provided a lot more than was required by the contract I signed with him. His work was of exceptional quality. I hired him many times after that. He never disappointed me, not once."

"You're retired now?"

"Retired." Henry grunted. "That's what they call it. I've been set aside, put out to pasture. It's been that way for more than two years now." His voice brightened. "But over that time, Chuck has maintained his contact with me. He told me he would, but I didn't believe him. I know the ways of the world. I know our relationship was based on his work for me and the Jicarilla people. But he still emails me, and he calls me when he's on the road, driving from place to place. He says we'll always be friends, which gratifies me."

"That sounds like Chuck. If he likes you, he likes you. If he doesn't, look out."

"That's the Chuck Bender I know as well."

"Why did you send the email to him about Ralph Hycum's death?"

"I knew most of the people who wrote about Ralph Hycum on the email, but I didn't see Chuck's name on the list. Although I expected Chuck would know about Ralph's death, I thought he would appreciate seeing the comments from the others nonetheless." A beat of silence passed, then Henry continued. "I have to tell you, there's something about the comments that concerns me. Now that I know Chuck is on the expedition, I also have to tell you that my concern is even greater than before."

18

Janelle sat up straight in Chuck's chair. "What is it you're worried about?" she asked Henry.

"There are a number of things," he said, drawing out the words.

"Of those things," she pressed, "what concerns you most?"

Rather than answering directly, Henry said, "There are always concerns in the world. Among them, it's difficult to determine which are the most concerning. That's the case with the Waters of the Southwest Expedition. You see, the people who are on the expedition will likely be making decisions that are of critical importance to the Jicarilla Apache people. The lands of the Jicarilla encompass the headwaters of the Navajo River, which is the easternmost tributary of the Colorado River. In the 1960s, the people who lived in the Rio Grande Basin convinced the US government to drill a tunnel underneath the Continental Divide, sending the waters of the Navajo River eastward through the tunnel to their lands along the Rio Grande."

Janelle bit her lip, forcing herself to remain silent. What did this history have to do with Chuck and the deceased professor, Ralph Hycum?

"The tunnel took the waters of the Navajo River away from my people," Henry continued. "We no longer could irrigate our grasses or provide water to our sheep and cattle, and we became poorer. Then, a few months ago, as if sent by the Creator, a water lawyer from Denver presented an idea to our tribal council. She explained that the Navajo River tunnel was on the verge of collapse. After half a century of use, she said, its walls were falling in and blocking the water's flow. She told us we could fight for our historic rights to the Navajo River by demanding that the tunnel be closed rather than repaired."

"What does all this have to do with Chuck?" Janelle asked, unable to remain silent any longer.

"It has everything to do with him."

"In what way?"

But Henry was not to be dissuaded from his story. "Our council voted to hire the lawyer," he said, his cadence still slow and measured. "Like Chuck, she's very good at her work. Already, she has had great success for us through the back channels of her world. She hasn't filed a lawsuit yet on behalf of the Jicarilla people. Instead, she has learned that engineers for the Bureau of Reclamation expect the Navajo River tunnel to fully collapse sometime soon, blocking the flow of water entirely. The engineers say repairing the tunnel will be very expensive. And for what purpose? The amount of water moved from the Navajo River to the Rio Grande is very little. Besides, the water would be of much greater benefit today to the growing desert cities of Phoenix, Las Vegas, and Los Angeles on the western side of the Continental Divide. For those cities, every drop of water counts, and they are willing to pay for it."

"How is it you know all this?"

"I'm a member of the Jicarilla council. If the lawyer wins back our rights to the water from the Navajo River—which was ours for centuries before it was taken from us—and if we can convince the government that the diversion tunnel isn't worth the cost to repair it, then the water will return to its original flow across our lands and on to the Colorado River. We could use the water ourselves, or we could sell it to the highest bidder downstream."

"Like Los Angeles?"

"Los Angeles has the most money. But Phoenix is the most desperate. It keeps on growing and growing, pretending its water will never run out. For us, high in the mountains, it's of little importance who we sell our water to, or if we use it ourselves. Whatever the case, the water will benefit us, and it will benefit the earth as well. We have determined that if we regain control of the water, we will make sure a portion of it flows all the way to the ocean, helping the plants and animals along the way, as it did before the white man came to this continent. At the same time, the water we use or sell will make for our young people a better future."

Janelle closed her eyes, recalling the friends of her youth she'd lost in Albuquerque's South Valley. "I hope you win back your water."

"The first thing we have to do is make sure the Bureau of Reclamation abandons the tunnel rather than repairing it."

"What does the expedition have to do with that decision?"

"One of the people on the trip is a water analyst for the Bureau of Reclamation named Joseph Conway. The decision to abandon or repair the tunnel rests with his office."

"What do you know about him?"

"I know that every proposed federal water project in the Southwest crosses his desk and that he approves almost every one of them. His approvals have made tens of millions of dollars for the construction companies that build the projects. I've been told he takes bribes to decide in favor of the companies."

"And you're saying his decision about the tunnel will be critical to your tribe's financial future."

"If my people could, we might be tempted to bribe Joseph Conway ourselves to get him to recommend the abandonment of the tunnel. But the construction companies have the money, we don't."

"What does the expedition, and Ralph's death in particular, have to do with all of this?"

"Ralph is, was, a friend of the Denver water lawyer. She asked him to write an article arguing that the tunnel should be abandoned, and that the water of the Navajo River should again be allowed to flow through the homelands of the Jicarilla Apache people. Ralph's article appeared in *WaterWest Journal* a month ago. In it, he said repairing the tunnel would be a waste of taxpayer money. He said only someone who was taking bribes would approve it. Everyone in the water-policy world recognized that his comment was aimed directly at Joseph Conway. And now, Ralph has died while on the expedition with Joseph."

"Was Chuck aware of the article?"

"I don't know."

"Someone has to warn him," Janelle said firmly.

"I doubt that there's any cell phone service where they're traveling in the canyon."

"There's a satellite phone for emergencies. Chuck left me the number. He said it would be checked for messages every twenty-four hours."

"Your message to him would be what, exactly?"

"I…I would…"

"If you send a warning to him and it's seen by Joseph Conway, that would not be good."

Janelle pressed her phone hard to her ear. "Do you believe Chuck is in danger, Henry?" she asked bluntly.

"I believe it's possible Ralph died a natural death."

"You're avoiding my question."

"The desert is a challenging place. It's not easy for older people like him or me."

"You're *still* not answering my question."

"When I heard Ralph had died, I sent Chuck the email that you've read. I wanted to be sure he knew about it. Now, I've learned from you that he's on the expedition. My direct answer to you is yes, it would be good to warn him, provided there's a safe way to do so."

"There is. Me."

"Not you," said Carmelita from the study doorway.

Janelle spun to face her.

"Us," Carmelita said.

19

Clarence gaped at the sheered oarlock resting in the palm of his hand. Half of a V-shaped divot, a quarter-inch deep in the bronze shaft, led directly to where the shaft had snapped in two. "Someone took a file to it, didn't they?" he said wonderingly.

"Looks like it," said Chuck.

"Why would they do that?"

Chuck freed the oars from beneath his legs and, gripping the handles, dropped the oar blades in the water. "Someone doesn't like me. Or, maybe, you."

"Me?"

"You're the one who's been chatting up Liza all week. I've certainly noticed. I'm sure others have, too. Maybe somebody's jealous."

"You honestly think someone would sabotage our boat in a fit of jealousy?"

"Stranger things have happened."

"That'd be strange indeed."

"Do you have any better ideas?"

Clarence shook his head. "Sorry, *jefe*."

Chuck sighed. "Neither do I."

"I guess we'll be keeping our eyes open, won't we?"

"I guess we will."

Chuck rowed the big raft backward across the eddy at the foot of Rapid 1.

Clarence wrapped his arms around his torso and leaned forward, shivering, in front of Chuck. "How can I still be this cold?" he moaned.

Despite the broiling mid-afternoon heat, Chuck shivered as

well. "The river was snow until just a few days ago. Its water temperature is in the fifties this time of year, even down here in the desert."

"I almost died, didn't I?" Clarence asked. For once, his seemingly eternal optimism was nowhere in evidence.

Chuck swallowed, his guilt intensifying. "But you didn't."

"This trip is supposed to be fun."

"What happened to us was scary, but we're okay," he said, attempting to reassure himself as well as Clarence. "Besides, judging by the look Liza gave you, I'm pretty sure there's some fun in your future."

Clarence looked over his shoulder at Chuck, his effervescent smile returning to his face. "Not the look. The slap."

Downriver, Liza and Torch floated around the bend in their kayaks. Just before they passed from view, they dug their paddles into the water, aiming for the right-hand shore. Chuck rowed the gear boat around the curve after them.

A long swath of tawny sand known as Betty Beach stretched for two hundred yards along the right side of the river. The sand built up below Rapid 1 whenever the river reached flood stage. The expedition rafts were nosed up to the shore in the middle of the broad beach. Lines ran from the boats to aluminum stakes pounded into the sand. The guides' PFDs rested over the tops of the metal stakes, serving as protection for errant feet.

The clients formed a line from the boats to the top shelf of the beach. Working in tandem, Maeve and Rocky loosened straps and freed dry bags and ammo cans in the fore and aft wells of one of the oar rafts. The two guides passed the items of gear up the line of expedition members, unloading the boat in bucket-brigade fashion. At the end of the line, Tamara and Vance dispersed the gear into piles, kitchen supplies in one mound, client belongings in another, the guides' camping gear in a third.

As Chuck rowed toward the secured rafts, Clarence remained

hunched forward, his body still shaking. "Thinking about Liza isn't warming me up as much as I thought it would," he said.

"I'm still freezing, too," Chuck told him. "We'll lie down on the sand as soon as we hit the beach. It'll heat us up in seconds."

"Sounds like just what I need."

Chuck angled the raft toward the river's edge. The group finished emptying the last oar raft and awaited the arrival of the gear boat. He nosed the raft up to the beach.

"Woo-hoo! You made it!" Rocky cheered. "You got dump-trucked." He aimed his finger at the picture of the dump truck silkscreened on the front of his ball cap. "That's what it's called when passengers get tossed out of a raft in a rapid, but the raft itself doesn't flip."

Rocky and Maeve hauled the bow of the gear raft onto the shore, its rubber bottom grating on the wet sand.

"The raft was hanging over me when I went under," Chuck said, shipping the oars. "It looked for sure like it was going to flip."

"You can be glad it didn't," Rocky noted, slapping the front thwart with the palm of his hand. "This beast would've taken forever to turn back upright if it had gone all the way over."

He set off up the beach with the bow line, unfurling it to the nearest sand stake. Chuck loosened straps over the mound of gear in the stern well of the boat. Maeve clambered into the front well with Clarence. Together, they unstrapped the load of gear stowed in the bow, passing stoves, tables, chairs, dry bags, water jugs, and aluminum dry boxes up the line of clients.

Maeve tapped Clarence on the shoulder when they finished unloading the front of the boat. "I'm glad you're all right," she told him.

"Thanks," he said. "I don't see how you run rapids like that every day for a living."

"With good PFDs and safety kayakers at the ready, drownings almost never happen these days."

"'Almost never.'" Clarence rolled his eyes, his skepticism obvious. "If you say so."

Maeve aimed a look down her long nose at Chuck, then smiled and said to Clarence, "You just need a captain who doesn't run your raft into a hole sideways."

"The oarlock snapped," Clarence said in Chuck's defense, making no mention of the V-shaped divot in the oarlock's shaft.

"Huh," Maeve responded. "That's weird."

When the gear boat was unloaded, Chuck asked Clarence if he was ready to lie on the hot sand.

"I'm good now," Clarence replied. "Unloading the boat warmed me up."

"Doesn't take long, does it?"

Clarence drew a deep inhalation of the superheated midday air hovering above the beach. "Give me a few more minutes and I swear I'll be ready for another dunk in the river."

While Chuck set up his and Clarence's tents, Clarence conducted his camp-arrival chores as the expedition swamper. First, he set up the portable toilet—a toilet-seat-topped ammo can known in the whitewater world as a groover—behind a screen of bushes out of smell distance at the far end of the beach. Next, he placed a pair of five-gallon plastic buckets in the sand outside the U-shaped camp kitchen. One bucket was empty. The other he filled with river water. He ran a length of surgical hose from the water-filled bucket to a metal spout clamped to the rim of the empty bucket, then placed a bottle of liquid soap in the sand beside the spout. A rubber foot pump halfway along the hose enabled users to pump water from the full bucket into the empty bucket while washing and rinsing their hands.

The CRA guides placed two heavy-duty aluminum stoves on one of the cook tables and ran hoses from the stoves to a twenty-pound propane tank resting in the sand beneath the table. They laid tarps over the sand in the kitchen to catch dropped bits of food that otherwise would attract biting red ants and marauding mice from the brushy hillside behind the beach. One by one, they took breaks from their work to approach Clarence and exchange a few words with him.

Tamara set out the afternoon snack—crostinis and peach chutney—on the table at the front of the kitchen. Vance placed a five-gallon jug of energy drink mixed from powder on the table next to the food, and Rocky arranged the group's webbed camp chairs in the customary semicircle facing the river.

The clients washed their hands and filled plastic cups from the refillable jug. Several topped off their drinks with alcohol from flasks retrieved from their personal bags. They loaded plates with crostinis and spoonfuls of chutney and downed the food quickly beneath the blazing sun. After returning their plates to the camp kitchen, they strolled to the river and stood knee-deep in the cool water, sipping their drinks.

Tamara addressed the group, speaking over the growl of Rapid 1 reverberating from upstream. "It's time for what we've all been waiting for." She added a dose of drama to her voice. "The Maze."

20

Chuck stood with Clarence upriver from the gathered clients. "What's this Maze place Tamara's talking about?" Clarence asked, his voice low.

"It's a bunch of slot canyons a couple miles from here, above the inner gorge," Chuck said.

"What's a slot canyon?"

"A narrow slit in solid rock, with just enough room to walk through. The Maze consists of a whole bunch of slot canyons cut into a single shelf of sandstone, all of them interconnected. There's no place else like it on earth. The only way you can get to it is by hiking up from the river or driving fifty miles on a rough four-wheel-drive road off the Hanksville highway. Hardly anybody attempts the drive, which means we're almost sure to have the place to ourselves when we hike to it this afternoon."

"What'll we do when we get there?"

"Wander around. Explore. Reflect. Contemplate."

"Like, ponder the true meaning of our existence in the vast universe of understanding?"

Chuck grinned. "Something like that. I know meditation isn't your thing. But you won't have to do it if you don't want to. You can just enjoy how beautiful it is. If nothing else, I guarantee you'll be impressed by the Doll House and the Chocolate Drops."

"The what and the what?"

"They're rock formations at the edge of the Maze. You wander through the slot canyons and then you pop out and, boom, there they are, towering over you. They'll take your breath away."

Clarence gazed at Liza, who was changing from her kayak

booties into running shoes in front of her tent. "You know what really takes my breath away? She does."

"She's capable, I know that much. And strong. She hauled you to shore like you didn't weigh a thing."

"That's what I'll be thinking about in the Maze—how glad I am to be alive."

"Is that what the guides talked with you about when they came up to you?"

Clarence nodded. "They know this is my first river trip. They offered me loads of reassurance. It was nice of them."

"It's almost as if they like you," Chuck teased. "Imagine that."

"Well, they appreciate the fact that I set up the toilet and wash dishes for everybody, anyway."

"Chuck!" Tamara called from down the beach. "You're up. Time for our geology lesson."

At breakfast, Tamara had asked Chuck to provide a brief overview on the area's rock formations before the group set out for the Maze. He left Clarence and joined her in front of the clients.

"Keep it short," she said in his ear. "We lost time with your swim. We need to get moving."

He nodded and faced everyone. "How many of you have visited the Maze before?" A third of the group members raised their hands. "Great," he said to them. "You know the treat you're in for." He addressed the others. "The rest of you are about to discover one of the most extraordinary examples of desert beauty on the planet. The Maze is a series of narrow canyons in a hard layer of Cedar Mesa Sandstone. Towering above the canyons is the Land of Standing Rocks—pinnacles of crumbly Organ Shale in fantastical shapes."

He pointed at the boulder-strewn hillside climbing from the beach to the base of the vertical wall of light gray sandstone that formed the inner gorge of Cataract Canyon, as well as the shelf into which the slot canyons of the Maze were cut. Directly behind the beach, the hillside rose to a square opening in the sandstone wall. A hiking trail zigzagged up the slope, past juniper and piñon trees, to the opening.

"We'll climb out of the gorge and hike to the Maze through Surprise Valley. Among the incredible geological formations in Canyonlands, Surprise Valley may be the most fascinating of them all. The valley is a graben, the German word for grave. It's a perfectly flat depression walled by vertical cliffs on both sides. It formed where underground salt deposits dissolved over time, allowing rock layers above to collapse along straight fault lines. In the case of Surprise Valley, the salt melted away beneath the shelf of Cedar Mesa Sandstone that contains the Maze. The valley is identical to several more collapsed grabens found in the park's Needles District on the east side of the river."

Chuck aimed his finger at the notch high in the canyon wall that marked the mouth of the valley.

"Beyond Surprise Valley is a super-rare geologic phenomenon known as a trapped graben. It's called Hidden Valley. A trapped graben is a graben that is collapsed on all four sides. Rain that falls into it has nowhere to go. The water soaks into the ground through openings called swallow holes, dissolving more of the salt underneath and furthering the collapsing process. The trail to the Maze passes right by Hidden Valley. We'll stop and check it out on the way."

He gave Tamara a thumbs-up.

She faced everyone. "Be sure to top off your water bottles before we leave. We'll tough out the hike in the midday heat so we can enjoy the Maze as the temperature drops this afternoon."

The clients and guides climbed the winding trail up the boulder-filled hillside away from the river one behind the other. Chuck and Clarence brought up the rear of the party. They reached the square mouth of Surprise Valley after a searingly hot forty-five minutes. The graben opened before them, half a mile long and a few hundred yards wide. Gray sandstone walls rose from both sides of the graben's pancake-flat floor. Chuck and Clarence trailed the group as everyone hiked the length of the valley and topped out at its head, emerging onto the sandstone shelf that contained the Maze.

Chuck took a deep slug of water. He tightened the cap on his bottle and turned a slow circle, gawking at the distant views. The La Sal Mountains, mantled with spring snow, punctuated the skyline fifty miles to the east. At the foot of the mountain range, well below the snow line, rocky desert surrounded the tourist town of Moab. To the north, the Island in the Sky massif rose two thousand vertical feet between the Green and Colorado Rivers, its immense prow of beige Navajo Sandstone slicing the blue sky.

The slot canyons of the Maze spread before him, sliced into the shelf of gray Cedar Mesa Sandstone. Crosshatched lines, dark with shadow, marked where the tight canyons cut into the bare stone shelf, often called slickrock. The Doll House, a hulking mass of rock pocked with window-like openings, rose at the far edge of the Maze. Beyond the Doll House were the Chocolate Drops, four pinnacles of mud-brown Organ Shale standing in a regimented line.

Chuck led the group west across the slickrock to the lip of Hidden Valley. The trapped graben was barely two hundred yards long and less than a hundred yards wide. Living up to its name, it was hidden from view until he reached its very edge. Its walls rose fifty feet straight up on all four sides, save for a single entry point a hundred feet to the right, where a steep ramp of stone led from the slickrock rim like a sloped diving board to the flat bottom of the tiny, four-walled valley. Ricegrass and stands of sagebrush covered the floor of the trapped graben. Swallow holes showed here and there between the brush as dark depressions down which water flowed when summer thunderstorms rumbled across the region, releasing rain in intense torrents.

Everyone gathered with Chuck and peered into the walled depression.

"This is a perfect example of graben formation," he said. "Geologic studies have found that the floors of grabens like this one and others in Canyonlands drop by as much as an inch in a single year of heavy rains."

At the back of the group, Tamara clapped her hands. "Okay, people," she said. "Time for the main event." Everyone turned to her as she continued. "At Wayne's suggestion, we're going to treat this afternoon as a meditative pause at the midpoint of our journey. Each of you will enter the Maze wherever you choose. For the next couple of hours, you'll wander through the slot canyons of the Maze in whatever state of reflection and introspection you choose." She looked at Wayne. "Have I got that right?"

He tipped his head to her and took over. "The idea is for each of you to take some time this afternoon to reflect on the conversations we've had over the last week, and to consider where you'd like the discussions to go in the week ahead. I know some of our debates have been testy, angry even. I would simply ask that, as you wander past each other in the confined space of the Maze this afternoon, you offer one another sincere greetings, with openness, kindness, and generosity of spirit."

A dismissive guffaw came from the center of the group, its source immediately recognizable to Chuck.

21

"I hear you, Leon," Wayne said without looking at the Consilla representative. "I suspect others of you are choking back laughter, too. I don't blame you for doing so." He scanned the group. "We're corporate managers and policymakers—not the sort of people normally given to spending time exploring our kinder, gentler selves. But we're here on this expedition on behalf of every citizen of the American Southwest, each of whom counts on the water from the Colorado River Basin for their lives and livelihoods. We're here for the plants and animals that depend on the river, too. As you walk through the Maze this afternoon, please join with me—in Ralph's memory, if for no other reason—to reflect on how each of us might help move our group forward, toward consensus and solutions, in the evenings ahead."

Silence followed Wayne's comments. Leon did not laugh again.

"Thank you, Wayne," Tamara said. She pointed across the slickrock at the crosshatched crevices and said, "Please, everyone, enter via any opening you like. We'll meet up outside the north end of the Maze, at the foot of the Chocolate Drops, in two hours."

She set out across the rock shelf toward the scattered entries to the slot canyons, leading the others.

Chuck followed, with Clarence at his side. "Hope you can handle being down there all alone for such a long time," he said.

"You and I aren't allowed to stick together?" Clarence asked.

"We're supposed to walk around on our own. Wayne's idea, not mine."

"To be honest, I'm looking forward to it. I bet it's nice and cool down there in the shade." He chuckled. "Besides, Liza's gonna be wandering around down there somewhere, too. We might run into each other."

Chuck split off from Clarence and crossed the bare sandstone on his own. Ahead were half a dozen Maze entrances—chutes sloping downward into the subterranean-like labyrinth. The majority of the slot canyons ran parallel to one another. Perpendicular cracks connected the parallel slots at numerous points, creating dozens of connections between the myriad passages.

Clarence waved farewell to Chuck and descended down one of the chutes. Chuck halted, allowing everyone else to disappear into the Maze as well. Alone on the slickrock, he did a slow rotation, soaking in the view one more time.

He strode to the head of the nearest entry point. A jumble of sandstone blocks sloped downward into one of the Maze's parallel slot canyons. He descended the heap of stone, squeezing past a boulder the size of a compact car wedged halfway down the slanted entry. The canyon that led away from the bottom of the chute was six feet wide, its floor flat and sandy, with sandstone walls rising fifty feet on each side. A sliver of blue sky showed high overhead, between the stone faces.

The temperature was at least fifteen degrees lower at the bottom of the slot canyon, which was shrouded in shadow for all but a few minutes each day, than on the sunbaked slickrock above. Chuck ran his fingers along the canyon wall. The stone was cool to the touch and worn smooth from centuries of wind and water erosion.

His eyes adjusted to the dusky light as he walked along the floor of the passageway. Footprints of group members who'd passed before him were imprinted in the sand.

He attempted at first to do as Wayne had requested, considering anything he might do to engender consensus among the group. But Wayne's instructions weren't necessarily aimed at him. Rather, they were directed at the members of the expedition tasked with solving the Southwest's vexing water issues. Instead, Chuck allowed his mind to wander aimlessly as he sauntered through the crevices of the Maze, taking right and left turns at canyon junctions without concern for direction. He passed other members of the group every few minutes as he strolled, nodding to them in greeting as Wayne had requested.

His thoughts turned to Janelle and the girls, and he came up short, a stab of panic cutting through him. What if something had happened to one of them in the last week? An accident, perhaps, or an illness. Why hadn't he tried to contact Janelle from up on the slickrock?

The likelihood that cell service reached the remote Maze area of the national park was extremely low, however. Besides, Janelle and the girls had been fine on their own before he'd come along. No doubt they were doing just fine without him right now.

He reminded himself he'd come on the trip to relive his river-rafting past, which included hikes through incredible places like the Maze. He exhaled fully, letting go of his concerns, and resumed his shaded stroll.

The sun fell in the west and the shadows climbed higher on the walls of the Maze's narrow canyons. Using the angle of the sun as a guide, he worked his way northward, turning left at a junction, then right, then left again, until one of the Chocolate Drops loomed above him in the narrow band of sky visible from the bottom of the slot canyon along which he walked.

He continued northward in the canyon until its walls fell away from one another. The air temperature rose as the canyon widened, and sagebrush and prickly pear cacti sprouted where more sunlight reached the sandy floor of the slot.

The passage ended at a swath of sand dunes and ricegrass extending two hundred yards to the foot of the Chocolate Drops. The four shale towers etched the sky like a quartet of soldiers standing at attention. Wayne and Tamara waited in the shadow of the nearest tower with a number of clients and guides gathered around them.

More people emerged from the mouths of other crevices that opened onto the sand dunes. Chuck accompanied them across the dunes to Wayne, Tamara, and the others. Everyone waited in the shade at the foot of the tower in silence, the solitude they'd experienced in the Maze maintaining its hold over them.

Clarence sauntered out of one of the slots and crossed the sand dunes with his hands in his pockets. "That was surprisingly nice in there," he said softly, stopping at Chuck's side.

"Any Liza sightings?" Chuck asked him.

"Nah. She probably would've punched me if I tried to talk to her in there, though."

"She's capable of it, I'll say that much."

As if on cue, Liza exited the same slot from which Clarence had emerged moments ago.

"She was stalking you," Chuck said in Clarence's ear.

"Can't say as I blame her," Clarence replied. As she crossed the dunes toward them, he whispered, "I told you she likes me."

He waved to her, but she angled away from him to the far side of the gathered group.

"Or not," said Chuck.

Clarence grinned, his round cheeks rising to his eyes. "She's just playing hard to get, that's all."

Wayne addressed the group. "I trust all of you appreciated your time in the Maze as much as I did."

Several people murmured their agreement.

"In the evenings ahead," Wayne continued, "I hope we'll take what we experienced over the last couple of hours and apply it to the good of our group as a whole."

He turned to Tamara, who stepped forward.

"We'll drop down to Spanish Bottom from here and loop

back to camp on the riverside trail," she said. "We'll be back in time for a late dinner."

"We're not all here yet," Vance noted. "Maeve hasn't come out."

Tamara scanned the group, her brow furrowed. "You're right," she said to Vance. She checked the bulky sport watch on her wrist. "She's ten minutes overdue at this point."

Vance tapped his own wrist. "She's as punctual as clockwork. I've never known her to be late for anything. Not once."

Tamara nodded, her neck stiff. "Neither have I."

22

"I'm beginning to wonder what on earth we're doing," Janelle said to Carmelita as she piloted Chuck's bulky Bender Archaeological crew-cab pickup truck through the midday heat on sunbaked Highway 95, north of the small Utah town of Hanksville.

They'd been on the road for hours now, with several more to go. Carmelita sat in the front passenger seat, while Rosie slumped in back, her head resting against the side window, her eyes half closed. The air conditioner roared, blasting cool air into the cab of the big truck. The highway was deserted, as were the scrublands stretching away from either side of the road. In Durango the previous day, Carmelita had remained steadfast in her determination to join Janelle in finding Chuck on the expedition and sharing with him Henry Lightfeather's warning about Joseph Conway.

"You absolutely, positively cannot head into the desert on your own," Carmelita said. "It wouldn't be safe."

"But we can't leave Rosie home alone," Janelle countered. "She's too little."

"She can come along. We'll surprise Chuck together, all three of us. It'll be fun."

"The idea is to warn him. I'm not sure where the word 'fun' comes into it."

"You're being overly dramatic. We just want to let him know about the phone call. Besides, who knows if we'll even be able to find him out there."

"If we leave first thing in the morning, I think the odds are pretty good. Chuck told me commercial river trips always stick to their planned schedules, 'come hell or high water' is how he put it. Tomorrow, the Waters of the Southwest Expedition is scheduled to hike through the slot canyons of the Maze, at the head of Cataract Canyon in the middle of Canyonlands National Park. They're supposed to camp at a beach below the Maze tomorrow night. According to the map, a road comes to within a mile of the river at that point—but the last stretch of the road is four-wheel-drive, and it's supposedly pretty rough."

"Which is why you can't go out there alone," Carmelita insisted.

"Okay," Janelle said, giving in. She forced a smile. "Maybe it'll be fun after all."

Now, Carmelita spoke over the low rumble of the truck's diesel engine. "You know exactly what we're doing," she said, twisting to face Janelle, her back to the passenger door.

Janelle let go of the steering wheel with one hand and waved at the empty desert stretching to the horizon on both sides of the highway. "There's nobody out here. We're all alone."

"So what. We're fine on our own. We'll drive to the end of the road, find Chuck and tell him what we need to tell him, give Uncle Clarence a hug, and go home." She dusted her hands together. "Done and done."

"You're not the least bit nervous, are you?"

"What's there to be nervous about? We've got food and water. Chuck made me change a tire on the truck before I got my license, so if we get a flat, I can take care of it. Besides, we're heading into a national park."

"According to what I read last night, Canyonlands is the most remote national park in the country outside of Alaska, and the Maze District is the most remote part of Canyonlands. The road from the highway to the Maze is sixty miles long, all of it dirt. At the forty-mile point, it drops down through something called the Orange Cliffs. That part is full-on four-wheel-drive, over rocks and along ledges."

"A perfectly great adventure," Carmelita said with a smile. "Like I said yesterday: fun."

Janelle smiled back at Carmelita, taken in by her enthusiasm. "Fine. I accept your confidence." She lifted an eyebrow. "I'm still not sure what I was thinking bringing you and your sister along, though."

"You were thinking of Daddy," Rosie said from the backseat. She leaned to the center of the truck and caught Janelle's eye in the rearview mirror. "I'm awake now."

Carmelita nodded. "Rosie's right: you were thinking of Dad. In fact, we're all thinking of Dad."

Janelle tightened her grip on the steering wheel. Carmelita's use of the word 'Dad' sealed it.

After six years with Chuck as the girls' stepfather, Rosie exclusively used the term 'Daddy' for Chuck, while Carmelita almost always called him by his name, calling him Dad only on rare occasions.

"Actually," Carmelita continued, "I can't wait to see the Orange Cliffs. I've only seen them in pictures. They have some of the best big-wall climbs ever—Air Drop, Pizza Slice, Rock 'Em Sock 'Em. Not to mention the four big towers of super-soft shale right next to the Maze called the Chocolate Drops. The routes up them are legendary—crumbly, exposed, totally rad. The Doll House is there, too, right next to the Drops. It'll be great to go back and tell everybody I saw the Drops and Doll House up close and personal."

"There's a doll house where we're going?" Rosie asked.

"Not a real one. A rock outcrop that looks like one, with holes in the sides that are like windows."

Janelle glanced at Carmelita. "You sure know a lot about Canyonlands."

"I learned about all the climbs in the park while I was studying up on the routes for Indian Creek."

Janelle groaned. "Chuck and I have made a monster out of you, haven't we?"

Carmelita crossed her arms. "I am *not* a monster."

But Rosie nodded emphatically in back. "Oh yes you are, Carm. You're a monster climber. You're the best for your age in almost the whole country."

"Not for long," Carmelita said, "if *Mamá* and Chuck won't let me go where I need to go to keep getting better."

"Indian Creek, Indian Creek, Indian Creek," said Janelle. "That's all you talk about anymore. Besides, we're not convinced that's really why you want to go."

Carmelita continued to address Rosie. "See? They don't trust me. Indian Creek is the best crack climbing in the world. It's a wall of cliffs that's miles long, right outside the Needles part of Canyonlands. It's only two hours from Durango. The whole climbing team goes there, like, all the time. But *Mamá* and Chuck won't let me go with them."

Janelle pressed the tip of her tongue against the back of her teeth. Older teenage climbers from Durango regularly drove to Indian Creek for weekend camping and climbing trips—without parent chaperones. As the top young climber in town, Carmelita had been invited along on the trips by her older teammates for more than a year now. So far, Janelle and Chuck had managed to put her off by insisting she was too young to join the weekend excursions.

"Your sister just finished her sophomore year of high school," Janelle explained over her shoulder to Rosie. "She's barely sixteen. The climbing team members who go over there are older. They camp with climbers who show up from all over the world and do whatever they want while they're there."

Carmelita straightened in her seat. "They're climbers," she said to Janelle. "They climb. At camp, they're so tired they just go to sleep."

"I'm not so sure about that. Besides, outdoor rock climbing scares me. It's not like the sport climbing you do in the gym, with top ropes all set to catch you when you fall."

Carmelita huffed. "I climb outdoors all the time with Chuck. Besides, crack climbing is the safest kind of outdoor climbing there is."

Rosie leaned forward. "What *is* crack climbing anyway, Carm?"

"It's where you climb cracks in the rock that go straight up in a perfect line, placing your protection as you go. It's the easiest kind of climbing to protect, but it's the hardest to do. There are only a few places where the cliffs have long, perfect splits in them like that. The walls above Indian Creek have the longest cracks in the whole world, going straight up for hundreds of feet. And there are lots and lots of them. Like, thousands."

"That sounds totally rad."

"Because it totally is. Or it would be, if I ever got to go there." Carmelita turned to Janelle. "I'm mature for my age. You always say so. I get straight As in school every single time. Plus, I've got my license now. Maybe I'll just drive over there on my own, no matter what you say."

Janelle pressed herself backward in the driver's seat, straightening her arms, her palms to the steering wheel. A sidelong glance at Carmelita revealed the same burning defiance in her daughter's eyes she remembered from her own teenage years.

Carmelita's mouth was clamped shut, holding back the commentary she clearly could have aimed at Janelle: that at seventeen, only a year older than Carmelita was now, Janelle had become pregnant with her oldest daughter—a far more significant act of rebellion than going rock climbing at Indian Creek.

Janelle relaxed her hands on the wheel. "I trust you," she said to Carmelita. "Chuck and I trust you, we really do. We'll revisit. We'll keep revisiting. It's just, we're scared for you, too. It's not like rock climbing is an entirely benign activity."

"Yeah," said Rosie. "It's not like my dancing classes. Nobody falls and dies from dancing, do they, *Mamá*?"

"No, they don't," Janelle acknowledged.

The resistance in Carmelita's eyes cooled to a simmer. "Fine," she said grudgingly. "We'll revisit." She smiled. "Every fifteen minutes."

Janelle scrunched her mouth. "That's what I'm afraid of."

23

Tamara directed everyone to form small groups and return to the Maze.

"We'll meet back here in thirty minutes," she said, tapping her watch. "That should give us enough time, between all of us, to cover every slot."

Rocky offered to climb the boulder-littered slope to the base of the nearest Chocolate Drop. "I'll have a bird's-eye view from up there. Maybe she got disoriented and came out on the wrong side."

"Good idea," Tamara said. "She could be wandering around up on the slickrock looking for us, for all we know."

"If she is, I'll be able to see her." Rocky climbed away from the dunes toward the base of the shale tower.

Chuck followed Clarence, who sidled through the group to Liza.

"Care to join us?" he asked her.

"Sure," she said.

"Great. You saved me once. If we get lost, you can save me again."

Her dark eyes shone. "I'd be happy to."

Chuck glanced at Liza as he hiked across the dunes with her and Clarence. "Are you worried about Maeve?"

"Nah. I'm sure she just got turned around in there, like Rocky said. They don't call it the Maze for nothing."

They entered one of the passages. The light grew dim and the temperature dropped. Liza led the way down the shadowed corridor. Clarence trailed a step behind her, while Chuck brought up the rear.

"How'd you come to be a kayaker?" Clarence asked Liza as they walked through the slot canyon.

"I started out as a rafting guide and picked up kayaking along the way. I've rowed rafts on trips lots more than I've safety kayaked."

"Well, you know what you're doing, I can vouch for that."

"Rescues in big water are fairly straightforward—get to the victim, get the victim to shore. Rescues in small water are a lot trickier."

"'Small water'?"

"Creek boating—steep, narrow streams with lots of waterfalls. It's for adrenaline junkies, which is not who I am."

"Could've fooled me. My adrenaline was pumping just watching you drop into Rapid 1 in your teeny, tiny, little boat."

"I was with Torch. That helps. Kayaking is a buddy sport." She reached back and rested her palm on Clarence's belly. "With your low center of gravity, you'd make a good kayaker yourself, you know that?"

"Would you be willing to give me lessons?" Clarence asked. "As in, one-on-one?"

She chuckled. "We'll have to see about that."

They came to a junction where a second slot angled off to the right.

"Which way?" Liza asked, turning to Clarence and Chuck.

"Right," Clarence said. "Because I always am."

"About what?"

"I'm right about you, that's for sure. About how beautiful you are. How humble. You saved my life, but you're totally modest about it."

Liza's cheeks grew red. "My people are not given to boastfulness."

Chuck slapped Clarence on the shoulder. "Unlike you."

Liza looked Clarence in the eye. "I'm fine with someone

boasting—when they've got something to boast about." She ran a hand down his swarthy forearm. "Like their strength."

"*Sí,*" Clarence said in instant agreement. "*Tengo mucho fuerte.*"

"*¿Fuerte?*"

"Power," he translated. "Strength."

She smiled. "I like that in a—"

A whistle sounded, its piercing screech echoing down the side canyon.

The blood drained from Liza's cheeks. She sprinted up the slot in the direction of the whistle. Clarence followed, also running.

Chuck walked quickly up the passageway after them, assuring himself Maeve had been located safe and sound, and the whistle was simply bringing everyone together.

The whistle came again. This time, it was three sharp blasts. A brief interlude was followed by three more whistle blasts—the international signal for help.

Chuck broke into a run. Liza and Clarence disappeared around a corner ahead. He rounded the turn after them, his shoes digging into the sand, then slid to a halt.

The slot canyon before him was wider and lower than most of those in the Maze, its walls twenty feet apart and less than thirty feet high. A narrow ledge climbed the right-hand wall. Sprigs of desert paintbrush and bunches of ricegrass sprouted on the ascending stone shelf.

Clarence and Liza stood with their backs to Chuck, Clarence's arm around Liza's waist. A dozen group members stood beyond them, also facing away from Chuck.

Three more whistle blasts came from the front of the group. Chuck rose on the balls of his feet, attempting to look past the people ahead of him, but could see nothing but the backs of their heads.

The ledge, a few inches wide, angled up the canyon wall beside him. He settled the sole of his shoe on the rock shelf at knee height, spread his hands on the face of the wall for balance, and stepped off the sandy canyon floor. He placed his other foot farther up the shelf and transferred his weight to it.

He was two feet off the ground now, head and shoulders above those in front of him. He peered past them, spotting Wayne at the front of the group.

Another half dozen people stood beyond Wayne, facing Chuck. Tamara knelt in the sand between the two groups, her head bowed. Wayne put a shiny metal whistle to his mouth and blew hard into it three times.

The ledge widened slightly as it ascended along the sandstone wall. Chuck took another step up it. From his higher vantage point, he saw that Tamara was crouched over something lying in the sand.

Or, rather, some*one*.

A pair of legs clad in multi-pocketed hiking pants extended, unmoving, from beneath Tamara's hunched frame. Next to the legs, a squared-off chunk of sandstone the size of a loaf of bread lay in the sand. On a corner of the stone a splash of liquid gleamed dark red—the color of blood.

24

Twenty miles north of Hanksville, Janelle slowed and turned onto a graded gravel road heading east from the highway. She braked to a stop at a weathered signpost that listed the Orange Cliffs as forty miles distant and the Maze as sixty miles away. The washboarded dirt road extended in a straight line across a vast sagebrush flat.

She dropped her hands from the steering wheel. Everything she knew about backcountry travel, all of it learned in her years since trading city life in Albuquerque for mountain-town Durango, told her venturing into the Maze District of Canyonlands came with a certain amount of risk.

She'd learned while reading about the national park last night that the other two of Canyonlands' three districts, separated by the Colorado and Green Rivers flowing through the heart of the park, were reached by paved roads. In contrast, the Maze District was accessible only by rafts floating through Cataract Canyon or by high-clearance vehicles via the dead-end dirt road stretching before her. The road into the Maze District was so rugged that only a handful of visitors ventured down it each week, and those who did were cautioned on the park website to come equipped with extensive tool kits and the ability to perform self-repairs as necessary.

Carmelita reached forward from the passenger seat and gave the dashboard a solid *thwap*. "We can do this, *Mamá*. The truck will get us there."

Janelle hoisted her water bottle from the center console, took a swallow, and wiped her mouth with the back of her hand. "*Bueno*," she said.

She took hold of the steering wheel with a double-fisted grip and let her foot off the brake. The truck rolled forward. The road was free of recent tracks; no other vehicles had driven down it for quite some time.

She accelerated. The highway receded in the rearview mirror. A cloud of dust rose behind the truck and was whipped away by the brisk afternoon wind.

She held the pickup at a steady thirty miles an hour, her teeth rattling as the wheels jounced over the washboards lining the road. An hour later, they passed Hans Flat Ranger Station, a small, single-story building beside the road just inside the park boundary. A white park-service pickup truck, caked with dust, was parked in front of the building.

Fifteen minutes after passing the ranger station, she pulled off the road at the scenic overlook atop the Orange Cliffs. The thousand-foot vertical escarpment of orange-red Kayenta Sandstone ran through the Maze District from north to south for dozens of miles. According to her research the previous night, this was where the road would get rough.

She and the girls climbed out of the truck. Heat rose from the sunbaked, gravel parking area, empty except for their vehicle. The wind swept over the top of the cliffs, whipping her loose hair. She gathered it in both hands and shoved it into the collar of her shirt.

A flat shelf of bare sandstone extended a hundred feet from the parking area to the unprotected edge of the escarpment. She halted with Carmelita and Rosie fifteen feet back from the drop-off and took in the expansive view before them.

"Why are we stopping so far back from the edge?" Carmelita asked her.

"This is close enough for me. I'm not exactly scared of heights, but I don't necessarily like them, either."

"Unlike me," said Carmelita.

The wall of cliffs fell away in a sheer drop to a stretch of desert scrubland far below. The lower expanse of sage and bunchgrass matched the broad flat they'd just crossed. The lower desert ended at a wide shelf of bare gray rock a mile from the base of the cliffs. The slot canyons of the Maze appeared as dark slashes in the rock shelf, as if a giant bear had clawed the canyons into the stone. The Doll House and Chocolate Drops towered above the Maze, every bit as impressive as Carmelita had predicted. Beyond the Maze, the inner gorge of Cataract Canyon was a deep, shadowed defile between vertical stone walls, the Colorado River out of sight at the bottom of the chasm.

On the far side of the inner gorge, the slender sandstone minarets that gave the park's Needles District its name rose above the surrounding desert. The spires' distinctive red and white bands, the result of sand layers deposited during the ebb and flow of the ancient sea that once had covered the region, shone in the afternoon sunlight. North of the Needles, the Island in the Sky plateau etched the horizon.

"*Caramba*," Rosie breathed, using one of Clarence's favorite words. She pointed over the edge of the escarpment. "Are we going all the way down there?"

"We *get* to go all the way down there," Carmelita said. She set off from Rosie's side toward the drop-off.

"Careful," Janelle warned, reaching a hand toward her.

"I won't get too close," she said over her shoulder. "That's the number one lesson of rock climbing when you're not roped up." She halted several feet from the precipice and peered left and right along the miles-long cliff face. "It's just like in the pictures. Route after route after route. I could spend my whole life here and never do the same line twice."

Rosie shook herself. "This place gives me the creeps, Carm."

"That's why it's so cool."

Janelle set her hands on her hips, taking in the vast view. "It's incredible, I will say that."

Carmelita pointed south, where the road angled downward

off the top of the escarpment on a narrow stone bench. "Is that where we're headed?"

"According to the map, yes. The road drops down the cliffs to the south, then turns back north to the Maze."

"I don't see how the truck will fit."

"I'm wondering the same thing myself."

Rosie performed a twirl on the bare rock. "Only one way to find out!"

Carmelita returned to her sister's side. "You sound just like Chuck."

"Because I am. Anyways, he's why we're here. Him and Uncle Clarence." She looked at Janelle. "Right, *Mamá*?"

"Assuming we can find them down there." She drew a breath, taking in the sweep of desert extending from the foot of the cliffs. "It's a lot more than I thought it would be."

"A lot more what?" Rosie asked.

Janelle swept her hand in a wide arc, taking in the bowl of blue sky overhead, the line of cliffs falling away before them, and the desert and bare rock and stone pinnacles stretching to the far horizon. "A lot more everything. This is just…it's…it's incredible."

"I'm glad we came," Carmelita said. She eyed the place at the top of the escarpment where the road descended into the abyss. "Assuming we can get down from here, that is."

Janelle retrieved the pair of binoculars stored in the truck glovebox and trained them on the slot canyons of the Maze. According to the trip itinerary, the members of the expedition would be hiking through the narrow canyons this afternoon.

As she spun the focus knob, three faint screeches floated to the top of the escarpment, riding the rising air up the face of the cliffs.

She lowered the binoculars and turned her ear to the sound.

"What the—?" Rosie began.

Janelle shushed her.

After a pause, three more faint whistles reached them at the top of the cliffs.

The wind picked up, humming as it swept over the escarpment and eliminating any chance of hearing more whistles from below.

Carmelita stared down at the slot canyons of the Maze. "Someone was whistling. Three blasts. SOS."

"What's SOS?" Rosie asked.

"It means help. Emergency."

"Daddy," Rosie whimpered. She wrapped her arms around Janelle's waist and stared down at the Maze. "Uncle Clarence."

Janelle put the binoculars to her eyes. The Maze came into sharp relief. She swung the binoculars across the expanse of crenelated stone, the shadowed canyons dark against the gray rock. The wind blasted past her ears, preventing her from hearing any more sounds from below.

She slowed her breathing, braced her elbows against her chest, and scanned the Doll House, then the Chocolate Drops.

Movement flickered in the viewfinder. She pressed the binoculars to her eyes. The movement resolved itself as someone heading quickly across a patch of sand dunes to the Maze from the base of the nearest Chocolate Drop.

"See that?" Carmelita asked.

"It's a person," Janelle said, staring through the binoculars. "Running."

The person disappeared into one of the slot canyons of the Maze.

Janelle swung the binoculars across the stone shelf that contained the narrow passages, then back to the Doll House and Chocolate Drops. She spotted no more movement.

The wind relented. She cocked her head, listening.

Nothing.

"The whistling stopped," Carmelita said.

Janelle lowered the binoculars. Had she imagined the person sprinting across the dunes?

No. Carmelita had seen the movement, too. Both girls had heard the whistles.

There was no doubt in Janelle's mind. Far below in the Maze—where Chuck and Clarence were scheduled to be right now—someone was in trouble.

25

Chuck scrambled higher on the ledge just as Rocky charged down the slot canyon from the opposite direction, arriving from his lookout station at the base of the Chocolate Drops. He muscled his way to the front of the group and stopped next to Tamara.

Chuck craned his neck to see the rest of the body lying on the ground. It was indeed the missing guide, Maeve. She lay on her back, unmoving, eyes closed and arms limp at her sides. Her face was ashen and her mouth slack. Blood soaked into the sand beneath her head, which was crushed at the temple. A lock of her blond hair stuck to the bruised skin of her forehead, soaked by a thick channel of blood.

Tamara, kneeling, performed chest compressions on Maeve, then pressed her fingers to Maeve's carotid artery. She looked up at Wayne, standing over her, and shook her head once, short and sharp. "Still no pulse." She leaned forward, bringing her face within inches of Maeve's lips. Seconds passed. She again looked up at Wayne. "She's not breathing." She placed her hands on Maeve's sternum, but Wayne gripped her shoulder and she did not resume the chest compressions.

"She's dead," said Wayne, his voice hollow. "She's been dead for a while now."

Tamara uttered an animal-like howl, half scream, half moan. She gathered Maeve's upper body in her arms and sobbed, rocking Maeve as the group stood vigil around her.

After a minute, Tamara's cries lessened. Sniffling, she laid Maeve back on the ground, cradling the back of the guide's head until it again rested on the sand.

"This was her seventh season with CRA," Tamara said, her tone solemn. "She joked with me just last week that she wouldn't be getting a seven-year itch, not this year or ever. She loved guiding. I loved working with her. We coordinated our schedules so we could do as many trips together as we could each year."

Tamara eyed the bloodied stone lying next to Maeve's head. She shifted her knees in the sand and peered up at the canyon wall. Her eyes found Chuck, perched on the ledge.

"What are you doing?" she demanded. Her voice rippled with fury clearly born of her grief. She scanned the portion of the ledge that climbed beyond Chuck to the top of the wall. "What's up there?"

"I'll look." He placed one foot in front of the other along the ascending shelf until his head reached the top of the wall. Scattered on the slickrock near the edge of the canyon were a number of sandstone chunks similar in size to the one that apparently had struck and killed Maeve.

He pulled himself out of the slot, picked up one of the stones, and displayed it to Tamara and the others below. "There are a bunch of these up here."

Tamara looked from the rock in Chuck's hands to the one next to Maeve. "It wouldn't have fallen. It *couldn't* have."

Wayne tilted his head. "We can't know that for sure."

"But we know the odds."

"All of us were moving through the slots, our steps setting off tiny tremors." He pointed at the bloodied rock beside Maeve's head. "If that was teetering on the very edge, ready to fall off…" He shrugged. "That's how these canyons were formed: wind, water, erosion, movement."

Rocky stood over Maeve, his chin trembling. "I don't buy it," he declared.

"We're not doing her any good by arguing like this." Wayne crouched and rested his hand on Maeve's shoulder. "We have to give her the care she deserves."

Rocky stared down at Maeve. Above his beard, his cheeks were pale, his eyes stricken. Squatting, he untied the blue bandanna from around his neck and draped it over her face.

Chuck stared at the place where the blue cloth covered Maeve's mouth, willing it to lift with an exhalation of her breath. But the cloth did not move.

Wayne's shoulders drooped. "We need the sat phone."

Tamara sighed and nodded. "It's in my pack. It won't work down here in the slot. I'll make the call as soon as I'm up on top. It's less than a mile from here to the end of the road that comes down from the highway. They'll want us to take her there. They won't send a helicopter, not with the road so close."

"I'll go," said Vance from the middle of the group, raising his hand.

Atop the wall, Chuck lifted his hand as well. "I'll go with Vance," he said to Tamara. "I'm sure Clarence will, too."

He and Clarence were outliers on the trip; their absence from the group over the next few hours would be missed the least.

"While the rest of you head back," Chuck continued, "we'll carry her to the end of the road. We'll hike back to camp after the rangers come for her."

At Liza's side, Clarence nodded his agreement.

Tamara looked up at Vance from where she knelt in the sand. "There's generally a ranger or two working out of Hans Flat. Assuming someone is there now, they'll be able to drive to the end of the road pretty quick. Can the three of you manage it? Do you need a fourth?"

"I'm sure the three of us will be enough," Vance replied. He turned to the rest of the group. "Who's got something to wrap her in?"

"I do," said Rocky. He pulled a foil emergency blanket from his daypack. "This should work." The blanket was folded in a tight square. He shook it out, its metal coating flickering in the shade of the slot.

Chuck slid his legs over the edge of the slot canyon and found the ledge with his feet. He faced the wall, pressed his palms to the stone, and edged along the shelf. Halfway down the ledge, a tuft of ricegrass grew from a crack where the horizontal ledge met the vertical wall. He noted as he stepped around the clump of grass that several stems in the bunch were crushed. The crushed stems, which had sprouted at the outside edge of the tuft, lay crumpled on the surface of the stone shelf.

Chuck stared at the broken stems of grass.

He was certain he hadn't stepped on the ricegrass on his way up the ledge. But if he hadn't, who had?

26

The roadbed on the sloped stone bench cut into the face of the Orange Cliffs accommodated the big truck's tires with only inches to spare. The road followed the bench downward across the cliff face, the sandstone wall of the escarpment rising straight up on one side and dropping away straight down on the other.

Janelle stopped the truck a hundred feet down the bench and sat behind the wheel, her foot pressed on the brake pedal, studying the road ahead. While the roadbed from the highway across the broad sagebrush flat had been dusty and washboarded, the roadbed angling down the face of the cliffs was bare rock strewn with pebbles and loose chunks of sandstone.

She eased up on the brakes and allowed the truck to roll forward, descending the bench at little more than walking speed. She sat forward in her seat, staring through the windshield, and clung tight to the steering wheel, which attempted to wrench itself from her hands each time the truck's big tires struck a rock or rolled through a pitted depression in the undulating stone surface. Where the road smoothed and widened for brief stretches, she accelerated as much as she dared, her thoughts on the emergency whistles that had come from the Maze.

"This is so frickin' cool," Rosie exclaimed, ogling the view out the window.

"No 'frickin',' please," Janelle said, her jaw set.

"I'm only saying it because you won't let me use the real f-word."

Carmelita peered up through the windshield at the cliff wall rising to the cloudless blue sky. "This is stupendously, awesomely, outrageously cool." She settled back in her seat. "See?" she said to Rosie. "There are lots of other adverbs you could use."

"Just because you know what adverbs are."

"They're modifiers. They make verbs more descriptive."

"Whatever."

Halfway down the escarpment, the road approached a perpendicular sandstone face extending outward from the cliff wall. The road appeared to come to an abrupt end at the stone face. As Janelle drove the truck nearer, however, she saw that the road actually seesawed backward and downward for a hundred feet along the cliff wall to another perpendicular face. At that point, the road seesawed forward once more, forming a giant letter Z against the vertical wall of the escarpment.

The two switchbacks were too tight for the big truck to negotiate. Instead, Janelle realized, her breath catching in her throat, the only way to continue down the cliffs would be to reverse the truck down the middle leg of the giant Z.

She inched the pickup to within a couple of feet of the first perpendicular face, then twisted and looked over her shoulder, preparing to back down the next section of road. But the descending roadbed was blocked from her view by the truck's eight-foot-long bed.

She put the truck in park and faced forward, her hands in her lap and her eyes closed. "I'm not sure I can do this," she said.

"I can," said Carmelita.

Janelle turned to Carmelita, her eyes wide open.

"I can do it," she insisted. "It's just backing up. You can guide me from outside."

"But you just got your driver's license a few weeks ago," Janelle said.

"That's why I can do it. Chuck made me practice reversing and parking in the high school parking lot, like, a kazillion times.

At this point, I'm better at backing up than I am going forward."

"Well, thank you, Daddy!" Rosie crowed from the backseat.

"Are you sure?" Janelle asked Carmelita.

She nodded, her pointed chin rising and falling with determination.

"You and I will both get out," Janelle said to Rosie. Then she said to Carmelita, "If there's any question, just hit the brakes and we'll figure it out from there."

Carmelita took Janelle's place in the driver's seat. Janelle and Rosie positioned themselves behind the truck, with Carmelita's face visible in the driver's side mirror.

"Make sure you keep it straight," Janelle called.

"Well, duh," Carmelita said through the open window.

She reversed the truck down the roadbed without hesitation, responding to Janelle's finger-pointed directions with adept turns of the wheel.

"I'll keep driving," she said after halting the truck at the bottom of the Z's middle leg.

"Fine by me," said Janelle.

She belted herself into the passenger seat while Rosie returned to her place in back. Carmelita proceeded forward down the final leg of the Z, the truck grinding in low gear.

Ahead, the road disappeared around a tight corner. Just before they reached the turn, the dust-covered park-service pickup from Hans Flat Ranger Station appeared above, on the top leg of the Z, descending the escarpment toward them.

"We've got company," Janelle noted, peering up at the truck.

The park-service pickup was several feet shorter than the big crew cab. Its driver performed a quick, four-point turn around the initial switchback and drove quickly down the middle leg of the Z.

"They couldn't possibly have heard the whistles from the ranger station," Carmelita noted.

"They're definitely in a hurry," Janelle said, her eyes on the oncoming truck and her thoughts on the expedition's satellite phone. "We need to find a place to get out of the way."

The road remained narrow beyond the corner. The ranger truck appeared behind them and rode their rear bumper until, after a few more turns, they came to a wide spot in the road. Carmelita pulled to the shoulder and the truck roared by. A pair of uniformed rangers, a woman and man, sat in the truck. They raised their hands in greeting but looked straight ahead as they passed.

The park-service pickup sped away from the crew cab, lifting a thin swirl of sand off the road. The particles of sand settled back to the ground in the park vehicle's wake.

Carmelita gunned the crew cab after the ranger truck, jouncing down the bumpy road. Janelle gripped the passenger door handle and said nothing, anxious to reach the Maze.

The road turned north at the base of the cliffs and again grew dusty and washboarded as it crossed the sage-covered desert stretching away from the bottom of the escarpment. Far ahead, the Doll House and Chocolate Drops rose above the shelf of stone that hid the slot canyons of the Maze.

Thirty minutes later, as they bumped across the desert, the ranger truck reappeared on the road, this time driving toward them. Carmelita pulled to the side to let the white pickup pass.

As the truck drew near, Janelle noted that three people now sat in the front seat, the two rangers and a new passenger in the middle. A flash of sunlight reflected off some sort of metal in the bed of the truck, though she was sure the truck's bed had been empty when it had passed earlier.

The truck slowed to a crawl as it went by, heading back to the base of the escarpment. The new passenger was a man in his twenties wearing a baseball cap. Beneath the bill of his cap, the man's face was drawn and pale, his eyes downcast.

Janelle relaxed. "It must've been some kind of minor medical emergency." She rolled her shoulders, loosening the muscles in her upper back. "Can't be too bad if the patient is sitting between the rangers." She exhaled with relief. "Whew."

"Good," Carmelita said. She aimed a finger ahead at the Doll House and Chocolate Drops, the sandstone expanse that contained the Maze spread below. "Let's go find them."

She pulled back onto the dirt track and accelerated.

"I'm going to hug Daddy so hard my arms will break," Rosie announced from the rear of the truck. "Uncle Clarence, too."

Janelle smiled back at her. "You and me both, *m'hija.*"

27

Chuck put his hand to his hat brim, shielding his eyes from the afternoon sun, and watched the departure of the white park-service pickup from the end of the road. Maeve's body, wrapped in Rocky's foil blanket, lay in the bed of the truck. Vance sat in front, between the two rangers from Hans Flat. He had insisted on accompanying Maeve's body out of the park, maintaining that Maeve's family deserved to hear the news of her death from one of her fellow guides.

Chuck had been tempted to join Vance and leave the park along with Clarence. But he couldn't bring himself to abandon Wayne and the expedition. The team of CRA guides was now down to five—head guide Tamara; senior guide Rocky; Leon's ex, Sylvia; and the safety kayakers, Liza and Torch—just as the group was heading into the heart of the canyon. Chuck needed to stick around with Clarence to help out.

Still, questions assailed him from all sides.

There were the questions surrounding Ralph's death and about the failed oarlock.

Now, there were the many questions concerning Maeve's death as well.

How could it be that the rock had tumbled from the edge of the slot canyon at the precise moment necessary to strike Maeve in the head and kill her? And what of the crushed grass stems on the ledge above her body? Was it possible the falling rock had struck the clump of grass on its way down, before going on to hit Maeve? Or had someone stepped on the clump of grass while climbing to the rim of the canyon, then waited there, rock in hand, for Maeve to pass below?

Frankly, the latter scenario seemed the far more likely of the two.

But why had Maeve been targeted? And by whom?

Moreover, given that everyone in the group had wandered through the Maze with no fixed routes in mind, how could anyone have known Maeve would pass by that particular spot?

From a broader point of view, if an unknown killer was on the loose within the expedition, what murderous intent could possibly connect Ralph to Maeve, and their deaths to the sabotaged oarlock?

And, if the filed oarlock had been an attempt on the lives of Chuck and Clarence, what possible connection linked one or both of them to Ralph and Maeve, and to the killer? Or was the slice in the shaft of the oarlock simply a factory defect?

Looking at the situation another way, what if the three mishaps on the expedition—two fatal, one potentially fatal—were some combination of murder and accident?

The three mishaps *so far*, that is.

Chuck shook his head, his nerves jangling, as the many questions swirled in his brain.

The park-service truck passed from view over a rise, dust trailing after it.

Clarence turned to him. "Are you thinking what I'm thinking?"

"What's that?"

"That somebody killed her."

Chuck squinted up at the sun, still above the Orange Cliffs in the afternoon sky. There was time enough to return to the site of Maeve's death for a closer look, with no one else around, and make it back to camp before dark.

"I think it's worth trying to find out."

They retraced their steps to the slot canyon. The place where Maeve's body had lain was trampled by countless feet, making any particular suspect's footprints impossible to decipher in the loose sand on the canyon floor. The deadly rock, with its bloodied point, lay on the ground next to the dark circle of blood from Maeve's head wound.

Chuck climbed up the ledge and squatted with his toes on either side of the clump of grass, scrutinizing it up close.

The crushed stems lay across the narrow shelf, broken off the front of the clump, while the stems at the back of the clump continued to stand, unbroken. He swung his fingers through the upright stems growing close to the canyon wall. Already, at the end of May, the stems were brown with the onset of summer. Even so, they retained their flexibility, bending beneath his sweeping hand and leaping back into place without snapping.

Given the flexibility of the grass stems, Chuck judged that while direct pressure from a shoe or sandal definitely would have broken the stems at the front of the clump, a glancing blow from a tumbling rock would have been far less likely to have done so.

He climbed out of the slot canyon and retrieved the rock he'd hefted earlier. Standing at the edge of the slot, he raised the rock above his head with both hands and sighted down at Clarence, thirty feet below.

Clarence ducked, protecting his head with his arms. "Looks like it would have been a direct shot from up there."

Chuck set down the rock. "She'd have been a sitting duck," he agreed.

Clarence lowered his arms. "Still, a kill shot would have been pretty unlikely."

"It didn't have to be fatal, just debilitating." Chuck pointed at the rock resting at Clarence's feet. "I'll show you what I mean."

He returned to the floor of the canyon, crouched over the rock with Clarence, and pointed at the jagged end of the stone, which was stained dark red with Maeve's blood. "If the initial blow from the rock wasn't fatal, the killer could simply have climbed back down and used the rock a second time to finish her off. Look at where it's bloody: right on its narrowest, sharpest point. The odds are astronomical that the sharpest part would have hit her when the rock first was thrown from above."

"*Por seguro*," Clarence agreed.

"The initial strike would have been a blunt-trauma blow, which wouldn't have caused much, if any, bleeding." Chuck pointed at the bloodied point of the rock. "The blood would have come from a finishing blow, or blows, up close."

"Even if she was conscious after the first hit, she wouldn't have tried to defend herself," Clarence reasoned. "She'd have assumed it was an accident, and that the person climbing down to her was coming to help."

"But why would someone have killed her? Why did someone want her dead?"

"Not just anyone," Clarence said ominously. "Someone on the expedition."

"Maybe it really was an accident."

"You mean, the rock just fell on its own?"

"No. I'm convinced the odds of that happening are just too extreme. But people accidentally kick rocks down on others all the time in the outdoors. Maybe somebody knocked the rock down on Maeve by accident. Then, when they climbed down and saw what they'd done, they panicked and finished her off."

"That's sick. Who would do something like that?" Clarence gazed at the bloodstained rock. "You know, it was Wayne who was doing the emergency whistling. Was he the one who 'found' her body?" He made air quotes with his fingers, looking at Chuck. "How well do you really know him, anyway?"

"I can't imagine him as a murderer."

"You keep talking about how important the expedition is to him. Maybe he accidentally hit Maeve with the rock, and then he figured it would ruin everything he's trying to accomplish. He thought it would put an end to the expedition, especially after Ralph's death, so he panicked, like you said."

Chuck shook his head. "First, I'm not sure he's even capable of climbing up the ledge. Second, I can't wrap my mind around him killing anyone. He's just not that sort of—"

He stopped, staring past Clarence.

A dull gleam shone from the shadowed place where the sandstone wall of the canyon met the sandy floor.

He scrambled to the side of the canyon. A penny rested in the sand, propped against the base of the wall. He leaned forward. The coin faced out, with Abraham Lincoln's profiled head aligned perfectly upright.

Chuck picked up the penny and studied it up close. The coin was scratched and worn, its copper surface dull brown.

"*Another* penny?" said Clarence. Chuck handed him the coin. He set it in his palm and gawked at it. "You said the other one fell out of Ralph's pocket, right?"

"I assumed it did," Chuck said. "But this one clearly was left here on purpose. I bet the first one was left with Ralph's body on purpose, too."

Clarence looked up from the penny. "This one's old. I can just barely make out the year. 1922."

"It's 1922? Really?"

"What year is the first one?"

"I hadn't thought to look."

Chuck unzipped his pocket and took out the coin. Like the second penny, the first one was dull with age. He rested it on his palm faceup and brought it close to his eyes. Beneath the Lincoln profile, the penny's mint year was clearly visible.

He looked at Clarence, his blood running cold. "1963."

"Not exactly new, either."

"There's more to it than that."

"What do you mean?"

"Glen Canyon Dam was completed in 1963, halting the flow of the Colorado River below Cataract Canyon."

"*Caramba.*" Clarence held up the penny in his hand. "What about 1922?"

"That was the year the Colorado River Compact was signed. The compact divided the water in the river between the upper and lower states. It's been hugely contentious the whole time it's been in existence."

"*Dios mio.*" Clarence tossed the penny to Chuck. "What do we do now?"

Chuck tucked both pennies in his pants pocket. "We get back to camp—and we keep a close eye out."

"For what?"

"For the murderer in our midst."

They were halfway down the path leading from the Maze to the river at Spanish Bottom, returning to camp via the main trail along the river rather than the alternative trail through Surprise Valley, when Clarence spoke up from behind Chuck.

"I don't understand why we're going back. Shouldn't we be getting the hell out of here and contacting the police or park rangers or somebody?"

They were in the deep shade of the inner gorge. The slanted rays of the late-afternoon sun struck the opposite canyon wall, giving the canyon a warm orange glow. The trail descended several hundred more feet to the river at Spanish Bottom. From there, it continued a mile downstream past Rapid 1 to the camp at Betty Beach.

Chuck answered Clarence over his shoulder without breaking stride. "We couldn't head out on our own even if we wanted to. It's more than twenty miles by road to Hans Flat Ranger Station. There's no way we could make it there with the little water we have in our daypacks." He stepped around a knee-high rock jutting from the trail. "Besides, we can't just leave everyone else in camp, clueless."

"What are you proposing we do—show up and announce that we know one of them's a killer? For that matter, do we even know for sure that's true?"

"The pennies are pretty damning evidence."

"Of what, though? A lot of people see pennies as charms, as *talismánes*. Maybe somebody in the group is leaving pennies wherever bad things happen, as little memorials."

"You think somebody could've snuck into Ralph's tent and left a penny on his body without anybody else noticing?"

"There was plenty of commotion at the time. Joseph and Greta were there. Then Wayne and Tamara came over. You were there, too. There was a lot going on."

"You're saying someone tossed a penny on Ralph in all the confusion?"

"It would've been easy enough for that guy Joseph to do, if no one else. He was the one who unzipped the tent, wasn't he?"

"And now you're saying he left another secret penny with Maeve?"

"Maybe. I don't know."

Chuck thought back, remembering that Joseph had reached out to him from the stern of Tamara's raft in the middle of Rapid 1. Joseph had withdrawn his hand at the last second, presumably to regain his balance. But what if that had been a ruse? What if he had pulled his hand away on purpose?

There was, as well, Joseph's odd accusation regarding Ralph's death, directed at Chuck in front of everyone else.

"I bet if we confront him, he wouldn't confess to having left the pennies," said Chuck. "Not if the pennies aren't innocent memorials..." He let the sentence dangle.

Clarence whistled softly. "...but markers of evil instead," he finished.

"We don't have enough information to risk confronting him. Not yet, anyway."

"But if we make a big announcement about the pennies to the whole group, we'll just freak everybody out."

"I can't see keeping it to ourselves, though."

"What do you think we should do?"

"Wayne's the trip leader. I think we should start with him."

"Do you really trust him?"

"I do. At least, I think I do. I've worked with him forever."

"We're talking about murder here, *jefe*. At least, the distinct possibility of it. And the expedition still has a week to go."

"A week is a long time. That's why I think I should go ahead and tell him. But I'll be watching him really close when I do."

28

Carmelita rolled the truck to a stop in the dusty turnaround at the end of the road and turned the key in the ignition, killing the engine.

"Well done, *niña*," Janelle said, climbing out.

She arched her back and stretched, extending her arms above her head, while taking in the scene before her.

Like the Orange Cliffs overlook above, the turnaround was empty of other cars. The broad shelf of bare rock that had been visible from above stretched away from the turnaround. The flat table of stone was crosshatched by the slot canyons of the Maze. The towering Chocolate Drops threw afternoon shadows across the rock expanse. To the east, the stone shelf fell away into the inner gorge of Cataract Canyon.

She unfolded the topographic map of Canyonlands National Park she'd taken from the extensive map collection in Chuck's study and spread it on the hot metal hood of the truck. Carmelita and Rosie studied the map along with her.

The Green and Colorado Rivers met at the center of the park, creating a giant Y on the map. The Colorado River formed the bottom leg of the Y as it coursed through Cataract Canyon below the confluence of the two rivers.

Carmelita pointed at a series of circular contour lines in the shape of a donut at the north end of the park. "That's Upheaval Dome. We studied it in physics. It's a perfect circle, five miles across and hundreds of feet deep, with a big, round hump of rock sticking up in the middle. It's way out in the wilderness, so hardly anybody ever goes to see it, but it's one of the coolest geological features ever."

Rosie perched herself on her tiptoes and traced the circular lines on the map with her fingertip. "That's so wild, Carm."

"It was formed by a massive collapse and rebound of sandstone after a layer of salt dissolved underneath it," Carmelita explained. "Although some people claim it was made by a giant meteor that hit the earth a long time ago."

"You sure are smart," Rosie told her sister.

Carmelita ducked her head. "I like science." She aimed her finger at parallel topo lines in the park's Needles District. The lines denoted three rigidly straight depressions. "We studied those, too. They're called grabens. They're basically square versions of Upheaval Dome, where the salt melted away underneath and the ground collapsed from above."

A gust of wind lifted the map. Janelle spread her hands, holding the edges in place. "What about us?" she asked Carmelita. "Where are we headed?"

Carmelita leaned forward, eyeing the map. "You said the itinerary calls for the expedition to be camped at Betty Beach tonight." She reached past Janelle's outstretched arm and traced the marked trail descending from the Maze to a flat spot next to the river labeled Spanish Bottom. "The hiking trail bypasses the slot canyons and goes down to the river here, then follows the river downstream to the beach."

"That's us, then," said Janelle. She folded the map and distributed daypacks loaded with food, water, jackets, and headlamps to Carmelita and Rosie. Before leaving the truck, she opened her pack and made sure it included the extensive medical kit she'd assembled over the course of her paramedic training.

They strode across the bare rock three abreast, their backs to the low sun and their shadows stretched before them.

Rosie flapped her arms. "Look," she said, her eyes on her fluttering shadow. "I'm a bird. I'll just fly there."

"Wouldn't that be nice," said Janelle.

"According to the map," Carmelita said, "it's only a mile

down to Spanish Bottom, and less than a mile from there to the beach. It shouldn't take us much more than an hour."

"That's good to hear," Janelle said as they crossed the stone shelf. "I want to get there as fast as we can. Those whistles are still stuck in my head."

"The emergency's all over with," Carmelita assured her. "We're right where we want to be, just like we planned. We'll find Chuck and Uncle Clarence, and then we'll head back up to the truck."

Rosie wove around a dry pothole sunk in the sandstone. "I can't wait to see them. I bet they'll be sunburned to a crisp."

A stacked pyramid of rocks known as a cairn indicated the place where the trail descended off the edge of the rock shelf. Janelle paused with the girls beside the cairn. Several hundred feet below them lay Spanish Bottom, a half-moon-shaped meadow of brown grass abutting the river. Nothing moved on the bottom, which was deep in evening shadow.

Beyond the river, the last of the day's sunlight painted the sandstone spires of the Needles District with deep red and blaze orange. The view was stunningly beautiful, but below the sunlit vista, the dusky inner gorge gave Janelle pause.

She glanced behind her. The sun was lower than she wished, hovering just above the horizon line of the Orange Cliffs. She looked back down at Spanish Bottom. "It's getting pretty late," she commented.

"We've got headlamps," Carmelita said. She scanned the clear evening sky. "The weather's fine. No storms."

"The landscape around here is just so immense. You don't get the sense of it from the map. Everything is so remote. We're definitely on our own out here."

"Chuck and Uncle Clarence can hike back to the truck with us after we find them," Carmelita reasoned, "so we won't be on our own anymore."

Janelle tucked Carmelita to her side. "You're right, *m'hija.* *Familia.* That's why we're here."

She straightened, keeping her arm around Carmelita's shoulders. The breeze, easing at the end of the day, sighed past her face.

"Okay," she said. "*Vamanos.* Let's go."

She set off down the trail, dropping off the sunny shelf of sandstone and into the shadows of the inner gorge via a break in the vertical wall of the canyon. Below the break in the wall, the trail wound down a steep slope strewn with house-sized boulders and spotted with piñon and juniper trees. She rounded a switchback and glanced down the hillside at Spanish Bottom and the muddy river beside it. As before, nothing moved on the open bottom. On the river, however, a flash of movement caught her eye.

A boat rounded a bend in the canyon, coming into view from upstream.

Janelle halted, her gaze fixed on the watercraft. The girls stopped behind her.

The boat was an inflatable rubber raft. No additional rafts floated around the bend behind it.

"It's pretty late for someone to still be on the river, isn't it?" Janelle asked.

"When we're backpacking," Carmelita responded, "we always make camp way before dark, just to be safe. That's got to be even more important on a river trip."

The boat floated closer, riding the current in the middle of the river. It was lemon yellow and oval shaped. Its oars were shipped forward, out of the water, the blades resting in the front passenger well.

"There's nobody in it," Rosie said. "It's going all by itself."

"I don't get it," Janelle admitted.

"Neither do I," said Carmelita. "But whatever it is, I don't think it's good."

Janelle took her lower lip between her teeth, watching as the boat turned a slow circle in the middle of the river. "We have to get down to the camp and find out what's going on."

"Maybe we can catch the boat and row it there," said Rosie with a chuckle.

Janelle summoned a smile. "Carm backed the truck down the cliff. She could probably swim out there and grab the boat for us, too."

She hurried down the trail with the girls, keeping a wary eye on the empty boat until it floated out of sight around the next bend downstream.

29

Silence and averted eyes met Chuck and Clarence when they returned to camp.

The clients sat in folding chairs facing the river. Some read paperbacks, others stared without expression at the brown water flowing past the beach and around the next bend in the river to Rapid 2. The remaining CRA guides clustered in the camp kitchen. Chuck was surprised and gratified to see Leon helping out in the kitchen as well. He stood next to his former wife, slicing vegetables on a cutting board, while Sylvia sautéed strips of chicken in an oversize skillet on one of the cookstoves.

The camp lay in deep shadow, the heat of the day giving way to the coolness of evening. The guttural rumble of Rapid 1 from upstream added a malign undertone to the high-pitched hiss of the gas stove.

Chuck dropped his daypack next to his tent, his thoughts on Maeve. It almost felt to him now, back in camp, that her death hadn't happened, that she'd never existed, and that the world to which her body was being returned, accompanied by Vance, didn't exist either. It was as if Chuck's entire existence had shrunk to the confined world of the expedition and nothing more.

But that feeling was good, he told himself. His concentration needed to be absolute, focused on the members of the expedition—beginning with his old friend Wayne.

Clarence headed to the camp kitchen to help with dinner while Chuck caught Wayne's eye and beckoned him out of his seat. Wayne trailed Chuck upstream along the shoreline. They stopped and faced each other out of earshot of the group.

"I found a penny," Chuck said without preamble, watching

Wayne intently.

"You found *what*?"

Chuck saw only sincere question in Wayne's eyes. "Pennies, actually. Two of them."

"You're telling me this because…?"

"One was left with Ralph in his tent. The other was left in the canyon with Maeve."

Wayne frowned. "They were left on purpose?"

"I'm certain of it." Chuck explained the circumstances of the coins—the first falling from Ralph's body, the second placed against the wall of the slot canyon upright and facing out.

"Sounds as if they're totems of some sort," Wayne said when he finished.

"Clarence thinks that might be a possibility, too."

"But you don't."

"There's more. The pennies are old, and they're very specific. The one with Ralph was minted in 1963."

"Glen Canyon Dam," Wayne said immediately.

"The one with Maeve is even older: 1922."

"Jesus," Wayne muttered, his voice low, glancing around. "The compact."

Chuck dipped his chin, his face set.

"But they still could be totems, couldn't they?" Wayne reasoned. "Just with the specific years. I mean, we're all a bunch of water nerds on the trip."

"The only other possible explanation…"

"I like my idea better."

"We're not doing ourselves any favors if we don't at least consider the alternative." Chuck gazed down the beach at the clients in their seats and the guides preparing dinner in the camp kitchen. He watched as Clarence poured a five-gallon bucket of settled river water into a stew pot on one of the stoves, beginning the process of heating dishwater for after the meal.

Chuck looked back at Wayne. "I spotted some crushed grass

stems on the ledge above Maeve's body. Maybe the grass was crushed by the rock as it fell from the top of the wall before it hit her—or maybe it was crushed by someone's foot."

"I don't like what you're suggesting."

"The sharpest end of the rock hit Maeve's head. The very sharpest end."

Wayne's jaw muscles twitched. "I know. I've wondered about the odds of that myself. I'm sure others have, too. How could they not?"

"There's something else I haven't told you. The shaft of the broken oarlock from the gear boat looks like it was filed at the spot where it failed."

Wayne cursed. "This is a lot to take in."

Tamara left the kitchen and strode up the beach toward them.

"Should we tell her what you just told me?" Wayne asked, glancing her way.

"I didn't know Tamara before the trip. I barely know her now."

"I'd never met her before the trip, either." Wayne turned his back to Tamara and leaned closer to Chuck. "I saw the way you were watching me just now, when you told me about the pennies."

"Trust but verify," Chuck said. "I told Clarence I've always trusted you. I trust you even more now."

"Why?"

"The look in your eyes—it was one-hundred-percent genuine."

"For the record, I trust you, too. You wouldn't have told me all this if you were some sort of stone-cold killer."

"Unless I was trying to throw you off my trail."

"If you're that good, I'm toast. We all are."

Tamara reached them. "What are the two of you talking about in secret?" she asked.

"We're not exactly hiding," Wayne said.

"What are the two of you talking about *in private*, then?"

"We're discussing the fact that two deaths on one trip is not at all normal."

"You mean, you're stating the obvious to one another?"

"And the not-so-obvious."

"Do tell."

Chuck held his breath. What would Wayne reveal to Tamara?

"We were talking about the fact that the pointed end of the rock hit Maeve," Wayne said, "perfectly and precisely."

Chuck exhaled. Wayne wasn't making any mention of the pennies. Not yet, anyway.

Tamara's face darkened. "I've certainly had the same thought. I just hope she didn't suffer."

Chuck caught Tamara's eye. "No one could have known Maeve would walk down that particular slot at that particular time," he said. "Or any other slot at any other particular time."

"That would rule out the idea of foul play—" Tamara looked at Wayne "—despite what you just said about the pointed end of the rock hitting her." She folded her arms over her chest. "I thought about it all the way back to camp. I believe Maeve's death was an accident. Even so, as you just said, Wayne, two deaths on one trip is awful. Horrible. And terrifying for everyone involved." She fell silent.

"What are you saying?" Wayne asked.

By now, the last of the evening sunlight had left the opposite canyon wall, leaving the inner gorge deep in evening shadow.

"We can end the trip right here and now," Tamara said. "I can use the sat phone to call in a bunch of vehicles. Everyone would hike to the end of the road, up by the Maze, and be driven out from there. My guides and I would take the empty boats on down the river."

"You'd pull the plug, just like that?"

"It's your trip, not mine. But you're the one who said it." She dropped her arms to her sides. "Two deaths. *Two*." She glanced at the seated clients and the guides at work in the kitchen, none of them speaking. "How does a trip recover from that? Should we even try?"

"Ralph would…he'd be…"

"Ralph's gone, Wayne," she said gently. "It's on you now, as trip leader, and me, as head guide. The decision is ours to make."

"We would hike out in the morning?"

"It'll take all night to arrange vehicles and drivers and get them headed this way. So, yes, we would camp here tonight and hike up and meet—"

Tamara stopped in mid-sentence and pointed upriver past Chuck and Wayne, her eyes growing large.

Chuck spun and peered upstream.

A raft rounded the bend below the rapid, riding the current in the middle of the river. The raft was upside down, its inverted thwarts bright yellow in the shadowy canyon.

"What on earth?" Wayne exclaimed.

"Check out the bow line," said Tamara.

Generally, the rope used to secure a boat to shore would be looped and secured on the front tube when a boat was afloat on a river. In the case of the upside-down raft, however, the bow line trailed off the front of the boat and disappeared into the water.

"It must've come loose from somebody's camp upstream," Tamara surmised. "That's why it's empty. It flipped in the Rapid 1 hole."

"It might not be empty," said Chuck, his voice tight. "Someone might've been on board. They might've gotten coiled in the bow line when it flipped."

He set off down the beach at a run.

"I hope you're wrong," Tamara called as she ran after him.

His toes dug into the wet sand at the edge of the river. After what he and Clarence had experienced in Rapid 1, he hoped he was wrong, too.

30

"Keep an eye out for any swimmers," Chuck hollered back to Wayne as he sprinted down the beach. "I'll go after the boat." Tamara's sandals pounded the sand behind him. "I'll send Liza and Torch after you."

"I'll only need one of them," Chuck called to her. "The other can help search for anyone who may have fallen out in the rapid upstream."

The overturned raft drew abreast of camp. Its thwarts rested on the surface of the water, revealing nothing of the interior of the capsized boat, or of anyone who might be trapped beneath it.

The expedition rafts, emptied of their loads, lined the shore ahead of Chuck. The weight of gear and passengers provided stability to whitewater boats. That meant the massive gear boat, heavy even when empty, was the best option for a hasty rescue mission to the overturned raft.

Rocky had already arrived at that conclusion. He crouched over the gear boat's knotted bow line, freeing the line from its sand stake. He straightened and gathered the rope in loops, hurrying toward the boat, his PFD slung over his shoulder. Chuck clambered over the bow and into the captain's seat. Rocky shoved the boat away from shore and leapt in after him.

Chuck unclipped his PFD from the seat stanchion and pulled it on. He rowed backward away from shore, spun the boat into the current, and pushed hard downstream after the overturned raft, which floated a couple hundred feet downriver from them, rounding the bend in the canyon below the beach.

"How far to Rapid 2?" he asked Rocky as he rowed.

Rocky crouched in the front passenger well, peering ahead.

"A quarter mile, maybe. No more than that. It's got two holes. The upper one is right of center, the lower one is to the left. An S-curve run takes you through it. You want me to take the oars?"

Chuck gritted his teeth. "I'll be okay with an empty boat." *And with two functioning oarlocks*, he thought.

The yellow raft passed from sight around the bend. Chuck dug the oar blades into the water. The roar of Rapid 2 filled the canyon as they rounded the curve behind the capsized boat.

He took deep breaths, pushing hard on the oars. The yellow raft was still well ahead of them. "We're not going to reach it before the rapid."

"We're gaining on her, though," Rocky said. "We'll catch her in the pool below." He pointed at the horizon line atop Rapid 2. "Enter on river left. Spin and pull to the right below the first hole." He tapped the front thwart. "It shouldn't take much to move this hunk of rubber, big as she is, seeing as she ain't got a load on her."

Chuck angled the nose of the boat to the left. The capsized raft disappeared over the lip of the rapid. The thunder of the whitewater increased. A surging maelstrom a few hundred yards long, about the same length as Rapid 1, appeared when they topped the horizon line. A massive, backward-breaking wave reared on river right, below the entry tongue. Chuck spun the boat and pulled on the oars, backing across the tongue to give the first hole plenty of leeway.

"Not too far," Rocky hollered over the roar of the rapid. "The second hole comes up mighty quick."

Sure enough, barely visible in the failing light, another recirculating wave stood tall on the left side of the river, its crown misty white.

Chuck shoved forward with the oars. The bow of the gear boat nipped the edge of the first hole and the boat blasted high into the air.

Kneeling in the front well, Rocky clung to the bow line and

swung his free hand above his head like a rodeo cowboy. "Yee-haw!" he cried as the boat reared skyward.

The raft flopped back into the water below the breaking wave.

"Right!" Rocky yelled. "Get right!"

Chuck spun the boat and pulled away from the second hole. Ahead, the upside-down raft spurted to the left, floated sideways up the vertical face of the recirculating wave, and toppled backward to the wave's base. The boat flipped violently in the hole once, twice, three times, slamming the water and overturning again and again with tremendous force. As the boat flipped, its oars wrenched free from the oarlocks and flew through the air like vanes on a windmill, still attached to the raft by nylon tethers.

Rocky stared at the spinning raft. "I don't see anybody," he hollered back to Chuck.

They drew even with the second hole at the same instant the yellow raft launched up and over the breaking wave. The raft resumed its unmanned run downstream, now upright in the whitewater, its oars dangling in the river.

The two rafts bounded side by side through the standing waves that made up the heart of Rapid 2. In the pool at the bottom of the rapid, Chuck rowed up to the yellow raft and nudged its side thwart with the bow of the gear boat.

Rocky leapt aboard the unmanned raft. He set the oars back in the oarlocks and rowed the boat to the right-hand shore. Chuck trailed him to the edge of the river. Liza powered through the rapid and paddled up to them. She clambered out of her boat as Rocky and Chuck secured the rafts on a narrow, rocky stretch of beach below the rapid, wrapping the bow lines of the two boats around a waist-high boulder protruding from the sand.

Liza stowed her kayak and paddle behind a rock well above the river's edge. She shimmied out of her spray skirt and shoved it into the cockpit of her boat.

"I'm glad you didn't need me," she said, returning to the shoreline. She tapped the yellow raft with her foot. "What do you think happened?"

"It's gotta be a runaway from an upstream camp," Rocky said. "Somebody didn't tie it in well enough."

"I hope you're right. Except…"

"Except what?"

"Except Maeve. And Ralph. There's way too much bad stuff happening on this trip for me to trust anything or anyone anymore."

Rocky rested his hand on the bow of the gear raft. "What are you thinking, Liza?"

"To be honest," she replied, "I'm too bummed about Maeve to even think straight at this point. I was all set to do shots after dinner—a bunch of shots—to help me forget everything. Instead, we're at least a mile down from camp and it's almost dark."

Chuck looked up. Liza was right. Already, a handful of stars glittered in the slice of darkening sky visible between the canyon walls overhead.

Liza pulled a headlamp from the pocket of her shorts. "I grabbed this before I jumped into my boat. It'll help us rock-hop back along shore."

"Aren't you the good Girl Scout," Rocky teased her.

"Be prepared," she replied with an earnest nod. "Oh, wait. That's the Boy Scout motto."

Rocky raised his hand and pressed his three middle fingers together, making the scouting sign. "Eagle scout, Troop 871," he said. "They allow girls now, you know."

"I heard that. But they still hate gay people, don't they?"

"They say they're getting over it."

"Let me know when they like all human beings—gay, trans, bi, queer, and everybody in between—would you?"

Chuck trailed Liza and Rocky upstream along the shoreline to a jumble of head-high boulders stacked at the foot of the rapid next to the river. The pile of boulders forced Liza, in the lead, to angle away from the shore. Chuck followed, at the back, as the three of them side-hilled along the steep slope between the river and the vertical canyon wall. Yucca and prickly pear cacti studded the hillside. Liza aimed the beam of her headlamp at the thorny plants as she passed them, alerting Rocky and Chuck to their presence in the gathering darkness.

They traversed a quarter mile of the slope, working their way upstream, as night enveloped the canyon. Liza held the headlamp in her hand like a flashlight and directed its beam forward and back, providing light for herself and Rocky and Chuck as they hiked. Rapid 2 rumbled below them. Betty Beach remained out of sight upstream around the bend.

Liza halted abruptly.

"Would you look at that," she said, directing the beam of her headlamp higher on the hillside.

The circle of light illuminated a black rectangular opening in a low rock wall at the back of a flat area dug into the slope. The opening, head high and half again as wide, led into the side of the canyon. A metal grid covered the mouth of the opening.

Liza's hand trembled, making the light quaver against the slope. "The gate's open. It shouldn't be, but it is."

PART THREE

"You are piling up a heritage of conflict and litigation over water rights, for there is not sufficient water to supply the land."

—John Wesley Powell

31

Janelle set a quick pace with the girls down the trail to Spanish Bottom. They arrived at the riverbank, turned south at a second cairn, and followed the trail alongside the river. The sound of a rapid reached them from downstream. Barely audible at first, the low-pitched rumble increased in volume as they hiked. Soon it became a full-throated growl, filling the canyon from wall to wall.

"That's Rapid 1," Carmelita noted from behind Janelle and Rosie. "It was marked on the map. It's the start of the whitewater in Cataract Canyon."

"It sounds scary," said Rosie.

"Because it is. That's why people run the canyon, to test themselves in the rapids."

"Like you do with climbing—except you've got ropes and helmets and stuff."

"Chuck and Uncle Clarence have helmets, too. But Chuck said river runners don't tie themselves into their boats with ropes. He said if they flip while they're tied in, they could get all tangled up and drown."

"Now I know why the people in the carnage videos Daddy showed me went flying all over the place."

Janelle frowned. "Carnage? He didn't show me any of those."

"I guess he didn't want to freak you out, *Mamá.*"

"I'll need to have a little talk with him about that."

"Oooo," said Rosie. "Daddy's in trouble."

The trail rounded a refrigerator-sized chunk of sandstone perched on the hillside above the river. In the fading evening light, Rapid 1 came into view—roiling waves, white spray, and dark current coursing downstream with the power of a freight train.

Janelle stared at the whitewater. Was it really possible that Chuck had rowed a raft through the rapid and taken Clarence with him?

"Yeah," she said, turning to Rosie. "Daddy's definitely in trouble."

The rapid ended in a calm pool. Below the pool, the river flowed down the canyon and out of sight around a bend. Both sides of the river were empty; the yellow raft had not spun out of the current and lodged itself against the shore anywhere Janelle could see.

"They should be right around the corner," Carmelita said. She held up her phone to Janelle. "Have a look."

Janelle squinted at the phone. A tiny map filled the screen, a red dot glowing at its center.

"I dropped a pin on the beach before we left," Carmelita explained. "We're almost there."

"The sooner the better," said Janelle.

Betty Beach came into view around the first bend below the rapid. More than two dozen tents lined the long stretch of sand, with several matching sky-blue rubber rafts snugged against the shoreline.

"*Buenísimo*," Janelle said, exhaling with relief. "Looks like they're here as scheduled."

She came up short, however, at the sight of numerous people hurrying across the beach between the tents and boats in the deepening twilight. The people were dark forms against the lighter sand. Some wore headlamps, others did not.

A large raft, the same light blue color as those tied along the shore, floated down the river below the beach. Before the raft disappeared around the next bend in the canyon, Janelle noted that a person sat at the oars in the center of the boat, while another perched in its bow.

A pair of kayakers shoved off the beach and into the river in their compact plastic boats. One of the kayakers paddled hard downstream after the blue raft. The other stroked to the middle of the river and ferried back and forth in the current, facing upstream. Someone dashed up the shore to the head of the beach, directing the beam of a powerful flashlight across the water above the ferrying kayaker.

"Check it out!" Rosie exclaimed, looking past Janelle at the commotion on the shore. "Something exciting is happening."

"It must have to do with the raft we saw," Carmelita reasoned.

"We'll know soon enough," Janelle said.

She hustled down the trail with the girls to the upstream end of the beach.

"Was that your raft?" the voice of a woman called to them from the shadowy darkness. "We've sent a boat after it. They'll nab it for you, I guarantee it."

"We saw it go by," Janelle called back, "but it isn't ours."

The woman approached and halted before Janelle and the girls. She studied them from beneath the brim of the battered, straw cowboy hat she wore low on her forehead. "Are you backpackers?" She leaned sideways, checking their backs. "No," she answered herself. "You're only wearing daypacks." She straightened. "What's going on? Are you lost?"

"Nope," said Rosie. "We're found."

"You are, are you?"

"Yep," Rosie declared. "We're here to see my daddy."

The woman's eyes widened, the whites showing in the dusky light. "Your...your daddy?"

Janelle put a hand to her chest. "I'm Janelle Ortega. These are my daughters, Rosie and Carmelita." She glanced at the kayaker still ferrying in the middle of the river. "We've obviously shown up at a bad time."

"This is a river trip. An expedition," the woman said. "We don't generally expect visitors."

Rosie bounced up and down on the balls of her feet. "That's what we are," she said. "We're visiting Daddy and Uncle Clarence."

"Clarence is your uncle?"

Janelle put her hand on Rosie's shoulder, stilling her. "He's my brother," she explained to the woman. "If you could just point me to him or Chuck Bender, we'll get out of your way."

"Chuck took off after the raft, but Clarence is here. Please, follow me."

The woman introduced herself as Tamara, the head guide for the expedition, as she strode down the beach with Janelle and the girls, taking long steps.

"You're sure a fast walker, Tamara," Rosie said, jogging to keep up.

"Sorry, hon. There's a lot going on and it's getting dark."

Carmelita shone her phone light on the sand in front of her. "What's with the empty boat in the river?" she asked.

"I wish I knew," said Tamara. "It most likely came loose from an upstream camp. Your father went after it with one of my guides."

"And a kayaker," said Carmelita.

"Yes. One of my safety kayakers, Liza."

"A woman kayaker? Cool."

"Not just any woman, I can assure you that."

"You're a woman, too."

"Last I checked."

"You said you're the head guide. That means you're the boss, right?"

"That's correct."

Rosie broke in. "Double cool."

"There's no room for sexism on the river," Tamara said. "Ever."

"We're three girls and we came all the way here," Rosie boasted.

"That you did." Tamara looked at Janelle. "Quite a surprise."

"We have good reason," said Janelle.

"I imagine so. Frankly, that's what worries me."

Janelle took in the scene as they walked. The tents occupied the back half of the beach. A hillside rose steeply behind the tents to the base of the vertical canyon wall. Above the wall, a few bright stars speckled the purple evening sky. Below, on the beach, campers stood along the edge of the river in front of a row of camp chairs. Between the chairs and tents, in the camp kitchen, blue flame glowed at the bottom of a steaming pot on a cookstove, and a rotund figure stood before the pot.

"Clarence!" Tamara called to the figure as she neared the tables with Janelle and the girls. "You're not going to believe who's here."

32

Liza led Chuck and Rocky to the level spot dug into the hillside. The flat dirt area extended thirty feet from the grid-covered opening in the rock wall to a plump juniper tree that shielded the flat area and rectangular opening from the river below.

Chuck gaped at the dark rectangle, gradually making sense of what he was seeing. Behind the metal grid, a tunnel disappeared into the side of the canyon. The grid was a gate over the tunnel mouth, with hinges on one side and a hasp on the other.

Liza directed the beam of her headlamp at the gate, which hung open a few inches from the rocky mouth of the tunnel. A padlock remained in place through the staple of the rusted hasp. The hasp was bent and twisted where someone had used a sledge or heavy rock to smash it free from its emplacement in the sandstone next to the tunnel opening.

Liza pushed the gate closed with a high-pitched *creak*. When she let go, the gate swung back to its original position.

"Is this what I think it is?" Chuck asked.

"It's an adit," Liza confirmed. "One of the test tunnels drilled by the Bureau of Reclamation back in the 1950s. I've brought groups here to check it out plenty of times, but the gate has always been closed and locked."

Rocky lifted the heavy padlock still hanging in place through the hasp's staple. "They really wanted to get in." He dropped the lock, which swung back into place with a *clang*. "I can't imagine there's anything to see in there, though."

"We should find out," Chuck said.

"You actually want to go in? *Now*?"

"It'll only take a couple of minutes. A quick check to make sure nobody's in there who might need help. As Liza said, with everything that's been going on…"

Rocky swung the gate, eliciting another sharp *creak*. "We came down here for the lost boat. This is just a distraction."

"I'll check it out myself if you want. You can wait outside."

"You'd never let me hear the end of it if I did that."

"I'm not the teasing type."

Liza chimed in. "Oh, but I am."

Rocky groaned. "Okay, okay." He aimed his chin at Chuck. "You can lead the way."

Liza handed her headlamp to Chuck and turned to Rocky. "I thought you were a big, brave Eagle Scout."

"Just for that," Rocky told her, "you can go second."

Chuck directed the headlamp at his feet as he walked down the tunnel. The downcast beam provided light to Liza and Rocky behind him while enabling him to see a few yards ahead.

The horizontal floor of the adit was bare stone strewn with gravel-sized rocks. The air in the passage was chalky, without a hint of moisture. White streaks appeared in the sandstone walls and ceiling fifty feet from the adit entrance. The streaks consisted of a granular material. Chuck touched one of the stripes, leaving an impression in the crumbly surface. He put the tip of his finger to his tongue and tasted exactly what he'd expected.

The streaks grew wider as he strode farther down the tunnel.

"See that?" he asked Liza and Rocky, pointing at one of the stripes.

Their footsteps crunched in the gravel behind him.

"Sodium chloride," Rocky said.

"You got it," said Chuck, his voice echoing off the walls of the passage drilled into the canyon decades ago. "Salt."

The percentage of salt comprising the walls and ceiling

increased as he proceeded down the adit. Mounds of salt ranging in color from white to dirty brown appeared on the floor, rising to ankle height.

He directed the light at one of the salt mounds. The top of the pile was crushed, leaving a footprint behind. The print was the size of an adult's, but otherwise was undefined in the loose grains.

"Looks as if they came back here after they broke open the gate," Chuck said.

"I don't like this," said Liza.

Chuck aimed the headlamp ahead. The tunnel extended as far as the light reached, at least another hundred feet.

"Whoever broke open the gate is long gone," he assured her.

He led the way farther down the tunnel. The piles of salt fallen from the walls and ceiling increased in size on the floor. He halted again, this time in front of the largest mound he'd yet encountered. The pile rose to his waist and covered the floor of the adit from wall to wall.

"What is it?" Liza asked from behind him.

He stepped aside, aiming the light at the pile of salt. "Check it out."

"Whoa," she breathed.

An inch-thick piece of wood, gray and cracked with age, poked two feet out of the top of the salt pile. Small bits of beige-colored fuzz and shiny flecks of dark, glassy material lay on the white surface of the salt at the base of the piece of wood.

"It's a stave," Rocky said. "A rib from a wooden boat. I'd recognize one of those anywhere." He leaned past Liza, peering at the pieces of fuzz and glassy flecks lying on the salt. "That's cotton and dried pine resin. I'd bet my whole kit and caboodle on it."

"Which means," Chuck said, "the rib isn't from just any boat. Cotton was used between the planks of wooden boats as caulking in the 1800s."

"The Powell expedition gathered pine resin to use as pitch to hold the cotton caulking in place between the planks of their boats." Rocky looked from the slender piece of wood to Chuck, his eyes gleaming in the light of the headlamp. "I've heard the rumor, too—the one Leon talked about at the beginning of the trip."

Chuck inspected the boat rib extending from the mound of salt. "In archaeology circles, it's legendary. I never believed it, though—until now."

The shimmering light of the headlamp threw disjointed shadows off the far side of the salt pile. He trained the light where the mound fell away to the rear.

"Strange," he said, craning his neck.

Stepping past the mound, he shone the headlamp at the back of the pile. Rocky and Liza leaned forward, looking on with him.

From his new angle, the light revealed a trough-shaped depression in the rear of the mound. The depression was two feet long, half a foot wide, and a few inches deep.

The trough was empty; whatever had previously lain there, buried in the salt, was gone—though, based on the size and shape of the depression, it almost certainly had been another boat rib like the one protruding from the top of the mound.

Chuck leaned closer.

No. Wait. The depression wasn't empty after all.

He brought the light close to the mound, squinting.

A small, round piece of metal rested in the bottom of the trough, precisely at the midpoint of the elongated hole.

He shuddered.

In the depression, facing him, was a copper penny.

33

Like the Lincoln penny left against the canyon wall near Maeve's body in the Maze, the penny in the depression sat perfectly upright.

Chuck plucked it from the trough and held it up, illuminating it with the beam of the headlamp. The coin was not a Lincoln penny. A Native American wearing a full headdress was profiled on the coin's face. It was an Indian Head penny, the type of one-cent piece produced by the US Mint in the late 1800s. With the aid of the headlamp beam, Chuck made out the production year stamped on its face: 1869.

His hand shook. He looked at Liza and Rocky, their faces indistinct in the dim light on the far side of the salt pile, and said, "JWP."

Rocky looked from the coin in Chuck's hand to the wooden rib protruding from the top of the mound. "It's true," he whispered. "The Powell Geographic Expedition."

They left the adit and gathered on the flat area outside the tunnel mouth. It was fully dark now, the stars bright overhead. A gentle evening breeze swept down the canyon, rustling the branches of the juniper and filling the air with the tree's piney scent.

Liza faced Chuck and Rocky. "What's with the penny?" she demanded. "What were you two talking about in there?"

"You tell her," Rocky said to Chuck. "You're the one who insisted we check it out."

"It all starts with the salt," Chuck explained. "That's why Canyonlands National Park exists. Cataract Canyon, too, for that matter. An ocean covered this area fifty million years ago.

When it receded, it left behind a thick layer of salt that's still in the process of dissolving, resulting in the fractured stone formations above it."

"I know all that," Liza said. "This is my fourth season guiding Cataract."

"Give him a chance," Rocky urged her. He turned to Chuck. "John Wesley Powell."

Chuck nodded. "The Green and Colorado Rivers provided passage through the desert for Powell and his team to explore the region. They were the first known explorers to run Cataract Canyon and check out the unbelievable landscape around here. But the same forces that created the beauty of this region also left Cataract Canyon filled with rocks and debris, producing nonstop rapids. After floating the calm waters of the Green River above Cataract, Powell's team thought they were home free. But they weren't."

"Yes, yes, yes. I know all that, too," Liza said. "Rapid 1 almost did them in."

Chuck inclined his head. "It was the first example of what they faced below the confluence of the Green and Colorado Rivers. One of their boats was tumbled and smashed in the Rapid 1 hole. They caught up with what was left of it above Rapid 2. It was in shambles. They hauled it above the shoreline and left it behind." Chuck cast his gaze at Liza. "I bet you know what the boat was made of."

"Wood. Oak, to be exact."

He nodded. "Thick oak planks secured by oak ribs, or staves."

She drew a breath. "You're saying the boat rib in the tunnel is from the Powell expedition's lost boat?"

"Almost certainly," Rocky said. "The smashed boat from the expedition sat above the river for decades. It became a big ol' tourist attraction—a mandatory stop for all boating parties down Cataract. Then, along about the time the Bureau of Rec engineers came here lookin' to put in a dam, the wreckage disappeared. The feds claimed a flash flood washed it away. But no floods at the time would have come close to reaching the boat. Instead, everybody figured one of the engineers had stolen the wreckage. There was a big uproar for a while about the boat's disappearance, but nothing turned up."

"Then came the rumor," said Chuck.

"The one Leon mentioned," Rocky confirmed.

"I couldn't help but be intrigued when I heard it," Chuck continued. "Lots of archaeologists, me included, are attracted by the treasure-hunting aspect of archaeology. Every time we stick a shovel in the dirt, there's the possibility we might unearth something incredible, which explains why my heart beats just a little bit faster every time I start a new dig. So, yeah, I was interested in the rumor."

"Which was what, exactly?" Liza asked.

"That the wreckage of the boat never left the canyon. That it simply had been moved for safekeeping, higher on the slope, or up or downstream, probably tucked under the branches of a tree or beneath a rock ledge. The rumor was that one of the Bureau of Rec engineers thought the wreckage would be stolen if it wasn't hidden away."

"But," said Rocky, "no one I know of ever hit on the idea that the remains might be hidden in one of the test adits."

"The engineers drilled the adits to check the solidity of the stone," Chuck said to Liza. "It didn't take long for them to learn that the permeation of salt through the sandstone walls of the canyon would have made building a dam in Cataract Canyon a tough proposition. Ultimately, however, it didn't matter, because Canyonlands National Park was created instead."

"That's exactly what I've told everyone when I've brought them here," Liza said. "But I never heard anything about the Powell boat."

"Somebody else did, though." Chuck held up the Indian Head penny between his thumb and forefinger.

He paused. How much should he reveal to Liza and Rocky? That is, how much did he trust them? The answer to both questions, he decided, was not very much. They'd seen him find the penny in the tunnel, but there was no need to tell them about the other two copper coins.

"This is an Indian Head penny, minted in 1869," he said.

Liza stared at it. "Powell couldn't have dropped a penny in the adit 150 years ago. The adit didn't exist back then." She shook her head. "I don't get it. Help me out here."

"It all goes back to the rumor that the wrecked boat from the Powell expedition was hidden in the canyon somewhere. From what we just saw, it would appear one or more of the Bureau of Rec engineers hid the wreckage in the adit when the tunnel was abandoned."

"Because they thought they were keeping it safe?"

"If the rumor is correct, yes. It would have been easy to cover the remains of the boat with salt from the walls. The salt would act as a preservative. The combination of that plus being stored out of the weather in the adit means the wreckage would be protected virtually forever. The engineer or engineers probably thought they were doing the world a favor. They didn't steal the boat, they just moved it. If two or more of them were involved, they swore each other to secrecy and went on with their lives."

"But somebody must've said something."

"Despite people's vows of silence, secrets have a way of revealing themselves."

Liza's eyes were bright in the light of the headlamp. "You think someone on the trip came up with the idea of the adit as the hiding place for the boat, is that it?"

Chuck nodded. "It looks like they dug one of the boat ribs out of the salt and took it with them. They'll verify its authenticity, then they'll publicize their discovery: the long-lost boat from the Powell Geographic Expedition."

"What would be in it for them?"

"Fame. Headlines. Notoriety. The wreckage wouldn't necessarily be worth a lot of money. But because none of the other original boats exist anymore, the cultural value of the wreckage, as the only surviving boat from the expedition, would be significant."

"What about the Indian Head penny?"

"They knew they wouldn't be able to repair the gate, so they left the penny, with its indicative year, as some kind of marker."

"And just what sort of marker would that be?"

"I'm not sure."

Rocky turned to Chuck. "For having no idea about the penny, you're awfully sure of yourself about the boat rib."

"You agree that the piece of wood and cotton batting and pine resin in the adit are from an old boat, almost certainly the one from the Powell expedition. The penny indicates that someone else—whoever broke into the adit and dug into the salt pile—agrees with you."

"Assuming that's the case, what do you suppose we should do next? Should we tell everybody what we found?"

Chuck considered the first two pennies—and the deaths of Ralph and Maeve. "I think it's best to keep this between us for now. I suppose it's possible someone from an earlier trip broke into the adit a while ago, but I doubt that's what happened. Our group is a pretty knowledgeable bunch."

"Besides which," said Rocky, "Leon mentioned the rumor at the beginning of the trip."

"He hasn't mentioned it since, as far as I know."

"Almost as if he regrets bringing it up."

"Whoever it was must have come down here and broken into the adit when we first got to camp. They wouldn't have been missed at that point, while everybody was putting up their tents and wandering around stretching their legs."

"Somebody might've spotted them coming or going, though."

"They might almost *want* to be found. They didn't dig up all the pieces of the wreckage and hide them somewhere else to come back for later. Instead, it appears they only took one of the staves. I think they just want to prove the rumor and reveal the boat to the world again. That would explain the gate being left open *and* the penny." Chuck squeezed the 1869 coin between his finger and thumb. How it related to the other two pennies, and to the deaths of Ralph and Maeve, he couldn't imagine. Not yet, anyway. "We should get back to camp," he concluded. "Everyone will be waiting."

"I'll be right behind you," said Rocky. He swung the barred gate, eyeing the bent hasp. Rusted screws extended through holes in its corners, broken free from their drilled seats in the sandstone wall beside the mouth of the tunnel. "I bet I can pound these back in place and resecure the door. I'm so pissed off at Leon or whoever did this. I don't want anyone else coming along and messing with the wreckage even more."

"But you won't have a light."

Rocky looked up at the star-filled slice of sky visible between the canyon walls. "I'll be all right. I'll pound in the screws and use the starlight to pick my way back to camp."

"Watch out for the cacti," Chuck warned.

"You bet I will."

"And falling rocks," Liza said, her tone suddenly grave.

Rocky wrapped her in a hug. "Maeve was the best," he said in her ear. "I cared for her, too. We all did."

They stepped back from one another.

A tear rolled down Liza's cheek, winking in the light of the headlamp. "Maeve," she said, pronouncing the name like an incantation.

"Maeve," Rocky repeated.

34

"*¡Jesu Cristo!* Is that really you, *hermana*?" Clarence asked.

Janelle couldn't make out much of her brother's shadowed face behind the cloud of steam rising from the pot in the camp kitchen, but the shock in his voice was obvious.

He spun a dial on the stove and the flame beneath the pot winked out with a breathy sputter. He stepped around the tables to Janelle, the girls, and Tamara.

Rosie stuck out her hip. "Yep, it's us, Uncle Clarence."

He rested his hand on her head and asked Janelle, "What are you doing here?"

Janelle shot a sidelong glance at Tamara. "We...came to see you."

"We have a warning for you," Rosie announced. "It's a big one."

"A *what*?"

"A warn—"

"Hush, please," Janelle cautioned her.

Tamara stood to the side, saying nothing.

Janelle said to Clarence, "We saw on the schedule that you'd be camped here tonight. It had been a whole week, and we thought..." Her voice died away.

"Yep, a whoooole week," Rosie said, filling the awkward silence.

"Where's Chuck?" Janelle asked her brother.

Clarence dropped his hand from Rosie's head. "He went after a raft that came floating by. It was upside down. They were afraid somebody might be trapped underneath it."

"It was upright and empty when we saw it above the rapid," Janelle said.

"Are you sure?" Tamara interjected.

"Fairly sure. It was a long way away, but we had a clear look at it from above."

"That's good to know," Tamara said. "I think I can begin to wind down the search at this point."

She left them, striding across the sand toward the kayaker still working the current at the head of the beach.

Janelle faced Clarence. "We heard about the death of your trip leader from Henry Lightfeather."

"The Jicarilla Apache dude?"

"That's right. He said he hired Chuck to do a lot of work for him in the past."

"He's a good guy. Chuck thinks the world of him."

"Henry said your trip leader's death seemed suspicious."

"Ralph's death, you mean."

"Yes, Ralph's. He wrote an article in support of the work Henry has been doing to get the water from a river in New Mexico returned to the Jicarilla people. Henry said there's a lot of money at stake, and the person who's going to make the decision one way or the other is on the expedition, someone from the Bureau of Reclamation named Joseph Conway."

"Henry thinks Joseph might have killed Ralph?"

"Yes."

Clarence swore beneath his breath. "If Henry thinks so, that makes what we've been thinking all the more clear."

"You were already onto him?"

"We suspected. But your information really helps. It puts Joseph at the top of the list." Clarence looked at the clients and guides lined along the river's edge. "We have to get the three of you away from here," he said. "Now, while everybody's still focused on the boat rescue."

"But Chuck isn't here."

"It's you and the girls I'm worried about. Tamara already knows you came here with a warning. Joseph will figure it out soon enough."

"But we just got here," Janelle protested. "It's almost dark."

"You don't understand. There was another death, just a few hours ago."

Janelle's stomach twisted, leaving her breathless.

"There have been *fuerzas* at work on the trip since day one," Clarence continued. "I've felt them. I've warned Chuck about them. Now, you've shown up with your own warning."

"But—" Janelle began.

"No buts," Clarence said firmly. "We have to get the girls out of here, right this minute."

"Okay," she said, relenting.

"The three of you must have driven down to the Maze, *verdad*?"

Rosie rocked her body from back to front in the affirmative. "There are some humongous cliffs. You won't believe it, Uncle Clarence, but Carm drove down them backward because *Mamá* was too scared."

"No," Carmelita corrected. "*Mamá* let me do it because I've been practicing with Chuck."

"Right," Rosie acknowledged. "Because you're already a pro driver." She faced Clarence. "But it was still totally crazy." She pointed at the canyon wall rising above the river. "We left the truck way up there. Waaayyyy up there."

"Well, then, that's where we're going." Clarence made a clicking noise with his tongue. "Do you have headlamps and water?" he asked Janelle.

"*Sí.* Both."

"*Bueno.* I've got my headlamp in my pocket. Follow me." He spun and headed around the cook tables.

"But the trail is in the other direction."

He turned back. "I know another way. It's shorter."

"How well do you know it?"

"Sheesh. Always with the big-sister routine." He rested his hand on the table beside him. "There's an unofficial trail to the Maze from the back of the beach. I went up it earlier and came back down the way you came, on the main trail via Spanish Bottom. The trail from the back of the beach is steeper, but it's more direct. It'll be quicker."

"Fine. Lead the way."

Clarence's fingers crept across the tabletop and curled themselves around the handle of a folding kitchen knife lying on a cutting board. He clicked the blade shut and dropped the knife in his pocket.

"Wait," said Janelle. She clenched and unclenched her hand. "I changed my mind. We can't leave Chuck here without doing what we came here to do. We have to warn him. He'll know we were here. He'll be confused if we don't."

"We could leave him a note," Carmelita suggested.

"A note?"

"Yeah, like, on paper."

"*Buena idea*," said Clarence. He flipped open a three-ring binder lying on the table, ripped an eight-and-a-half-by-eleven-inch sheet from it, and pulled out a pen tucked in the binder sleeve.

"It's the recipe planner," Clarence explained of the binder, handing the sheet and pen to Janelle. "One page for each meal, with all the ingredients and cooking instructions printed out. Tamara and Rocky call it the bible."

There was room enough in the margin for Janelle to jot a quick note to Chuck explaining Henry Lightfeather's concerns about Joseph Conway, urging him to be careful, and letting him know she and the girls were heading back to the truck with Clarence.

She folded the note. "Now what?" she asked.

"Chuck's personal dry bag," Clarence said. "I'll wrap your

note around his headlamp and leave it at the top of the bag. That'll be the first thing he'll go for when he gets back to camp."

Clarence disappeared into the darkness.

"Done," he reported when he returned a minute later. "*¿Estáis listo?*" he asked the girls. "Are you ready?"

"I was born *listo!*" Rosie declared.

They switchbacked up the hillside away from the beach, the roar of the rapid gradually diminishing below. Clarence walked quickly in front of Rosie and Carmelita, his breaths coming in harsh gasps. Janelle brought up the rear. She wore her headlamp along with the others. Their four beams flitted across the steep slope as they hurried single file up the path. Above them, evening gave way to night and the moonless sky filled with stars.

Even after dark, the air remained warm. Sweat built on Janelle's forehead. A drop of perspiration curled past her brow and into the corner of her eye. She knuckled the stinging saltiness away without breaking stride.

Far below, a single headlamp moved upriver along the shore toward the expedition campsite. "See that?" she called ahead to Clarence.

"That'll be Chuck on his way back."

She groaned. He was so close.

"He'll be okay," Clarence assured her from the front of the line. "He'll find your note."

After a few more minutes of hustling up the trail, Rosie announced she was exhausted.

"I am, too, *bambina,*" Clarence told her.

"Can't we stop for just a second?" she begged, breathing heavily.

"What do you say, *hermana?*" Clarence asked Janelle.

"I'd like to get out of the canyon first. It'd be good to be out of sight of camp."

Below, the light reached the beach and joined with other

lights as campers moved about on the open expanse of sand.

"If we can see them," Carmelita noted, "they can see us."

"Why are we being so secretive?" Rosie asked.

"Because of the other death Uncle Clarence talked about."

"Who else died?"

Carmelita raised her head, lighting Clarence's back.

"One of the guides on the trip," he said.

"That's too bad," said Rosie. "Did he drown in the river?"

"*She*. And, no. A rock fell on her in the Maze."

"Ew."

Janelle peered guiltily down the slope. Clarence was right—the girls' safety came first. Still, she was leaving Chuck on his own in camp with Joseph Conway while she fled.

A light breeze sifted across the hillside. She wrapped her arms around herself. What if Chuck discarded the menu sheet without seeing her scribbled note? What if Tamara didn't tell him about her and the girls' arrival in camp?

She dug her fingers into her sides. What if Tamara was in on it? Whatever *it* was, that is.

Carmelita aimed her headlamp up the trail. "There were some emergency whistles," she said to Clarence. "Were they for the guide who got hit by the rock?"

"You heard them?" he asked.

"The sound reached us when we were on top of the cliffs. Was her body in the ranger truck that passed us?"

"That'd be right."

"It's so sad," said Rosie. "I still don't understand why we're running away, though."

"There are pennies involved," Clarence said.

"Pennies?"

"It's confusing. The first person who died on the trip, Ralph, had a penny that—"

He fell silent when the distinct *chock* of two stones striking one another echoed up the hillside from below.

35

When he returned to camp, Chuck dropped his PFD next to Clarence's life jacket in the sand between their two tents and opened his personal dry bag in search of his headlamp. Oddly, he found the light rolled up in a sheet of paper at the top of the bag.

He unwrapped the headlamp, flicked it on, and directed its beam at the sheet, which turned out to be a printed recipe for stove-top lasagna ripped from the menu binder in the camp kitchen. He knit his brow, confused—until he spotted Janelle's familiar handwriting in the margin. His knees nearly buckled. He read what she'd written, the paper trembling in his grip.

The fact that she and the girls had been in camp worried him far more than her warning, relayed from Henry Lightfeather, that he should be wary of Joseph Conway.

He looked up from the sheet of paper. Four lights bobbed along the trail above the beach—those of Janelle, Carmelita, Rosie, and, obviously, Clarence. Beyond the lights, a square section of star-speckled sky marked the mouth of Surprise Valley. The sight of Janelle and the girls with Clarence comforted him. They were well away from camp and drawing farther away with each second that passed.

He found Tamara at the edge of the river. In the darkness, she directed her headlamp at Torch as he stepped out of his kayak and dragged it onto the shore.

Chuck tapped her shoulder. "My wife and kids were here?"

"Here and gone," she confirmed, turning to him.

"I'm going after them."

"I need you to stay, Chuck." She directed her light at Torch. "You all set?"

"I'm good," he said, tugging his spray skirt from his waist.

Tamara led Chuck away from the shoreline. "Your wife had a warning for you," she said when they were alone. "She wouldn't tell me what it was, and she left with Clarence—as near as I can tell, anyway. He's gone, and he didn't ask my permission to leave."

Chuck eyed the four lights on the slope above camp.

"I've never had a swamper ditch me in the middle of a trip before," Tamara continued. "Then again, I've never had somebody's whole family show up in one of my camps, either. Or two deaths on one trip, for that matter." She blinded Chuck with the glare of her headlamp. "And now you want to leave, too."

Chuck raised his hand, blocking her light. "I don't have any choice."

"That's what Wayne predicted you'd say. He and I decided to pull the plug on the expedition. I'm about to get on the phone and arrange for vehicles to head this way. I'll make the announcement after everything's in place. Everyone will hike out in the morning." She trained her light downriver. "How'd it go with the boat?"

Chuck lowered his hand. "We caught up with it below Rapid 2. It was empty."

"Good. Whoever lost it will track it down in the morning. There wasn't anyone in the river, either." She aimed her light at Chuck's feet. "I'm sure Clarence is accompanying your family to their car. He'll be back down here with their warning for you soon enough. In the meantime, I really do need your help. I'm severely shorthanded. I didn't just lose Maeve, I lost Vance, too. And now your brother-in-law has ditched me." She put her hand on Chuck's arm. "You can get out of here in the morning with everyone else. You'll be back with your family in no time."

197

She lowered her hand. Behind her, headlamps crossed the beach toward the camp chairs as the clients congregated, awaiting dinner.

Chuck laid his fingers over the three pennies in his pants pocket, pressing the coins against his thigh. Janelle had succeeded in warning him about Joseph, and she and the girls were safely headed back to the end of the road with Clarence.

If he left camp now, he'd be abandoning everyone on the expedition to a potential double murderer, someone who also had filed the oarlock to make it fail and presumably had broken into the adit and stolen the boat rib besides.

He looked up at the lights. Janelle, the girls, and Clarence were approaching the notch in the canyon wall, where they would pass from sight. From there, it was a straight shot through the valley to the end of the road.

"Okay," he said. "I'll stay. For now, anyway."

"Just help with dinner, that's all I ask."

A propane lantern hung from a pole above the camp kitchen, lighting Liza and Sylvia at the cook tables, and the backs of the clients in their chairs facing the river.

Before Chuck joined Liza and Sylvia in the kitchen, he invited Wayne up the beach for another private conversation. When they were away from the bright light hanging over the kitchen, he stopped and pointed up the slope at the four headlamps nearing Surprise Valley. "I think Tamara told you those are my wife and daughters."

"Yes, she did. You're not going after them?"

"Clarence is with them."

"Tamara told me that, too. Why'd they come—and leave so quickly?"

Chuck pressed his lips together. Should he tell Wayne about Joseph? No, he decided. Not quite yet. "I'll find that out from Clarence when he gets back."

"You really think he'll come back?"

"If he doesn't, I'll head out after them."

"We'll all be going out in the morning."

"For what it's worth, I agree with your decision."

"It was an easy one to come to, actually. There really was no other choice."

Chuck unzipped his pocket, dug out the three pennies, and sorted them in his hand. He dropped the first two pennies back in his pocket and placed the copper Indian Head coin on his palm. "This will assure you even more that you're doing the right thing."

Wayne leaned forward, lighting the coin with his headlamp. "My God. Another one?"

Chuck described the adit break-in, the discovery of the 1869 penny in the otherwise empty depression dug into the salt pile, and the presumption that a rib from the Powell boat wreckage had been removed from the depression.

Wayne took the penny from Chuck's palm and examined it up close. "This makes three." He folded his fingers over the coin. "Ralph's death, Maeve's death, and now a theft, all marked by pennies." He opened his hand. "This one, from 1869, makes obvious sense, given what you're saying about the missing boat rib."

"The thief must've planned on breaking into the adit all along. Why else bring the 1869 penny?"

Wayne counted on his fingers. "We've got Glen Canyon Dam, marked by the 1963 penny with Ralph's body; the Colorado River Compact, marked by the 1922 penny with Maeve's body; and now, the Powell expedition as well."

"Someone on the trip has a real penny fetish."

"And a real history fetish, too." Wayne shook his head, his headlamp's light sweeping back and forth across the sand. "All I know is, I won't be sleeping much tonight, and I can't wait to get out of here in the morning."

He handed the Indian Head penny back to Chuck, who returned it to his pocket and looked up at Janelle, Carmelita, Rosie, and Clarence climbing the hillside, the star-filled mouth of Surprise Valley just above them. As Chuck watched, their four headlamps winked out one after another.

Where seconds earlier their lights had moved steadily up the trail, now there was only inky blackness.

36

Janelle froze and clicked off her headlamp. Ahead of her, the girls and Clarence stopped and did the same. Janelle stood still, holding her breath. To her ear, the *chock* clearly had been that of two rocks kicked together by someone following them up the trail.

"We're sitting ducks on this slope," she whispered to Clarence in the sudden darkness.

"Agreed," he replied softly from the front of the line.

He set off, his body a broad, black shadow in the trail. The girls stepped nimbly behind him.

As her eyes adjusted to the dark, Janelle could just make out the dusty path snaking between brush and boulders beneath the stars.

She settled into her stride behind Carmelita, struggling to quell the rising tide of fear inside her. Why would anyone be sneaking up on them in the dark? It certainly wasn't Chuck, who would be using a light and calling up the trail to them.

She halted, allowing the girls' and Clarence's footsteps to fade ahead of her. She listened for several seconds while staring down the slope with unblinking eyes.

No sound reached her from the trail below, nor did she spot any signs of movement along the path.

Had the person who'd kicked the rocks turned back? No, she told herself. Whoever was following had come this far; they wouldn't give up just because they'd accidentally revealed their presence.

She resumed her ascent, moving as quickly as she dared beneath the faint starlight.

* * *

Clarence and the girls waited for her at a wide notch in the wall of the inner gorge. Ahead, the trail crossed a level expanse walled on both sides by vertical sandstone cliffs so uniform beneath the starry sky that they appeared sliced by a giant cleaver.

"This is Surprise Valley," Clarence whispered to Janelle when she reached him and the girls, their forms shadowy in the gloom. "The trail goes to the far end and climbs on up to the Maze."

She peered past him at the open, treeless valley bottom. "There's no place to hide."

"The sooner we get across it, the sooner we'll be across it."

"Okay," she said, her chest tight.

As before, Clarence set out first, followed by the girls. Janelle brought up the rear of their small procession. They wound through low stands of sagebrush, the pungent scent of the bushes filling the night air, their footfalls nearly silent on the soft dirt floor of the valley.

Clarence moved fast. The girls swung their arms and took big steps, matching his speed. Janelle hurried behind them. She glanced back every minute or two and was relieved to see no signs of movement in the notch or on the valley floor.

The trail angled upward at the head of the valley. A single switchback deposited them on the broad pan of bare rock containing the slot canyons of the Maze. Beyond the flat table of stone, the Doll House rock formation and Chocolate Drop towers rose against the night sky, blotting stars.

They gathered where the path vanished on the rock surface. Clarence bent forward, his hands on his knees, gasping for air. Unlike the point where the main trail dropped off the stone shelf to Spanish Bottom, no cairn marked the spot where the less frequented trail leading up from Betty Beach left Surprise Valley.

Carmelita pointed at the Orange Cliffs to the west. "The truck is that way, past the slot canyons."

Janelle eyed the dark wall of cliffs rising to the horizon

beyond the Maze. The escarpment was their salvation. They had only to reach the truck and drive back up the face of the cliffs and on out of the park from there.

She took deep, bracing breaths, assuring herself yet again she'd been correct to leave camp with Clarence and the girls. As Clarence had said, Chuck was already on alert. He would find her note and be doubly warned. He would be all right on his own.

"Almost there," she said to the others as she caught her breath.

But Rosie pointed back down into Surprise Valley. "What's that, *Mamá*?" she whispered.

A dark form moved toward them on the trail across the valley floor, less than a quarter mile away.

Janelle stared at the approaching apparition, her eyes wide.

"Ohhhhh!" Rosie cried softly, putting a hand to her mouth. "They're coming."

"We have to get out of here. *Now*," Janelle whispered to Clarence.

"I'm on it." He turned north, toward the Maze.

"No," Carmelita hissed. "We have to go around the slot canyons."

He faced her. "Sorry. You're right. You lead."

Carmelita strode west across the slickrock. After only a few steps, however, she stopped and shot out her hand, halting Clarence, Rosie, and Janelle beside her. "Someone's coming," she whispered, peering ahead, her voice shaking.

"We already know that," said Rosie. "They're coming after us."

"No. Someone else, from the other direction."

Janelle followed Carmelita's gaze. A second dark form— another person, also moving through the night on foot—was heading toward them across the slickrock from the west. The person was less than a hundred yards away, terrifyingly close.

Janelle whirled, her eyes darting, searching for an escape route. But the silent forms were coming at them from in front and behind.

"We're trapped," she moaned.

"No," Clarence whispered. "Follow me."

37

Chuck grabbed Wayne's shirtsleeve and pointed at the dark place on the slope where, seconds earlier, the headlamps of Janelle, the girls, and Clarence had moved along the trail leading out of the inner gorge. "We need to get up there."

"What are you talking about?"

"They turned off their headlamps."

"So?"

"Ralph. Maeve. The break-in. The *pennies*, Wayne."

Wayne clucked his tongue. "If someone on the trip is up to no good—and that's still a big *if* in my mind—the last thing they would do is leave camp to go after your wife and daughters."

"But something made them turn off their lights."

"What is it you're worried about, exactly?"

"They're hiding, that much is clear." Chuck held out his hands, pleading. "We're talking about my wife and daughters. I have to make sure they're okay. You're the only one I trust on the expedition. I'm asking you, as my friend, to come with me."

Wayne looked up at where the lights had blinked out a moment ago. "All right. Just let me pull on my hiking boots."

Chuck found Tamara in the camp kitchen. He drew her aside and told her what he'd seen.

"Their lights went out?" she asked. "You're sure?"

"All four of them, one after the other," Chuck confirmed. "They must have turned them off."

"But why?"

"That's what I'm going to find out."

"Agreed," she said with a firm nod.

* * *

Twenty minutes later, Chuck reached the spot on the trail above camp where the four lights had gone out. He slowed, catching his breath, and peered about, his headlamp lighting the slope.

Wayne, trailing behind, caught up a minute later.

Chuck directed his headlamp at the empty trail. "Nothing."

"They must've kept going," Wayne said.

"It'd be possible with just the starlight. They'd have to move more slowly, though."

"Do you think we should turn off our lights, too?"

"We could give it a try, see how much it limits us. We're almost out of the gorge. If we go dark now, we'll be able to climb on up to the valley and cross it without being seen."

"You really are worried, aren't you?"

"Yes," Chuck said grimly.

"For the record, having had more time to think about it while we've been hiking, so am I."

They turned off their headlamps and resumed the climb. Chuck placed his feet on the rocky trail with care, allowing his eyes to adjust to the dark. Wayne stayed close behind.

They stopped at the point where the path broke out onto the flat expanse of Surprise Valley. Chuck studied the valley floor, hoping to see the four lights turned back on and weaving through the sagebrush ahead. Only darkness greeted him.

He scanned the place where the valley topped out against the moonless night sky, searching without success for human silhouettes on the edge of the slickrock shelf that contained the Maze.

He berated himself. Janelle, Carmelita, and Rosie had been so close. Now, they and Clarence had vanished.

Why hadn't he headed out after them as soon as he'd found Janelle's note? Why had he agreed to remain in camp?

Moreover, why had Janelle, the girls, and Clarence turned off their headlamps?

He was sure of only one thing at this point: whatever they'd seen or heard had indicated danger.

It had been thirty minutes since they'd gone dark. A lifetime.

He cursed. Enough with creeping slowly through the night. He needed to find his family quickly, and he needed light to do so.

He reached for his headlamp, fumbling for its switch.

Before he clicked it on, however, a terrified screech filled the night, echoing from the head of the valley, followed an instant later by a second scream.

38

Janelle followed Clarence and the girls across the bare rock, angling away from the silent figures approaching through the darkness from opposite directions.

"Careful. Slow, now," Clarence whispered after less than a minute. "We're almost there."

"Where's there?" Rosie asked.

"Hush," Carmelita admonished her before Janelle could do the same.

"But I'm scared, Carm," Rosie whispered plaintively.

"So am I," Carmelita whispered back, pulling her close as they trailed their uncle.

Clarence halted, his arms spread wide. Janelle and the girls stopped beside him. In the dim starlight, Janelle could just make out a yawning void a few feet ahead, where the flat stone shelf ended at a precipice.

"It's a trapped graben," Clarence whispered. "It's collapsed on all sides. We can hide in it. There's a way to get down into it somewhere near here."

"There!" Carmelita cried softly, pointing.

To the right, the sharp line of the cliff gave way to a ramp of stone extending downward into the darkness. Carmelita scurried along the clifftop, leading the others to the head of the stone ramp.

"I'll check it out," she whispered. She plunged over the edge of the graben, the soles of her trail-running shoes gripping the rough sandstone surface of the sloped rock.

"Wait for me," Rosie implored, following.

"Okay, sis?" Clarence asked Janelle.

"*Sí*," she said.

He descended after the girls, the blackness swallowing him after only a few steps.

Janelle looked back along the edge of the cliff. A flicker of movement signaled the approach of the pursuer from Surprise Valley, now coming toward the trapped graben. She looked the other way. Another flutter in the darkness was the person approaching from the direction of the Maze and the end of the road.

She spun and headed down the ramp after the girls and Clarence. She descended quickly, her mouth parched. Vertical walls of stone rose like ramparts on both sides of the incline as she neared the bottom of the ramp.

The sage-covered floor of the graben spread before her. She stepped from the end of the tilted stone to the flat ground, fighting the urge to reach beneath the ramp and somehow lift it like a drawbridge to cut off their pursuers.

Carmelita took Janelle's hand. "This way, *Mamá*," she whispered.

She led Janelle around the stone ramp to the base of the cliff, where Clarence and Rosie squatted in the shadows.

"Quiet," Clarence instructed. "Not a word."

Janelle crouched with the girls. She drew them to her, her arms around their shoulders, and stared up at the sharp edge of the graben slicing the starry sky fifty feet above.

The shuffle of feet sounded on the rock at the top of the cliff.

"You!" a gruff, male voice declared. "I should've known."

Harsh breaths followed. Feet scrabbled on the stone surface atop the graben. A human form plunged off the cliff, blotting the sky. The person cried out, a screech of terror that filled the night, before striking the ground with a dull thud.

Rosie screamed. Janelle released her hold on the girls and darted toward the victim. Sage branches ripped at her legs and she fell, her shoulder slamming the ground. She twisted and looked ahead from where she lay. Ten feet in front of her, the person who'd fallen from the top of the graben lay still and silent.

She crawled to the victim and turned on her headlamp, lighting the face of a man in his forties with light-colored hair. The man lay faceup on the ground, his eyes open and glinting in the starlight. His head was twisted so far to one side that his ear was pressed to his shoulder, indicating a broken neck. The man's eyes were unblinking and his pupils did not constrict in the sudden light of her headlamp. She checked for a pulse, finding none.

She sat back, helpless. Nothing in her medical kit would aid the victim.

Rosie approached from the bottom of the cliff, dropped to her knees beside the man, and stared at him, her hands clasped.

"Is he dead?" a male voice asked from above, the same voice that had spoken before.

"Yes," Janelle acknowledged.

Clarence approached and crouched next to the victim. He turned on his headlamp. "*Dios santo*," he breathed. "It's Leon."

"Thank God I followed you," the man said from the top of the cliff. "I spotted him sneaking out of camp after y'all left. He headed up the river in the dark. He never turned on a light."

"Rocky?" Clarence asked, looking up. "Is that you?"

"Alive and well. Barely."

"You killed him. *Jesu Cristo*. You killed Leon."

"That's exactly what I did. Before he killed you. He almost managed to take me with him."

"Why...what...?"

"He must've figured y'all were going to spill the beans on him once you got out of here."

"You think he's...he's a...?"

"A murderer? I'm sure of it. Maeve without question. Ralph, too, most likely. He came at me with a knife."

Clarence's headlamp lit the top of the cliff. "What happened up there, Rocky?"

"Come on up and I'll show you."

Janelle gripped Clarence's arm.

"It's okay," he whispered to her. "Rocky's the senior guide on the expedition. He saved us."

"He only *said* he saved us," she whispered back.

"Wrong," Clarence said. "Look at this." He directed his light at the ground next to Leon's body. A glimmer of steel shone in the sand—a knife, just as Rocky had said.

Janelle rose. "I'm sorry you had to see that," she said to Rosie, pulling her to her feet.

"So am I," Rosie said gravely. "But he wanted to hurt us, didn't he?"

"Yes, he did," Carmelita said as she arrived from the base of the cliff. "Come on, *hermana*. Let's get out of here."

The girls ascended the stone ramp together, their headlamps lighting the way. Janelle hurried after them with Clarence at her side.

"I was prepared when he went for me," Rocky explained when they met him at the top of the cliff. "I turned the tables on him, lucky for me."

"Lucky for all of us," Rosie said.

"You got that right, sweetie." He turned to Janelle and Clarence, his bearded face a shadowy oval beneath his headlamp. "We need to get back. Tamara will be worried."

Janelle shook her head, the beam of her light swinging from side to side. "No, absolutely not. My daughters and I are getting out of here. Our truck is parked at the end of the road, next to the Maze."

"Who are you, anyway?"

"I'm Chuck Bender's wife, with our two daughters."

"What are you doing way the heck out here?"

"We came to visit," said Rosie.

"Huh," Rocky said, his bewilderment apparent in his voice.

Janelle didn't offer a follow-up to Rosie's response.

"What about you?" Rocky asked Clarence.

"I was thinking of leaving with them. But now, with this—" Clarence pointed over the edge of the cliff at Leon's body "—I'm not sure. I'll definitely go with them as far as their truck, though."

"I'll join you," said Rocky. "You and I can head back to camp together if you decide to come."

"Rosie and I will lead," Carmelita said, taking Rosie by the hand.

"Yeah," said Rosie. "We know the way."

"Janelle!" a voice called from the darkness.

39

"Daddy!" Rosie cried out.

Chuck clicked on his headlamp as she ran to him. He wrapped her in his arms and looked past her at Janelle and Carmelita, joined by Clarence, their faces lit by the downward rays of their headlamps.

"We heard the screams," Chuck said, approaching with his arm tight around Rosie. He embraced Janelle with his free arm and stepped back. "I thought..."

"We're all right," Janelle said. "But he's dead."

"He?"

"It was Leon," Clarence said.

Chuck stiffened, dropping his arm from around Rosie. "Leon?"

"He came after us."

Next to Clarence, a man's voice issued from beneath the beam of his headlamp. "I saw him leave camp."

"Rocky? Is that you?" Chuck asked.

"In the flesh," Rocky replied. "I figured he was up to something, and that whatever he was up to wasn't exactly copacetic. Turned out I was right."

"Rocky?" Chuck repeated. "I thought you were working on the gate at the adit."

"It only took a couple of minutes. I almost caught up with you and Liza before you made it back to camp. When I got there, I spotted Leon leaving the kitchen. Dinner wasn't ready yet, so I wondered why he was taking off. I trailed him to the end of the beach. He headed up the trail along the river."

"Toward Spanish Bottom?"

"Yep. He wasn't using any sort of light at all. I saw the head-lamps of four people moving up the trail to Surprise Valley. It was obvious Leon was circling around in the dark to head them off for some reason. I never trusted the guy, not from day one. And I was right. He tried to kill me."

"But he didn't," said Clarence, directing his headlamp into the graben.

Chuck stepped to the edge of the precipice and looked down. The beam of his headlamp illuminated Leon's broken body sprawled in the dirt among sagebrush plants.

Wayne joined Chuck at the edge of the cliff. "Dear God," he said. "He's…?"

"He tried to kill me," Rocky said. "See the knife?"

Chuck scanned the area around Leon's body. A metal blade, lying in the dirt, glittered in the light of his headlamp. He turned to Janelle.

"We have to get the girls out of here," she said.

"You're absolutely right." He shook his head, his gaze drawn back to Leon's body. "I can't even…this is…it's just…"

Carmelita lit his face with her headlamp. "The truck is parked at the end of the road."

He turned to her. "Good. It's close."

Wayne directed his light off the edge of the precipice at Leon. "Are you sure he's…he's…?"

"Yes," Janelle said. "I confirmed it."

"We can't just leave him there, can we?"

Rocky stepped to Wayne's side. "We got no choice, the way I see it. You and me, Wayne, we gotta get back to camp and Tamara and the sat phone. These folks—" he flicked his head-lamp at Janelle, the girls, Clarence, and Chuck "—can head on to their car. They'll be able to report in at the ranger station on their way out of the park." He aimed his headlamp at Chuck. "Do you agree?"

"I do," said Chuck. "Leon will have to wait."

"After what he did to Maeve, he can rot down there forever, far as I'm concerned."

Rocky and Wayne headed for camp, their headlamps lighting the slickrock before them.

Chuck took Janelle in his arms.

"You're coming back to Durango with us, aren't you?" she asked.

Ralph's admonition that Chuck never take Janelle and the girls for granted echoed in his head. "Of course."

He crossed the stone shelf with his family. The moon, more than three-quarters full, rose behind them as they walked.

The truck glinted in the moonlight where the slickrock gave way to desert scrubland. The crew cab sat low to the ground— too low, Chuck realized with a start.

He hurried forward. The truck rested on its rims, its tires flat.

He put his hand to a cut in one of the sidewalls. "Slashed," he reported to the others. He circled the truck. "All four of them."

Clarence unleashed a string of curses in Spanish, the words coming one after the other in a rapid-fire burst.

Chuck stared at the truck. "Leon sure didn't want you to leave."

"What do we do now?" Janelle asked.

"We don't have any choice but to head back to camp. There's a whole bunch of vehicles headed this way in the morning to evacuate the expedition clients. We'll go out with them."

Chuck brought Janelle up to speed as they trailed Clarence and the girls back across the slickrock. He told her about the sheered oarlock and his and Clarence's swim in the river. He chronicled the deaths of Ralph and Maeve, and the discovery of the adit break-in and theft of what likely was a length of wooden rib from the missing Powell boat wreckage. He concluded with the discoveries of the three pennies with their specific mint years.

Janelle related Henry Lightfeather's concerns about the Bureau of Reclamation water analyst, Joseph Conway, that had led her to drive to Canyonlands with Carmelita and Rosie. "I'm glad, somehow, it wasn't the Bureau of Reclamation water guy," she said.

"Leon was a water guy, too," Chuck replied. "In the Southwest, everything comes down to water these days."

"Henry talked about how much the Jicarilla people stood to gain from the water of the Navajo River being returned to them after all these years."

"If they get it back, I bet they'll sell it downstream. It's so valuable to cities in the desert that they won't have much choice."

"Is it really that valuable? I mean, is it really worth killing over?"

"It has been for a long time."

"Do you think Ralph was murdered?"

Chuck considered Leon's body lying at the bottom of the graben, the knife beside him. "I'd agree with Rocky that it's a distinct possibility. And that's before adding in Maeve, too."

"Why would Leon have left the pennies?"

Chuck tapped the coins in his pocket. "The years are clearly symbolic. Take the last one, 1869. Water was on people's minds clear back when John Wesley Powell came through here. One of the things he was trying to determine was how much development was possible—that is, how much money people could make—in the Southwest, given that the Colorado River was the region's only plentiful source of water."

Janelle snapped her fingers and turned to Chuck. "That's it," she said. "Money. How much do you suppose the boat wreckage is worth?"

"In dollars and cents? Not that much. But to the right people, it would be worth a whole lot culturally—assuming the wreckage is proven to be from the Powell expedition."

"That would explain the empty divot in the salt pile, wouldn't it? When it comes to archaeology, you always say everything comes down to where something is found."

"The term for that is provenance," Chuck said, nodding. "That's why stratification is so important during a dig—archaeologists evaluate every artifact they discover based on the layer it's found at underground and what other artifacts it's associated with."

"Maybe that's the answer, then. You said Leon took the rib from the adit to prove the Powell boat's provenance, which in turn would assure its value."

"But he essentially announced what he was up to by leaving the pennies behind. I can't for the life of me figure out why he would've done that. Besides which, I can't imagine why he came after you and the girls, either."

Camp was quiet when they returned, the clients and guides retired to their tents after dinner.

Only Tamara waited to greet them when they reached the beach. Chuck joined her beneath the propane light at the camp kitchen, along with Rocky and Wayne, while Clarence led Janelle and the girls to his and Chuck's tents.

"We had a big group meeting while you were gone," Tamara reported. "Everyone agrees with the decision to get out of here tomorrow. In fact, I'd say there would have been an uprising if we'd have tried to keep going."

"After what's just happened," said Rocky, "they'll agree all the more."

He described again how he'd grown suspicious when he'd spotted Leon exiting the kitchen and sneaking up the beach.

Chuck recalled that before he'd leapt into the gear raft and chased the yellow boat down the river, he had observed Leon in the kitchen next to Sylvia. But after Chuck had returned to camp, he'd spotted only Sylvia and Liza at the cook tables.

"My nose was twitchin'," Rocky said. "Leon sneaking off like that just didn't pass the smell test. Folks with headlamps were heading up the slope toward Surprise Valley. After what happened to Maeve, and then seeing what Leon was up to, I wasn't about to take anything for granted. I figured I'd trail along behind the lights, just to make sure everything was okey dokey. And, boy, am I glad I did." He described the altercation that ended with Leon's fall from the cliff. "I guess it'll be best to wait and head back up there in the morning to deal with his body," he concluded.

Tamara moaned. "I can't believe it. Leon? Really?"

Wayne wagged his head. "Whatever he was up to, I have to think Rocky's right: it'll turn out to have been related to Maeve's death. Ralph's, too, if I were to wager anything on it."

"I worked a lot of trips with Leon over the years, before he got on with Consilla and quit guiding," Tamara said. "He wasn't the easiest person to get along with, but he didn't seem evil to me, either."

Chuck lifted an eyebrow. "How well did you know him *off* the river?"

Tamara's voice took on a hard edge. "What are you saying, Chuck?"

"One of the nights I visited with Ralph, he and I discussed the fact that river guides don't make much money. After Leon switched to the corporate side, he was probably making more than as a guide, but I don't imagine he was getting rich."

"What money was there for Leon in killing Maeve? Or Ralph? Or in going after your wife and daughters?"

"Ralph's death came first. It stands to reason Maeve's death was somehow connected to his. Maybe she got wind of something."

"Let me get this straight," Tamara said. "You honestly want me to believe Leon murdered Ralph for money, and then killed Maeve to cover it up?"

"Ralph was clear about his anger at Consilla's wasteful use

of Colorado River water in the Imperial Valley. Maybe Leon thought Ralph would convince the policymakers on the trip to stop Consilla from irrigating crops in the desert. If that was the case, Leon might've thought he was doing his employer a favor. He might've threatened Ralph in his tent. Maybe Ralph tried to cry out, and Leon suffocated him or choked him, just trying to keep him quiet."

"That's...that's nuts. That's absolutely bonkers."

"I'm just trying to figure this out along with you. Three deaths on one trip don't just happen. I'm willing to bet the broken oarlock on the gear boat didn't just happen, either. There's a pattern here, that much is certain."

"I'm with Chuck," Wayne said to Tamara. "You can defend Leon all you want, but facts are facts."

Tamara turned to Rocky. "Maybe I owe you my thanks," she told him grudgingly. Then she said to Chuck, "Or maybe we'll find out this was all a tragic mix-up of some kind."

"It wasn't," Chuck insisted. "Leon was trying to keep Janelle and our girls from leaving. He had already slit their tires."

"You can't possibly think he was going to kill the whole lot of them, can you?"

"He snuck out of camp and circled around via Spanish Bottom to the end of the road. After he slashed their tires, he came back toward them. Why else would he have left camp without telling anyone?"

"Clarence didn't check in with me before he left, either."

"He figured you'd shut him down if he did."

Rocky bobbed his head up and down, his headlamp beam following. "To be honest," he said to Tamara, "that's what I thought, too. With everything that was going on—and with Maeve's death, in particular—I didn't want you telling me my suspicions about Leon were all in my head. I was afraid you'd make me stay in camp."

"That's exactly what I'd have done," Tamara admitted.

"Well, there you go, then," said Rocky.

Chuck drew a breath. "The question is, what's next?"

"I made the phone calls," Tamara said. "The vehicles are coming tomorrow."

Wayne cleared his throat. "We're doing the right thing by ending the expedition, Tamara. Now, with Leon's death, there's no question whatsoever."

"I know you're right," she said. "Everybody else agrees with the decision, too. I just hate to admit it."

She and Rocky excused themselves and headed for their tents.

Chuck turned to Wayne. "Are you going to be okay?"

"Of course not," Wayne snapped.

"I'm sorry. I really am. About Ralph. About the expedition. About everything."

"No, I'm the one who's sorry," he said, softening his tone. "I shouldn't have spoken to you like that." He turned his head away. "The truth is, I won't be okay until we learn for sure what Leon was up to."

Chuck and Clarence divided their sleeping gear between Janelle, the girls, and themselves. Chuck spread his and Clarence's sleeping bags in his tent for Carmelita and Rosie. Janelle handed energy bars from her daypack to the girls, then accepted Clarence's sleeping pad at his insistence, unrolling it in front of Chuck's tent.

"I'll build padding for myself out of my extra clothes," Clarence said. "Anyway, the sand's pretty soft."

Chuck zipped the screen door closed behind the girls and lay facing Janelle on his sleeping pad in front of his tent, still fully clothed.

"I never should've come," she whispered.

He slid forward on his pad until his face was inches from hers. "I'm glad you did," he said quietly.

She put her hand to his cheek, her palm warm against his skin. "I'm just glad we found you."

"We're together. We're safe. That's all that matters right now."

"Do you really think we're safe?"

"Leon's dead. You witnessed it. You saw his body."

"It's not just Leon I'm worried about. I came here because of the Bureau of Reclamation guy, Joseph. There are millions of dollars at stake with the Navajo River decision. What if he and Leon were in cahoots somehow?"

"Cahoots?" Chuck teased.

She punched his arm. "This isn't funny. It's the furthest thing from funny. There's no way I'm going to be able to sleep tonight."

"I'm sorry," he said. "You're right. How about if we take turns on watch?"

Clarence rustled in his tent. "You can include me on that."

"You were listening in on us?" Chuck asked him.

"I couldn't help it. For what it's worth, I agree with everything both of you just said. I'm glad Leon's out of the picture, but I'm with Janelle—I'm not convinced we're entirely out of the woods yet."

40

For a moment, when she opened her eyes, Janelle didn't know where she was. Gradually, however, the gray light above her resolved itself as the dawn sky, and the low rumbling in her ears as the roar of Rapid 1 from upstream.

She rolled to face Chuck, the sleeping pad squeaking beneath her. He lay on his back beside her, his eyes open, looking at the sky.

Reaching out, she rested a hand on his chest. "Thanks for taking the last watch."

He shifted to face her. "I'm glad we took turns doing it—and I'm really glad it turned out to be unnecessary."

"Are we really where I think we are?"

"You're the one who decided to come all the way out here to the middle of nowhere," he said, smiling.

She narrowed her eyes at him.

"Which I totally appreciate," he hurried on.

She returned his smile. "That's the correct answer."

The temperature was cool but not cold. Birds chirped in the bushes behind her. She raised her head, checking on Carmelita and Rosie through the screen door of Chuck's tent. They were curled close together in the sleeping bags inside. Beyond the tent, barely visible in the dawn light, folding chairs and cook tables occupied part of the beach. No one worked at the tables, and the chairs were unoccupied.

"Looks like we're the first ones awake," she said.

Chuck looked around. "Good." He settled his head back on the wadded jacket serving as his pillow. "Things will happen fast when Tamara gets up. Before that, I need a few minutes to make sense of everything from last night."

Janelle shivered as the image of Leon plummeting from the edge of the graben to his death rushed back to her. "The way he screamed. He came right down past us."

"Are you worried about how Carm and Rosie are going to take it?"

She glanced at the sleeping girls. "Only a little. They seemed okay last night. Besides, awful as it was, he got what he deserved."

"I still want to find out for sure why he did what he did. Tell me again what Henry had to say."

Speaking softly, she repeated Henry's story of the failing tunnel and Joseph Conway's position as decision maker for the federal government, and, finally, Henry's concern, after learning about Ralph's death, that Chuck was on the trip with Joseph.

"That's the thing," Chuck said when she finished. "It feels like Joseph's the key way more than Leon. It all started with Ralph, and the connection between Leon and Ralph is tenuous at best, whereas the connection between Joseph and Ralph is rock solid. In the article Ralph wrote, he came out publicly in favor of shutting down the Navajo River tunnel and returning the water to the Jicarilla tribe. If his view proved successful, no bribery money would have come Joseph's way. Talk about a clear motive."

"What about your oarlock?"

"That came next, after Ralph but before Maeve. Joseph saw the friendship that had developed between Ralph and me. At one point, he even accused me of being responsible for Ralph's death. It was almost as if he was trying to shift the blame over to me. Maybe he was worried I would put two and two together."

"That still doesn't explain Maeve. Or the adit break-in. Or Leon's sneaking out of camp last night and slashing the truck tires."

Chuck grunted. "You're right, it doesn't."

Movement caught Janelle's eye. Beyond Chuck, Tamara walked across the beach toward the camp kitchen. She held a small, black object in her hand.

"The day begins," Janelle said.

Chuck followed her gaze. "She's got the satellite phone."

Janelle sat up, her eyes on Tamara. "Should we find out the latest?"

Tamara held the phone to her ear, her free hand resting on one of the cook tables, when Chuck and Janelle approached the camp kitchen. She lowered the phone as they reached her. Wrinkles cut dark lines in her sallow cheeks and her eyes were rimmed with red.

"The search and rescue folks are getting ready in Hanksville," she reported. She rolled her bloodshot eyes. "They *love* this sort of thing."

Rocky headed toward them from his tent. In the absence of sunshine this early in the morning, he wore his ball cap backward on his head. He yawned and scratched himself through the thin cotton of his river shirt.

"I'll get goin' on some water for coffee," he said, entering the horseshoe of tables.

Tamara nodded and turned to Janelle. "Please, join us for breakfast."

"Thanks. Do you have a sense, yet, how long it'll be?"

"We'll have plenty of time to eat before we head out. The sheriff's office has been busy all night. The Jeep brigade is assembling as we speak. They'll be leaving Hanksville in an hour or so. They should get to the end of the road around midday." She addressed Chuck. "You and Clarence are free to leave along with everyone else. With the paddle rafts deflated and Liza and Torch out of their kayaks, I'll have enough guides at the oars, even without...without..." Her voice caught in her throat.

"I'm sorry for what happened," Janelle said.

Tamara squared her shoulders. "Thank you. Maeve was... she was a wonderful person. And a close friend. I thought Leon was a good person, too. I feel terrible about what he tried to do to you." She rubbed her nose, looking from Janelle to Chuck. "Why? That's what I want to know. Why did he do what he did?"

"Like I said last night," Chuck said, "there's so much money at stake for Consilla, and for all the corporations." He studied the line of client tents at the back of the beach. "Although I will say, Leon came across as a river guide almost as much as a corporate water person."

Tamara glanced at the guides' tents grouped behind the camp kitchen. "All river guides are water people, too. Every last one of them. They don't do what they do for the money, that's for sure. They do it for their love of the rivers—for the water flowing between the canyon walls."

Chuck put a finger to his lips. "Hmm. You could be right."

"About what?"

"About keeping water in the rivers. In their debates this past week, the policymakers and corporate reps focused almost exclusively on how the Southwest's water should be used by people. They barely addressed the most important question to rafting guides—making sure the rivers don't end up high and dry and empty."

"But Ralph was as dedicated as any guide to keeping water in the rivers. Why would Leon have had it in for him? Or Maeve, for that matter?"

Wayne joined them at the cook tables.

"How about you?" Tamara said to him. "Have you come up with some new idea for why Leon did what he did?"

"I only know one thing for sure," said Wayne. "Ralph and I never should have allowed him to come on the trip in the first place. I feel awful about that."

Chuck unzipped his pants pocket and tucked his hand inside. Janelle watched as he fingered the pennies—but made no move to take them out.

He had mentioned to her last night that he'd told Wayne about the pennies left behind by Leon. Why wasn't he telling Tamara about them as well?

41

Chuck noticed Janelle's gaze on his pocket. He withdrew his hand and zipped the pocket closed. "We should check on the girls," he said to her.

They left Tamara and Wayne at the cook tables and walked up the beach together.

"Why haven't you told Tamara about the pennies?" Janelle asked when they were out of earshot.

"I didn't know her before the trip."

"Wayne hasn't told her yet, either."

"So it would seem."

"It sounds as if she's genuinely shocked by what Leon did."

"I'm surprised, too. We just need something to prove for sure it was him and not Joseph."

Janelle stopped abruptly. "Like some sort of *physical evidence*?"

Chuck halted and raised his eyebrows. "That's it. The boat rib."

"*Exactamente*. Leon didn't have it with him last night. It has to be here in camp somewhere."

"The question is, where would he have hidden it?"

"Does everyone on the trip have a personal dry bag, the same as you?"

"Yes."

"Leon's personal bag would make a good hiding place, wouldn't it?"

"God, you're smart."

"No, Clarence is. He's the one who thought to hide my note in your bag."

"Team Ortega strikes again." Chuck frowned. "But how do we get a look inside Leon's bag? Everything's out in the open."

Janelle's eyes lit up. "Got it," she said.

Ten minutes later, after Janelle had prodded Rosie and Carmelita awake, Rosie directed a surreptitious smile at her mother and Chuck, and set off across the beach.

Chuck tracked her progress from where he knelt in front of his tent, stuffing his sleeping bag into its stuff sack. Janelle observed Rosie while she crouched in the sand behind Carmelita, combing out Carmelita's long, tangled hair with her fingers. Clarence sat in his tent, looking on through its open door.

Leon's name was written on a strip of waterproof tape affixed to his dry bag, which rested on the ground in front of his tent. As instructed, Rosie walked straight up to the bag, unclipped its side straps, and rooted around inside it.

By now, a handful of clients sat in camp chairs beneath the milky morning sky. They faced the river, unaware of what Rosie was up to behind them. Tamara and Wayne continued to converse at the camp kitchen, oblivious to Rosie's endeavor.

Within seconds, she pulled a slender piece of weathered wood from Leon's personal bag. The length of wood was an inch thick and a foot and a half long, rounded at one end and snapped at the other.

Rosie grinned across the beach at Chuck, Janelle, Carmelita, and Clarence, and thrust the piece of wood into the air in triumph. The movement caught the attention of Tamara and Wayne. They watched as Rosie tucked the length of wood beneath her arm and hurried back to Chuck and Janelle, who rose along with Carmelita.

"I found it, just like you said I would!" Rosie crowed, handing the broken boat rib to Chuck.

He balanced the stave on his palms, marveling at it. The broken rib was sanded smooth and gray with age, matching the length of wood that had protruded from the top of the salt pile in the adit last night. Evenly spaced lines of dark flecks stuck like glue to the broken rib every few inches along its length, and bits of fuzz clung to the flecks.

"Fine work," Chuck praised Rosie. "This answers a lot of questions." He handed the boat rib to Janelle. "Here you go," he said to her. "You're the one who figured out where to find it."

Janelle flushed as she examined the piece of wood. Carmelita looked on with her. Clarence scrambled out of his tent, and she offered the stave to him.

"What do you have there?" Tamara asked, striding up to them with Wayne at her side.

"Exactly what we'd hoped," Janelle said.

Clarence gave the piece of wood to Tamara, who turned it over in her hands.

"What is this?" she demanded.

"The rib of a boat," said Chuck. "It's more than a century and a half old."

Wayne took the stave from Tamara and studied it, then looked at Chuck, his eyes growing large. "By God, you were right," he said. He waved the rib at Tamara. "This is from the wrecked Powell boat."

Tamara looked at Leon's personal bag in front of his tent and shook her head, her brows a tight V. "I don't get it."

"Neither do I," Chuck admitted. "Not entirely."

He described coming upon the broken gate to the adit with Liza and Rocky the night before. "We found what almost certainly is the wreckage of the Powell boat preserved in a pile of salt," he explained. "But a piece of it had been dug out." He pointed at the stave in Wayne's hand.

Tamara's brow remained knotted. "You're saying Leon broke into the adit and took it?"

"He stole it," Chuck said with a nod. "To prove the boat was there, I think."

"Why didn't anyone tell me about this last night?"

"There was too much going on. This is the first chance any of us have had."

"I want to see Leon's body and verify his death for myself," Tamara said. "I'll head up there as soon as breakfast is over." She pointed at the broken boat rib in Wayne's hand and asked Chuck, "How do you see this as fitting in with what he did to Ralph and Maeve? If he did anything to them, that is."

"I'm convinced it all comes down to money. It has to."

"If that's the case, why did he go after your wife and daughters last night? That doesn't seem money-driven at all."

"He didn't actually go after them. He went after their truck. He went around on the trail via Spanish Bottom, the opposite of the way they were headed. Rocky said he was moving fast, almost running. He obviously was rushing to get to their truck before them and slash its tires. By sabotaging it, he must have figured they'd have to float down the river with us."

"Why would he have wanted that?"

"I think he was buying himself time. Over the last days of the trip, he would have set up someone else to take the blame for the adit break-in and the deaths of Maeve and Ralph, after which he would've killed whoever he set up, putting himself in the clear. He needed to keep Janelle and the girls away from civilization until he'd set everything up. But on his way back from the truck to the campsite, he ran into Rocky and freaked out."

Tamara eyed the stave. "I can't believe it." She looked into the distance. "What on earth were you thinking, Leon?"

"Like Janelle said, he took the rib to prove the boat's provenance," said Chuck. He pointed out to Tamara the lines of dark flecks on the wooden stave. "That's pine resin. Powell's team used it as pitch to secure cotton batting between the planks of their boats. A spectrometer would carbon-date the resin—and, therefore, the boat wreckage—to within a decade. With the age of the boat verified to the 1860s, Leon would have announced his find to the world, putting another layer between himself and whoever he set up for the murders. He couldn't have imagined that a lost boat would float by and that Liza would spot the broken gate when she was leading us back from—"

Chuck stopped at a cry of "Ahoy!" from upstream.

A lithe, brunette woman in strap sandals, short shorts, and a skintight tank top bounded down the trail from Spanish Bottom. "Did any of you see a yellow boat float by here last night?" she called to the group as she reached the beach.

Tamara lifted a hand. "Yes, as a matter of fact, we did."

She crossed the sand to the woman, who was in her late twenties and had a pixie nose and full lips. The woman pointed up and down the canyon as she spoke. Tamara added a few words here and there. After a minute, she led the woman back to Chuck and the others.

The woman threw herself at Chuck, wrapping her arms around him in a bear hug. "Thank you, thank you, thank you," she proclaimed.

Chuck staggered backward, his hands extended from his sides.

"Sorry," the woman said, stepping back. "It's just, you saved our trip when you went after our boat last night."

Chuck tugged his shirt back into place. "I'm glad we were able to catch up to it for you."

"I was telling Tamara, we stopped at that little beach above Spanish Bottom yesterday just before dark," the woman explained, addressing Chuck as well as Wayne, Janelle, Clarence, and the girls. "It was getting late and we were afraid the Spanish Bottom campsite would be taken. We didn't tie off our boats well enough, and Mellow Yellow pulled loose."

She opened her arms to again launch herself at Chuck. He raised his hands, fending her off. "Your boat is waiting for you at the bottom of Rapid 2."

"Great." She looked past him and her eyes grew large. "Hold the phone!" she exclaimed. "Is that who I think it is?"

Chuck turned to find Rocky approaching across the sand.

"Maybe it is, and maybe it ain't," Rocky replied to her. A grin parted his dark beard and mustache. "Heavens to Betsy, but ain't you a sight for sore eyes."

The woman hugged Rocky and turned to the group, her arm around his waist. "This rapscallion and I go all the way back to my start as a river guide."

"We worked together in Grand Canyon for a couple years," Rocky explained, tucking the woman to his side. "This here's Marlene." He cast a sidelong glance at her. "Marlene, this is... uh...everybody."

Janelle, Clarence, and Wayne nodded to her. Carmelita and Rosie raised their hands in greeting.

"I was just a kid on the Grand," Marlene said. "I didn't have a clue what I was doing. Lucky for me, Rocky took me under his wing. I never would've made it without him."

"I'm not sure I taught you well enough," Rocky said, smiling. He bumped her hip with his. "I assume you're here because you didn't manage to secure your boat last night."

Marlene smiled sheepishly and looked at her tanned feet. "It's a private trip, with a bunch of friends. You know how *that* goes."

"I do. It gets a little difficult to tie decent knots in your bow lines when you're toasted by ten every morning, doesn't it?"

"You haven't changed a bit, Rocky, you know that? Still giving everybody a hard time." Her smile faded. "I heard about your dad. I'm sure sorry about that."

"Yeah, well." Rocky looked away, his grin disappearing behind his beard.

"I hope it wasn't an accident on his job. You were always saying how much he loved what he did."

"The mine laid him off, actually."

"I'm sorry, Rocky, I really am. I know how much you cared for him."

He cleared his throat. "Thanks. Good of you to say that." He threw back his shoulders. "Long as you're here, would you care to join us for our last breakfast?" He looked at Tamara. "If it's okay with you, that is."

Tamara nodded. "Of course."

Marlene furrowed her brow at Rocky. "What do you mean by 'last breakfast'?"

"You thought you had it bad with your lost boat," Rocky said, "but our trip is a lot worse off than that. We're losing people right and left."

"People?"

Tamara raised a hand to Rocky, but he continued nonetheless.

"Three deaths so far on the trip."

"*Three*?" Marlene exclaimed, stepping back from him.

"Afraid so. We're throwin' in the towel this mornin'. Everybody's hiking out to the end of the road at the Maze after breakfast. The guides will take the boats on down the river. The *surviving* guides, that is."

Marlene gawked at Rocky. "You lost a *guide*?"

He inclined his head. "Falling rock, yesterday, in the Maze. The first to go, a customer, died of a heart attack a few days back."

"What about the third?"

"Another accident." Rocky arced his hand, imitating a person falling off a cliff, and whistled a descending note. He made no mention of the suspicions swirling around Leon, or his own role in Leon's death.

Marlene managed a weak smile. "I'm not so sure I want to have breakfast with you after all."

"Just be careful you don't choke on a piece of bacon." He extended his hand in the direction of the camp kitchen. "Shall we?"

The two headed down the beach together. Rocky's ball cap still faced backward, his dark hair falling to the tattered collar of his shirt beneath the cap's brim.

Rosie looked after Rocky and Marlene. "What did she mean about his dad?" she asked Tamara.

"Rocky's father died a while back," Tamara replied.

"My daddy died, too," Rosie said. "But it was a long time ago, when I was little, so I'm all over it now. I call Chuck Daddy, but Carmelita doesn't. Except sometimes."

Carmelita flushed.

"What she calls me," Chuck explained to Tamara, "depends on what she thinks of me at any given moment."

Tamara smiled at Carmelita. "I've never had kids, but I was a teenager once myself. I hesitate to recall some of the names I called my father."

Carmelita glanced at Chuck. "He's not so bad, all things considered."

"He taught you how to drive," said Rosie. "That's why you could back the truck down the cliff." She looked at Tamara. "But before he left, he wouldn't let Carm go to a party in her friend's car. That made her really mad."

Carmelita tightened her arms at her sides. "I'm over it now, Rosie."

Rosie tossed her thick hair. "If you say so."

42

Janelle joined the end of the breakfast line with Chuck, the girls, and Clarence. The smell of fried bacon wafted from the camp kitchen, making her mouth water.

"That smells sooooo delicious," Rosie said, sniffing the air. "I'm starved."

The front table was set as a buffet. Clients soaped and rinsed their hands at the wash station and worked their way along the table, loading their plates with toasted bagel halves, slices of bacon, and scrambled eggs with sautéed vegetables. They settled in their camp chairs, their plates balanced on their knees.

Chuck pointed at a woman in her thirties seated in one of the chairs. Her face was pale, her eyes blank. A small amount of food rested uneaten on her plate. "That's Sylvia, one of the river guides," he said in Janelle's ear, his voice low. "She's divorced from Leon. She looks pretty bad, doesn't she?"

"I'd be in shock, too, if I was her," Janelle whispered. She scrutinized the rest of the group. "What about the Bureau of Rec guy, Joseph Conway?"

Chuck aimed his chin at a heavyset man with a crewcut seated on the opposite side of the semicircle from Sylvia, his plate piled high with food. "That's him."

Joseph dug his fork into his eggs and shoveled a big bite into his mouth.

"If he's guilty, either instead of Leon or along with Leon," Janelle said, keeping her voice low, "it sure isn't affecting his appetite." Joseph chewed, his cheeks bulging. "I wonder if we should approach him."

"What, just walk up and ask him if he's a murderer?"

"Why not? He's out in the open with everybody else, so it wouldn't be dangerous." Joseph took another bite, a fleck of eggs sticking to his lower lip. "We could watch him real close while we question him."

"Maybe we should do that," Chuck said, pursing his lips and nodding. "Before you got here last night, I did the same thing with Wayne. In his case, his eyes told me he was one-hundred-percent innocent, no question."

Marlene displayed her full plate to the girls as she passed them in line. "You're gonna love this," she said with a wink.

Rosie stared at the bacon on Marlene's plate with round eyes. "All we had for supper last night was energy bars. I'm gonna eat a ton!" she exclaimed.

Trailing Marlene, Rocky lifted his plate to Rosie. "I made sure and left plenty for you."

"*Gracias*," she said.

Marlene and Rocky headed for the chairs.

Rosie watched Rocky as he walked away. "That's sad about his dad."

"You're nice to feel sorry for him," Janelle said.

"That's what we're learning in improv. We have to be in touch with people's feelings. We're not allowed to make any jokes that make people feel bad. Just good."

"Dying's no joke, that's for sure. Like last night—are you feeling okay about what you saw?"

"The bad guy who fell?" Rosie nodded. "Oh, yeah." She pointed at Rocky. "He's the one who saved us."

"I guess you could say that."

"I'm going to thank him."

Before Janelle could react, Rosie scurried after Rocky. She exchanged a few words with him, and he handed her a strip of bacon from his plate. She returned, chewing, to the breakfast line.

"I just knew how good this would be," she declared, her

mouth full. She held up the remaining half of the bacon slice. "He gave me some. Can you believe it?"

"I can see that." Janelle tilted her head. "Well?"

"Well, what?"

"What did he say when you thanked him?"

"He asked if I was okay about what happened last night, the same as you."

"That was thoughtful of him."

Rocky settled in one of the camp chairs. Marlene lowered herself to the ground and sat cross-legged in front of him, plate in one hand and fork in the other.

Rocky's backward ball cap faced Janelle. She studied the logo on the cap's crown—the letters CSM and a black, line-drawn dump truck over a circle with rays extending from it in all directions. The rayed circle behind the dump truck was obviously a sun, and its color—brown tinged with red—could be considered copper.

Her heart quickened. She turned to Chuck. "Tell me again, what reason did Rocky give you for following the girls and Clarence and me up the trail in the dark last night?"

"He said that when he saw Leon sneaking out of camp, it didn't pass the smell test."

"The smell test? That doesn't seem like a lot."

"It was enough, obviously."

"According to Rocky, you mean." She squeezed her chin with her finger and thumb. "All he said was that Leon's leaving camp looked suspicious to him? Nothing more?"

"Right. That's all."

"How did he explain the fact that he followed us up the trail to Surprise Valley without using a light?"

Chuck frowned. "He didn't really explain that part. Not very clearly, anyway."

She dropped her hand. "Why didn't he follow Leon? That's who he was suspicious of. Why did he follow us instead?"

Chuck's frown deepened. "I think he said something about making sure everything was okey dokey."

"Okey dokey?"

"Uh, yeah."

Janelle cocked her eyebrow at Marlene. "You heard what she said, right? She hoped Rocky's father didn't die at his job, because she knew how much he liked it."

Chuck nodded. "That's right. At a mine. Rocky said his father got laid off or let go or something."

Janelle squinted at the logo on Rocky's cap. "Copper."

"What?"

"We're out in the open right now, all of us." She tousled Rosie's nest of black hair. "Hold my place in line, would you?"

"Sure, *Mamá*," Rosie said, her mouth still full.

Janelle rounded the line of chairs and approached Rocky and Marlene. "I'm sorry about your father," she said, stopping next to Marlene and looking down at Rocky.

He squinted up at her from his seat. "You're Chuck's wife, right?"

"Yes." She did not proffer her hand.

Rocky's eyes tightened, his pupils black specks between his slitted eyelids. "Well, Chuck's wife, why is it you're so keen to offer me condolences about my dear old dad?"

"Because I care." She did not explain *what* she cared about—which, in this instance, was her *familia*...her daughters, husband, and brother.

"My father was a good man."

"I'm sure he was." She put her hands on her hips, waiting.

"He worked as hard as he could for as long as he could," Rocky said, filling the silence. His voice hardened. "He would've kept going, except for the damn permit."

Marlene set her fork on her plate, observing the exchange between Janelle and Rocky.

"He worked for a mine, right?" Janelle asked.

"Yes'm. He was a reclamation guy. He started in Texas, where I grew up, then he got on with CSM." Rocky spun his cap forward and pointed at the crown. "I wear this to remember him by."

"CSM?"

"Copper Sun Mining. They've got the big pit outside of Globe, up in the mountains above Phoenix, but it's pretty near shut down now."

"Pit? As in an open-pit mine?"

"That's what a pit is. They were doing it right, reclaiming every inch they uncovered. My pop was the foreman on the reclamation squad. He'd been at it for more'n twenty years. They'd worked their way through the grasses and finally settled on less intensive coverage—sage and prickly pear."

"Less intensive how?"

"Water, of course. They were getting better at it every year. The mine was producing real good, too. The whole operation was solid. But Dad got the call—the phoned-in pink slip. It wasn't CSM's fault, though. They lost their permit, and that was that."

"Permit?"

"They thought it was forever, but it wasn't, not with all the houses and golf courses they're building down in Phoenix."

Janelle glanced at Chuck, who watched her in wary silence. She looked back down at Rocky. "Did the mine lose its water rights, or did it sell them?"

"The parent company sold the rights. Mining's just like agriculture these days. The water's worth a lot more to others, so you might as well just sell it on down the line."

Rocky held her gaze, his head tipped back. Within its emanating rays, the copper-colored sun on his cap was perfectly round—the same shape as a penny.

Janelle's face grew hot. "What happened to your father?"

"Globe was a dead-end street. No jobs, nothin'. But he'd been there too long to make a go of it somewhere else. He took to playing with that nine millimeter of his, and one day it just went off."

Rocky put a finger to the side of his head and pulled his thumb like a trigger.

43

Chuck kept his eyes on Janelle as she finished her conversation with Rocky and returned to the breakfast line. She walked stiff-legged, looking at the ground.

"The circle on Rocky's hat is a copper-colored sun," she said when she reached him. She eyed Chuck's pants pocket, where the three pennies rested. "Rocky's father killed himself after he lost his job at a copper mine that sold off its water rights."

It took a moment for Janelle's words to sink in. When they did, Chuck swallowed, his throat suddenly dry. He turned to face Rocky, who watched Chuck over his shoulder from his camp chair, his plate in his lap.

"You said Rocky tried to talk you out of going into the adit last night," Janelle continued. "And that he stayed behind to hammer the gate closed again."

Chuck curled his hands into fists. "He's been right in front of me the whole time."

Leaving the line, he stalked across the sand toward the half circle of chairs.

Rocky rose, set his plate in his seat, and stroked his beard, watching Chuck. Then he spun and walked to the boats at the river's edge.

Chuck bypassed the chairs and approached Rocky, who bent over the front of one of the oar rafts, working with its bow line.

"Ralph Hycum was my friend," Chuck said to Rocky's hunched back, halting behind him.

Rocky straightened and turned. "I have no idea what you're talking about."

Chuck glowered at Rocky. "Ralph didn't deserve to die."

Rocky's bearded cheeks drew tight over his cheekbones. "My father didn't deserve to die, either. But Ralph killed him. Ralph and all the other paper pushers who make sure the water goes to whoever's got the most money."

"Ralph was a good man," Chuck said. "One of the best."

Rocky's face loosened. "All I did was dribble some oleander extract in his scotch. It was only supposed to make him sick."

"You killed Maeve, too," Chuck spat.

Tears rose in Rocky's eyes. "That was an accident. I just wanted to mess with the people on the trip, that's all. I signed on to work the expedition as soon as I heard about it. I wanted to give everybody a taste of what they deserved."

"You didn't give Maeve a taste of anything. You murdered her."

"It wasn't like that." Rocky held out his hands to Chuck. "You have to believe me. I was up on top of the Maze, all set to put a scare into one of the corporate sleazeballs, and along came Greta in her baggy pants with all the pockets. She works for Amalgamated Mining. They're nothing like CSM. They waste so much water." Tears slid from Rocky's eyes and disappeared into his beard. "It turned out Maeve's pants were just like Greta's. But I didn't realize it until after I dropped the rock. She was conscious when I got down to her. She looked me right in the eye. I could tell she knew who I was and, well, I did what I had to do."

"You mistook Maeve for Greta?" Chuck asked, aghast.

"I didn't even mean to hit her with the rock in the first place. I was just trying to scare her—or, Greta." Rocky lifted and dropped his shoulders. "I told you," he insisted. "It was an accident."

"You murdered Leon," Chuck growled. "He did what you said *you* did—he followed my wife and daughters, didn't he?"

Rocky's lips flattened. He began to speak more quickly. "I talked to him when I got back from the adit. He told me your wife and daughters had shown up in camp but that they left right after they got there. He said that added to the doubts he was already having about what had happened to Maeve. He told me he was going back for a closer look at where she got hit. He followed the lights of your family and stayed in the dark himself so Tamara wouldn't see him." Rocky shook his head sharply, as if absolving himself of responsibility. "Everything was happening at once. Your family was getting away, but I needed to make sure they stuck around until I had everything set."

"It was you who slashed the truck tires," Chuck snarled.

Rocky's tears were gone now. His rate of speech continued to accelerate. "I didn't have any choice. I went around on the main trail via Spanish Bottom. I ran the whole way to make sure I beat them there. But they spotted me on my way back and headed for the graben. Leon surprised me at the edge of the cliff—but I surprised him even more." Rocky lifted the cover of the knife holster at his waist. The holster's pouch was empty. "Luckily, I thought to toss my knife in after him."

"You filed the oarlock, too," Chuck said, his voice hard.

"Late the other night," Rocky admitted, nodding. "I figured the gear boat was the most likely to have problems if it lost an oar in the rapids. And, man, was I right. That was back when I was still on Plan A."

"Plan A?"

"To mess with the trip, nobody the wiser." Rocky leaned back against the bow of the oar raft. The boat slid a few inches, its rubber bottom scraping on the wet sand. "My dad's life was all about doing right with water, the same as me. I brought along the pennies in his honor, for the policymakers and the corporate jerks."

"The pennies were messages?"

Rocky nodded. His words flew from his mouth as he answered. "Somebody has to make people understand what's going on. My dad was so proud of how little water he was using to reclaim the mine, how much he was leaving in the rivers instead. 'Rivers gotta have water in 'em,' he'd say, 'or they ain't rivers no more.' Even Powell knew that, way back when." Anger flashed like bolts of lightning in Rocky's eyes. "Leon sold out when he went over to Consilla. He got what he had comin' to him last night—which gave me the chance to switch over to Plan B. I stuck the stave in his bag and blamed him. Perfect." Rocky shot a look past Chuck at the breakfast line. "Until your wife had to get all smartypants on me, that is." He looked back at Chuck. "Which brings me to Plan C."

Chuck glanced over his shoulder at Janelle. She stood next to Clarence, watching from the end of the line with her arms crossed. He turned back just as Rocky leaned harder against the bow of the oar raft. The boat slid into the water, and Rocky flopped backward into its front well. Chuck grabbed the bow line, but its end slipped through the D-ring on the front of the raft and plopped into the water.

Rocky righted himself. "Whoa, did I just untie that?" he asked, his surprise clearly feigned. He sat in the captain's chair, grabbed the oars, and stroked backward away from shore.

Chuck dove off the beach and threw an arm over the front of the raft. Rocky swung one of the oars across the bow. The oar blade struck Chuck in the forehead. He lost his grip on the boat and fell into the water. His feet found sand beneath him, and he rose and stood waist-deep in the river, blood pouring into his eye from a slice in his temple.

"People have to know," Rocky blurted as he backed away in the raft, facing Chuck in the captain's seat. "Tell everyone I did what needed doing, nothing more. As for me, I know where I'm headed. I've got it all mapped out. Y'all will find my boat floating on down the river somewhere, but I'll be long gone by then."

Chuck swiped blood from his eye. When Rocky reached the eddy line, he would spin the boat into the current and power it downriver, getting farther away with each stroke of the oars.

Chuck bent his legs, preparing to dive into the river in pursuit. But he hesitated. Like Rocky, he wasn't wearing a PFD. But Rocky was in a boat and Chuck wasn't.

Something struck him in the back. He stumbled forward, scrambling for purchase on the river bottom.

44

"*¡Vamanos!*" Clarence cried as he raced past Chuck and leapt into the river.

Chuck's PFD floated beside him in the water, where it had landed after Clarence's toss. Chuck shucked the life jacket on, zipped it tight, and launched himself into the water behind Clarence, who stroked across the eddy in his PFD, his big arms windmilling.

The raft reached the eddy line and Rocky turned it downstream. Clarence lunged after the boat like an attacking shark. He opened a folding kitchen knife he held in his outstretched hands and slashed the blade downward, slicing a six-inch gash in the raft's inflated rear thwart.

Rocky swung an oar in an arc above the water's surface, aiming for Clarence's head.

Clarence kicked, propelling himself straight up out of the water like a porpoise. Rather than strike his head, the oar blade slammed him in the chest. The thick padding of his PFD absorbed the blow. He wrapped his arms over the oar and sank back into the water beside the raft, drawing the blade down with him. Keeping one arm folded over the oar, Clarence slashed viciously at the boat with the kitchen knife, opening long gouges in its side thwart.

Chuck swam downstream, trailing the raft, as Clarence released the oar and grabbed the boat, spinning it and lacerating its air chambers with repeated cuts. The raft spewed air and settled visibly in the water as the current swept it around the bend below Betty Beach.

Clarence shoved himself underwater, disappearing beneath the boat.

"No!" Rocky howled, kicking at the inflated floor from the captain's chair.

Spouts of air and water shot from the floor of the raft when Clarence sliced it from underneath. He reappeared behind the deflating boat, pressed his feet to its stern, and shoved it downstream with a powerful thrust of his legs.

The raft sagged as it plowed through the water toward the head of Rapid 2, the leaking thwarts collapsing inward on all sides. Rocky stood up from the captain's chair and immediately sank to his knees, the weight of his body driving the lacerated floor beneath the surface.

The nearly submerged raft floated over the horizon line at the top of Rapid 2. Chuck stroked downstream to Clarence. They hooked arms and faced forward, neck-deep in the water, as they crested the horizon line and plunged down the rapid's smooth entry tongue behind Rocky's boat.

"Hang on!" Chuck hollered over the roar of the rapid.

"You know it, *jefe*," said Clarence through clenched teeth.

The raft sped to the bottom of the tongue, struck the rapid's initial standing wave, and folded in on itself. Rocky cowered in the captain's seat, his arms above his head, as the oars lifted into the air above him. The counterweighted shafts drove downward, slamming him out of his seat to the floor of the raft.

The deflated tubes sank into the river until only the raft's aluminum frame rested on the surface. The hydraulic force of the rapid's second wave sucked the boat fully underwater, frame and all. Rocky raised his hand, grasping at the sky, before he, too, disappeared beneath the surface.

Chuck mentally replayed yesterday's run through Rapid 2 as he and Clarence shot down the tongue. The rapid's two holes sat a few feet on either side of the river's main channel, leaving a potentially safe, if harrowing, run straight down the middle of the rapid.

He drew a breath before they reached the first wave at the foot of the tongue. The wave drew him and Clarence underwater and spit them out its downstream side. Chuck shook his head, clearing water and blood from his eyes, as he and Clarence shot past the first hole, on the right, with inches to spare.

The rapid's next two standing waves drew them underwater. Both times, their PFDs returned them to the surface. They surged past the second hole, on the left, with several feet to spare.

Chuck caught a glimpse of the end of the whitewater ahead. The gear raft and recovered yellow raft were tied at the side of the river, but Rocky and his deflated boat were nowhere to be seen.

Chuck floated with Clarence into the pool at the bottom of the rapid. He spun in the calm eddy on his back, his face to the sky, filling his lungs with air.

He straightened in the water when his heart rate slowed and stroked with Clarence to the edge of the river. They hauled themselves onto the shore and sat beside the secured rafts, facing the river. The rapid roared menacingly upstream, but the pool before them was placid and silent in the shaded morning light.

Chuck shook himself, chilled by the freezing water. He scanned the river as far as the next bend, two hundred yards downstream, for any sign of Rocky. Nothing. "The river took him," he said, gritting his teeth to keep them from chattering.

"I'm not so sure about that," Clarence replied. He wrapped his arms around himself, shaking.

"Rocky drowned," Chuck insisted. "But at least we're safe now. Janelle and the girls are safe. Everybody's safe."

"I'd rather be sure." Clarence directed his blocky jaw downstream, where the river disappeared around the next curve in the canyon. "He definitely could have made it that far. You said I was underwater for a long time in Rapid 1 before you got to me."

"But you were wearing a PFD that brought you back to the surface."

"He could've grabbed a big breath before he went under. He might've resurfaced around the bend, even without a life jacket."

"You honestly want to go look for him?"

"He could've made it to shore. He might need our help."

"Why should we care?"

"He's crazy. He's messed up in his head. Besides, if he's alive, he deserves to be brought to justice." Clarence stood and swung his arms in circles. "Brrr. We can head downstream along the edge of the river to warm ourselves up. Just to the first bend. If we don't see anything, we'll go back."

Chuck groaned. "Okay." He rose to his feet. "But we'd warm up just as fast heading straight back up the river to camp, you know."

They made their way along the narrow band of sand lining the shore below Rapid 2. At the bend in the river, they climbed a slanted rock the size of a two-story house and stood atop it together, peering downstream.

Chuck touched the wound on his temple as he looked down the river. His head ached from the oar blow, but fortunately the bleeding had stopped.

Beyond the bend, the river ran straight for a quarter mile to Rapid 3, which thundered downstream. The wall of the inner gorge was broken at the head of the stretch of whitewater by a narrow side canyon coming in from the west. Blocks of sandstone littered the mouth of the side canyon, forming a stack beside the river at the top of the rapid. In the water next to the rocks, a patch of sky-blue rubber bobbed against the shoreline.

"*Jesu Cristo*," Clarence exclaimed. "See that?"

They clambered off the rock and hurried downriver to the deflated raft, but when they tugged the waterlogged boat onto the shore, they found it empty.

"You were right, the river took him," said Clarence, gazing at the surging rapid.

But Chuck eyed a flat chunk of sandstone the size of a refrigerator on shore next to the raft. "No," he said, pointing at the rock. "You're the one who was right."

Wet footprints splashed across the bare surface of the stone. The footprints led toward the side canyon climbing away from the river's edge. Piñons and junipers grew among boulders in the tight, V-shaped ravine, which turned a corner and disappeared from view a hundred yards from the river.

Clarence stared at the watery prints on the chunk of stone, then up the ravine. "Do we go after him?"

Chuck shook his head. "He's got too much of a head start. Besides, the sat phone's a lot faster than us."

"In that case, the quicker we get back to camp and the phone, the better."

"And the quicker we get back to Janelle and the girls."

EPILOGUE

Chuck drove the truck away from the Maze. Janelle sat across from him in the front passenger seat of the crew cab, while Clarence was wedged between Carmelita and Rosie in back.

"And we're outta here!" Clarence crowed. He bumped fists with Rosie, his wide, toothy grin filling the rearview mirror.

Calls by Tamara on the satellite phone after Chuck had returned with Clarence to camp had alerted the National Park Service and local sheriff's office to Rocky's attempted escape. Within thirty minutes, a park-service helicopter had begun a series of sweeps over the Rapid 3 side canyon and the stretch of desert above it.

Another call, this one by Chuck, had resulted in the leader of the Southeast Utah Search and Rescue Team picking up four mounted wheels in Hanksville for the disabled Bender Archaeological truck and delivering them to the end of the park road.

Ahead, the personal four-wheel drives of the rescue team members—the vehicles' extra seats occupied by the Waters of the Southwest Expedition clients—raised a cloud of dust as they headed for the base of the Orange Cliffs.

Chuck slowed, falling back from the team members' vehicles to allow the dust to dissipate behind them. He caught sight in the mirror of the gauze bandage covering the wound on his forehead. His temple was bruised and swollen from the blow by Rocky's oar, but a pair of butterfly bandages applied by Janelle had closed the split in his skin.

"I don't get it," Rosie said from the backseat. "Why did that guy kill everybody?"

"He was avenging his father's death," Janelle explained. "He thought the people on the expedition were responsible for it."

"But his dad shot himself in the head. He blew his brains out. That's what you said."

"I probably shouldn't have told you that."

"But you did, *Mamá*."

Janelle sighed.

"His father's death and water were all mixed up together in Rocky's mind," Chuck said. "Rocky told me he only wanted to mess up the trip. It doesn't sound like he set out to kill anybody. Not at first, anyway."

"All you really need to know," Carmelita said to Rosie, "is that people are weird."

"Which is probably why he cut up our tires," Rosie responded. "Because he was a weirdo."

Chuck caught Rosie's eye in the rearview mirror. "Rocky told me the tires were part of his first backup plan—his Plan B—which was to blame Leon for the deaths of Ralph and Maeve. He knew Leon was following you up the trail through Surprise Valley to the Maze, so he went around the other way and slashed the truck tires to make Leon look even more guilty after he died—or, I should say, after Rocky killed him." Chuck glanced out the window at the cloudless midday sky. "Deep down, Rocky was a water geek. I'm sure he was the same as a lot of us who live in this part of the country, wondering every year if this could be the summer it never rains and everything dries up and blows away. Each time I turn on the water in the sink at home, I wonder if that will be the time nothing comes out."

Rosie chortled. "Like that would ever happen. I mean, there's always water."

"Every year, less water is reaching Durango and the desert lands south of us. So far, we're okay up in the mountains. Down here in the desert, though?" He shook his head. "Not so great."

"But the river is huge. There are rapids and everything."

"The pipelines that suck the water out of it are even huger. I'd say that's the real reason Rocky turned into a killer—he didn't think the corporations and policymakers were leaving enough water in the rivers."

"What are policymakers?"

"The people who make up the rules. They came on the trip along with businesspeople to discuss who gets what shares of water."

"They'll figure it out," said Rosie.

"What makes you say that?"

"Because they always do."

"You mean, just like there's always water when you turn on the faucet in the sink?"

"Yeah, like that."

"Until there isn't."

"If that ever happens, I could do a rain dance." She wiggled in her seat. "Maybe that would work."

"Nothing has worked so far. The drought in the Southwest just keeps getting worse. People are starting to get desperate. In fact, Rocky is a perfect example of that."

"What I don't get," said Clarence, "is the pennies. And why he broke into the tunnel."

"I think they were one and the same to him," Chuck said. "The meaning behind the years of the pennies is obvious. All the biggies: Glen Canyon Dam, the Colorado River Compact, the Powell expedition. He told me he wanted people to know what's going on with water in the Southwest—that the rivers are being sucked dry. He said John Wesley Powell knew clear back at the start what was going to happen. That's why he couldn't help but go after Powell's wrecked boat. I'm sure he would've used the rib from the boat as another message of some sort. But when everything started to fall apart on him, he stuffed it in Leon's personal bag to make Leon look guilty instead."

"And I found it!" Rosie crowed.

"Yep, you flushed him out into the open." Chuck extended his hand over the front seat for a high-five.

She slapped his palm. "I solved the crime."

"Well, we all did." He glanced at Janelle. "Your *mamá* most of all. She went right over and confronted him."

Janelle's cheeks reddened.

"But I talked to him first," said Rosie.

"You set the wheels in motion, that's for sure."

"Like I always do."

"A truer statement has never been stated."

The road turned west and entered the deep shade of the Orange Cliffs.

Chuck braked to a stop at the foot of the towering escarpment. To the east, the helicopter flew low over the desert, continuing its search.

"Will they catch him?" Rosie asked.

"Without doubt," Chuck said with an assured nod. "According to Tamara, a bunch of ground personnel are on their way. The helicopter will keep him pinned down until they get here. They'll have drones, tracking dogs, the works. It won't take long for them to round him up. He told me he had an escape route figured out farther down the river. That was what he called his Plan C, after his first two plans didn't work out. He might have gotten away if he'd managed to float as far downstream as he wanted, but your uncle Clarence made him abandon the river a lot sooner."

"Way to go, Uncle Clarence," Rosie commended him. "You're, like, a real river person now."

"I'm never getting in a river raft again if I can help it," Clarence said. "I've got someone who's going to teach me how to kayak instead."

"Not just someone," Chuck prodded.

"Her name is Liza," Clarence told Rosie, "and she's as good a kayaker as you are a dancer."

"Which means," Chuck said, "she's really, really good."

"We're meeting up after she gets off the river," said Clarence. He patted his belly and said pridefully, "She says I've got what it takes to be a great kayaker."

Chuck hooked his thumbs over the bottom of the steering wheel and leaned forward, eyeing the rescue team vehicles snaking up the narrow road along the rocky face of the escarpment. The road was far more exposed than he'd imagined, falling straight down to the desert floor from its outer edge.

He bit the inside of his cheek. The drive up the cliff wall would be much more precarious for the big, wide Bender Archaeological crew cab than for the smaller vehicles of the rescue team members—though, he reminded himself, Janelle and the girls had successfully descended the road in the truck on their way to the Maze yesterday.

"Want me to drive?" Carmelita asked from her seat behind him.

"Yeah!" Rosie cried. "Carm should drive! She already did it once!"

"Backward," Janelle added.

Chuck dropped his thumbs from the wheel and put the truck in park. "Sure," he said, unclipping his seatbelt and reaching for the door handle. "That'd be great."

ACKNOWLEDGMENTS

As with each National Park Mystery, I owe a huge debt to my early readers, who this time around included Roger Johns, Margaret Mizushima, Chuck Greaves, Sue Graham, John Peel, and Pat Downs. They read my woeful early versions of *Canyonlands Carnage* and offered key suggestions that improved the substance and form of the story immensely.

I owe great thanks to the brilliant and tireless team at Torrey House Press—Kirsten Johanna Allen, Anne Terashima, Michelle Wentling, Rachel Buck-Cockayne, and Kathleen Metcalf—who provided their tremendous editing and design skills to *Canyonlands Carnage*, and their unceasing encouragement to me.

The masterful, eye-popping artwork of David Jonason graces the cover of *Canyonlands Carnage*. I cannot thank David enough for lending his talent to my series, and to the Torrey House Press mission of promoting environmental conservation and social change.

FURTHER READING

Canyonlands Carnage is full-on fiction, but its story line is based on the very real conflicts erupting today over water allocation in the increasingly arid Southwest.

Readers interested in exploring nonfiction books about those conflicts would do well to begin with Kevin Fedarko's *The Emerald Mile*. Fedarko's heart-pounding book uses a record-breaking 1983 boating trip down the Colorado River at flood stage as the basis from which to tell the geological and political history of the river, and of the use and abuse of water in the American West over the last century.

The opposing-views plot line of *Canyonlands Carnage* is borrowed from John McPhee's classic *Encounters with the Archdruid*, which follows famed environmentalist David Brower on a rafting trip down the Colorado River with dam builder Floyd Dominy. During the trip, the two debate preserving the river and its irreplaceable ecosystem vs. drowning the river behind a string of concrete edifices for human development and financial gain.

Numerous nonfiction books explore the life of explorer John Wesley Powell and his two scientific expeditions down the Green and Colorado Rivers in the mid-1800s. All make for informative reading, with Wallace Stegner's *Beyond the Hundredth Meridian* and Edward Dolnick's *Down the Great Unknown* at the top of the list. Powell's *The Exploration of the Colorado River and Its Canyons* is the explorer's fascinating and surprisingly readable firsthand account of the expeditions.

ABOUT SCOTT GRAHAM

Scott Graham is the author of eleven books, including the National Park Mystery Series from Torrey House Press, and *Extreme Kids,* winner of the National Outdoor Book Award. Graham is an avid outdoorsman who enjoys whitewater rafting, skiing, backpacking, and mountain climbing with his wife, who is an emergency physician. He lives in southwestern Colorado.

TORREY HOUSE PRESS

Voices for the Land

The economy is a wholly owned subsidiary of the environment, not the other way around.
—Senator Gaylord Nelson, founder of Earth Day

Torrey House Press publishes books at the intersection of the literary arts and environmental advocacy. THP authors explore the diversity of human experiences with the environment and engage community in conversations about landscape, literature, and the future of our ever-changing planet, inspiring action toward a more just world. We believe that lively, contemporary literature is at the cutting edge of social change. We seek to inform, expand, and reshape the dialogue on environmental justice and stewardship for the human and more-than-human world by elevating literary excellence from diverse voices.

Visit www.torreyhouse.org for reading group discussion guides, author interviews, and more.

As a 501(c)(3) nonprofit publisher, our work is made possible by generous donations from readers like you.

Torrey House Press is supported by Back of Beyond Books, the King's English Bookshop, Maria's Bookshop, the Jeffrey S. and Helen H. Cardon Foundation, the Sam and Diane Stewart Family Foundation, the Barker Foundation, Diana Allison, Klaus Bielefeldt, Patrick de Freitas, Laurie Hilyer, Shelby Tisdale, Kirtly Parker Jones, Robert Aagard and Camille Bailey Aagard, Kif Augustine Adams and Stirling Adams, Rose Chilcoat and Mark Franklin, Jerome Cooney and Laura Storjohann, Linc Cornell and Lois Cornell, Susan Cushman and Charlie Quimby, Betsy Folland and David Folland, the Utah Division of Arts & Museums, Utah Humanities, the National Endowment for the Humanities, the National Endowment for the Arts, and Salt Lake County Zoo, Arts & Parks. Our thanks to individual donors, members, and the Torrey House Press board of directors for their valued support.

Join the Torrey House Press family and give today at www.torreyhouse.org/give.

SAGUARO SANCTION

A National Park Mystery
By Scott Graham

Coming next in the National Park Mystery series

TORREY HOUSE PRESS

Salt Lake City • Torrey

1

Rosie Ortega inhaled deeply, and noisily, through her nostrils. "I've never smelled anything so good," the chunky fourteen-year-old declared.

"You sound like a horse," said Carmelita, Rosie's lean sixteen-year-old sister.

"Neeeiiigh!" Rosie whinnied. She shook her head, her thick, curly, black hair bouncing around her face. "If I was going to be a horse, I'd be a wild horse. Especially around here. The desert smells sooooo delicious."

"Hard to eat, though, with all the thorns."

Rosie stopped in the middle of the rocky path she and Carmelita were traversing with their mother, Janelle Ortega, and stepfather, Chuck Bender, along the top of a ridge in the Sonoran Desert of southern Arizona.

Chuck halted behind Rosie, Carmelita, and Janelle. The granite-studded ridge snaked ahead of them beneath the clear, blue, mid-October sky. Desert greenery blanketed the slopes dropping steeply away from either side of the long promontory. Multi-armed saguaro cacti, some more than thirty feet tall, towered above prickly pear cacti with flat, thick pads the size of dinner plates; stout barrel cacti as thick as fire hydrants; and tall, spindly ocotillo plants, their stiff, gray branches thrust toward the sky.

Mimicking Rosie, Chuck sniffed the air. It had rained the day before, when a low pressure system had passed through Arizona. This morning, with the precipitation gone and the sun heating the ridge, the strong scent of the drying desert filled the air. The odor—sweet and tangy, with an earthy undertone of pine—came from the many creosote bushes that dotted the hillside among the cacti. The pores of the bushes' tiny, resin-coated leaves, wide open to absorb as much of yesterday's moisture as possible, emitted the unique smell, as distinctive as any in nature.

The pleasing odor invigorated Chuck, putting him in mind of the full, captivating life he'd been privileged to share with his family since becoming husband to Janelle and stepdad to Carmelita and Rosie six years ago, after far too many years as a lonely bachelor.

Over the course of his two-decade career as an independent archaeologist, it was the scent of the drying Sonoran Desert, even more than the stunning desert scenery itself, that had led him to bid regularly for contracts in southern Arizona. He drove south from Colorado once or twice each winter to work the bids he won, escaping the cold and snow of the Rocky Mountains to complete the fieldwork portion of the contracts and to enjoy the desert warmth and beauty—and, after the desert's infrequent rainstorms, that wondrous Sonoran scent.

"I'm with you, Rosie," he said. "If you ask me, there's no better smell on earth."

He'd left the first autumn cold snap in their mountain-ringed hometown of Durango, in southwestern Colorado, a week ago to complete his latest archaeological contract in the desert, scheduling his two weeks of on-site work to coincide with the girls' week-long fall break from Durango High School, which fell in the middle of his stint in southern Arizona. Janelle and the girls had driven the five hundred miles south from Durango yesterday, joining him in the small campground in Saguaro National Park available to scientists and maintenance contractors working temporarily in the park. The campground's half-dozen barren, sun-bleached sites were shoehorned between the park's maintenance yard and the base of the ridge along which Chuck and his family now hiked.

Chuck and Janelle had rousted the girls before sunrise. In

order to enjoy the desert at its daybreak, after-rain best, the four of them had set out up the ridge as the stars faded from the sky. Neither Chuck nor Janelle had shared with the girls the additional reason for their dawn departure.

"I'm glad we got up so early," Rosie said, gazing at the cactus-studded slopes falling away from the ridge top. "Even if everything's so prickly."

Out of sight behind them, beyond the next ridge to the east, the suburbs of Tucson ran hard up against the national park boundary. Ahead, the park gave way to the undeveloped and largely uninhabited desert lands of the Tohono O'odham people stretching from the outskirts of Tucson all the way to the US-Mexico border. At 2.8 million acres, the sprawling Tohono O'odham reservation, the second largest in Arizona after the Navajo reservation to the north, was roughly the size of the state of Connecticut.

"I guess I wouldn't want to be a horse around here after all," Rosie continued.

In her eighth grade Colorado Environment class last year, she'd studied the herd of wild horses living in remote Disappointment Valley, west of Durango near the Utah border.

"You'd be surprised," said Chuck. "The desert looks inhospitable, but it supports an amazing amount of wildlife, including wild horses. Well, wild burros, anyway."

"Burros?"

"Donkeys," Carmelita interjected. She glanced at Chuck. "Right?"

"Yep. Burros are small donkeys with extra-long hair. They were brought to America by the Spanish conquistadors along with horses."

"*Sí, burro,*" Janelle said, emphasizing the double r's in the word with the rolling trill of a native Spanish speaker. "That's Spanish for donkey."

"Well, then," said Rosie, "hee-haw!"

"In some parts of the Sonoran Desert," said Chuck, "feral burros are so plentiful that they're destroying the plant life and driving out the native animals like desert bighorn sheep."

"Is somebody going to round them up, like they did to the horses in Disappointment Valley?"

Rosie had learned in class, and reported to Chuck, Janelle and Carmelita, the story of the federal government's controversial roundup of the burgeoning herd of nonnative equines in western Colorado a number of years ago. The feds had used helicopters to chase the feral creatures for miles across the sagebrush-covered floor of Disappointment Valley, resulting in injured and terrified horses, and fiery protests by animal-rights organizations.

"The desert is too rugged for that. They're using contraceptives instead."

"I know what those are. So does Carmelita." Rosie's mouth turned up in a sly grin and she adopted a sing-song tone. "Don't you, Carm?"

Janelle had told Chuck of a recent visit she'd made with Carmelita to the local family planning clinic in Durango.

When Carmelita did not respond to her younger sister, Chuck filled in the awkward silence. "Prophylaxis is an excellent tool when it's used for the right reasons."

Carmelita's back stiffened. She thrust out her chin, her mouth clamped shut.

"The *right* reasons," Rosie said, giggling. "I know all about those, too."

"We're talking about burros," said Chuck.

Rosie laughed harder. "No, we're not."

"Enough of that," Janelle said. "Let's stick with where we're at, shall we? We're in the middle of the desert, a whole different world from the mountains. It's sunny and warm and beautiful."

Chuck pointed at the highest point on the ridge, half a mile ahead. "The trail tops out up there, then drops into a drainage.

There'll be some shade under the palo verde trees that grow in the bottom of the wash."

Rosie set off once more, followed by the others. "Is that where the pictographs are?" she asked from the front of the line.

"Yes," said Chuck. "But they're not pictographs, they're petroglyphs. Pictographs are ancient pictures painted on stone; petroglyphs are pictures chipped into stone."

"Pet-ro-glyphs," Rosie said, breaking the word into individual syllables. "You try it, Carm."

"Pet-ro-glyphs," Carmelita repeated. "And pic-to-graphs. They're two different things, whereas hieroglyphs are both."

"How come you know so many words?" Rosie asked her.

"From studying vocabulary for my SAT."

"Your what?"

"Scholastic Aptitude Test, for college."

"You're already doing that?"

"Sure. I already took my Pre-SAT last spring."

In April, Carmelita had scored in the highest percentile range on the preliminary version of the college entrance exam given to all Durango High School sophomores. Now, at the start of her junior year, she'd added several hours a week of college-entrance-exam studies to her already packed schedule.

"I'm going to miss you when you leave," said Rosie.

"Whoa," Janelle cautioned. "Carm's not going anywhere for a long time."

"But when I do," said Carmelita, "I'm going a long way away."

"Depending on how much it costs," Janelle said.

"Which is why I'm studying so hard for my SAT. So I can get a scholarship."

"Why don't you define hieroglyph for us, then?" said Chuck.

"A hieroglyph is a symbol painted on a wall, chipped into stone, or pressed into clay that has a message—that is, some sort of meaning. Hieroglyphs tell stories. They're an early form of writing most commonly associated with the ancient Egyptians."

"*Perfecto*," Chuck complimented her.

"Yeah, Carm, *perfecto*," Rosie said.

"Do you remember, Rosie," Chuck asked, "why I'm doing the work I'm doing here in Saguaro National Park?"

"Nope. But I bet it has something to do with hieroglyphs and petroglyphs."

"*Correcto*," he said. He vibrated the tip of his tongue against the roof of his mouth, practicing the hard trill Janelle had given the double r's in *burro*. "Like Carm said, the ancient Egyptians developed an entire written language based on hieroglyphic symbols. Other ancient peoples communicated with hieroglyphs, too, including the Obijwe in the northern US and the Mayans in Central America. I've been hired to study whether the petroglyphs chipped into rocks around here by predecessors of today's Tohono O'odham people might, in fact, have hieroglyphic qualities. That is, are they more than just pictures chipped into rock for the artistic fun of it?"

"I bet they have all kinds of secret meanings," Rosie said.

"You're not alone." Chuck glanced back along the trail, where a team of seven people hiked along the ridge a quarter mile behind them. "The park's lead anthropologist, Martina Carmarello, is convinced that at least some of the petroglyphs found in the park are symbolic in some way or another. Ronald Little Boy, the cultural preservation officer for the Tohono O'odham people, is on her side. But others disagree, including Wilma Longworth, the dean of the Anthropology Department at the University of Arizona in Tucson. Ron Blankenship, the superintendent of Saguaro National Park, is on the fence about it. He brought me in to study the petroglyphs and let him know what I think. My findings could help determine how the park proceeds in its preservation efforts. If the petroglyphs in the park are just pictures, they'll continue to be protected and appreciated, and that will be that. But if they're part of an ancient language developed by the predecessors of the Tohono O'odham, then that's a whole other thing entirely. A finding of that sort would lead to much more extensive study of the petroglyphs in the national park, and on the lands of the Tohono O'odham, too."

"So you're, like, a judge?"

"Sort of. Ron wants me to give him my honest opinion as an outside observer."

"Chuck is known for being a straight shooter," Janelle explained to Rosie. "Nobody ever accused him of bending to the will of anybody else, that's for sure. He won't even bend to my will—and believe me, I've tried."

Chuck grinned. "I do the dishes, don't I?"

"Sometimes."

Rosie looked back at Chuck as she walked. "Mostly, you make me and Carm do them."

"That's my prerogative."

"Your what?"

"Carm, would you like to take that?" Chuck asked.

"Prerogative," Carmelita stated. "A right or privilege of an individual or group."

"Wow," said Rosie.

"It basically means I'm the boss," Chuck said.

Janelle shot him a smile over her shoulder. "Not with me."

"Not with me, either," said Rosie.

From the high point, the trail descended into a dry wash that drained westward away from the ridge. Palo verde trees sprouted on both sides of the gravel drainage, their needled branches extending from the trees' vibrant green trunks. In the distance, the dry creek bed petered away into the flat scrubland of the Tohono O'odham reservation. Directly below, at the edge of the wash, a dark blue flag attached to a flexible aluminum pole fluttered in the gentle morning breeze.

They followed the trail to the foot of the slope. Beneath the flag, a sky-blue plastic barrel the size of a beer keg with a spigot at its base sat on a waist-high metal frame. The opaque plastic barrel was half full of clear liquid.

"What's that?" Rosie asked as they approached the container.

"Water," Chuck said. "It's for unauthorized migrants—people crossing the border from Mexico and traveling north through the desert."

"You mean, *sneaking* through the desert?"

Chuck glanced at Janelle and nodded to Rosie. "They move mostly at night and hole up in the shade during the day." He waved his hand at the gravel channel descending to the west. "They follow open drainages like this one as much as possible, to avoid the cacti and thorns."

"Is that how Grand-*papa* and Grand-*mamá* got here?" Rosie asked, using the Spanglish names she and Carmelita had adopted for Janelle's parents, who lived in Albuquerque, New Mexico.

"Your *abuelos*," Janelle said, "came to the US on work visas a long time ago, when they were teenagers. They applied to become citizens after that."

"How come there's water for the people coming through here?"

"Humanitarian groups put it out," Chuck explained, "to keep the migrants from dying of thirst. But others sabotage it—they drain the barrels or shoot holes in them or, worse, add gasoline to the water to sicken or kill the people who drink it."

"Why would they do that?"

"They don't want anyone else coming to America after their own ancestors came here."

Janelle clucked her tongue. "There's more to it than that," she told Rosie. "Lots more. We could talk for hours on the subject. But suffice to say, most people believe anyone coming to the US should do it through legal channels, like your *abuelos* did."

"Except," said Chuck, "gaining citizenship is a lot harder today than it used to be. Almost impossible. Meanwhile, the governments of the countries south of here are so messed up that people are willing to risk crossing the desert to get away from the tough lives they have there."

"Like I said," Janelle said, "it's complicated."

Chuck looked at her. "Very," he agreed.

She held his gaze, apprehension showing in her eyes.

The sound of hiking boots striking rocks on the trail above reached the drainage, signaling the approach of the research team.

Chuck pointed beyond the water barrel at a line of dark, volcanic boulders, each the size of a small refrigerator, lining the opposite bank of the wash.

"Those are what we came here for," he said. "I hiked in here on my own a couple of days ago and checked them out. The petroglyphs are chipped into the rocks."

"Cool beans," said Rosie. She rounded the blue barrel and strode halfway across the dry channel before coming up short in the middle of the drainage. She aimed a finger into the speckled shade under the palo verde trees on the far side of the line of rocks. "Someone's there," she said, her voice trembling.

Chuck hurried with Janelle and Carmelita to Rosie's side. Beyond the boulders, a man lay on a patch of bare, sandy ground beneath the trees. One of the man's arms rested at his side, the other lay across his stomach. Above his draped arm, the man's chest was still.

"Stay here," Chuck told the girls, his heart racing. Leaving them, he hurried with Janelle on across the wash.

He stepped between two of the dark rocks, taking no note of the spirals, rayed circles, and human-like stick figures chipped into the stones. He and Janelle entered the shade beneath the spreading palo verde branches and stood over the unmoving man.

Up close, he saw that the man was young, in his late teens, clearly not yet twenty. Long, black lashes curled upward from his closed eyes. The bare skin of his face was silky and unblemished.

He was short and slight and wore jeans, boots, and a plaid, cotton shirt with snap front pockets and cowboy-motif embroidery across its upper chest. A ball cap pulled low over his dark eyebrows featured on its crown the words "*Cemento Majestuoso*" in flowing, cursive script above a picture of a concrete mixer truck. He lay on his back, his body contorted over a daypack strapped to his shoulders, its top unzipped.

In the calm air beneath the trees, the piney smell of the desert was overridden by the metallic taint of blood. Two small holes punctured the teenager's chest. Stains spread around the holes into the cotton fabric of his T-shirt, the dark red circles spotted by buzzing flies. The teenager's eyes were open and sunken in their sockets, staring unblinkingly up at the tree branches.

Chuck's breath caught in his throat. The teenager was dead.

"There's someone else!" Rosie hissed from the center of the wash.

Chuck whipped around to find her pointing downstream.

Janelle sprinted from Chuck's side back into the channel. Her hiking boots dug into the loose gravel as she charged down the drainage. She slid to a stop beside a second person, who lay beneath the wiry branches of a creosote bush at the edge of the wash.

She dropped to her knees, staring down.

"He's breathing!" she cried out. "He's alive!"